RAVES for IZZY BALLARD

The Alaska Girl & The Spy:

"The Alaska Girl & The Spy is another dizzying descent into the delightful world of Abigail Vertuccio and the charming crew of Alaska Virgin Airlines. Izzy Ballard stays true to form with her unique fusion of sexy comic adventure."

Stephen Evans, author of *The Marriage of True Minds*

Temptation, Alaska:

"Ballard takes readers back to Alaska in her humorous look at politics, family and a young woman's journey to regain her memory and her life. Engaging characters and charming small-town dynamics provide a fast-paced, entertaining read."
Romantic Times Book Review

Fearless in Alaska:

4.5 Stars: Romantic Times nominee for best Indie Press Romance

"This fun, entertaining romance is the second book to bring readers into the humorous world of Alaska Virgin Air. Abigail is a beyond-funny woman who knows the difficulties of living in Alaska, even more so because she has the gift of clairvoyance. But when she sees her own "ending," Abigail is sent on a mission that will truly captivate readers. The humor, charm and intoxicating characters make this novel a must-read!"
Romantic Times Book Review

Alaska Virgin Air:

"Alaska Virgin Air is a comic romp through a northern landscape rich with quirky characters, the adventurous culture of Bush flying, and romantic intrigue. Snappy dialogue, strong characters, and plot surprises make this a compelling read for those who like their mysteries served with humor."
Sherry Simpson, author of The Accidental Explorer

"Izzy Ballard is a rare talent."
The Anchorage Press

ENLIGHTENED

by

Izzy Ballard

40 BELOW INK
Anchorage, Alaska

First 40 Below Ink Printing, 2021
Copyright (C) 2021 by Izzy Ballard

Library of Congress Control Number: 2019948023

Ballard, Izzy.
Enlightened: A young woman inherits a defunct lighthouse and runs away to Alaska to discover age-old family secrets.

1st ed.
1. Alaska - Fiction. 2. Contemporary- Fiction. 3. Women - Fiction 4. Prince of Wales Island, Alaska. - Fiction 5. Humorous - Fiction. 7. Mystery - Fiction

ISBN: 978-0-9818267-8-3
Printed in the United States of America

Not All those
who wander
are lost

J.R. Tolkien

Books by Izzy Ballard

Alaska Virgin Air

Temptation, Alaska

Fearless in Alaska

The Alaska Girl & The Spy

FOR

AMY, DYLAN, ETHAN AND LOGAN

Prologue

July 21, 2019

My head slammed against the side of the rusty Jeep door and I bit back a word I shouldn't repeat here, wondering how I had ever managed to land in this predicament—blindfolded and stuffed into the back seat of a Jeep—one reeking of rotting fish and damp seaweed, mind you, blasting over bumpy, unpaved roads for what felt like hours, although it was likely minutes. But soggy undies translate like dog years in time. Trust me. At least I wouldn't fall through the hole in the rusted out floorboard, because one wrist was handcuffed to the door handle, which also meant that jumping was out of the question. Sounds of the sea and birds in trees gave me no hints as to where I was beyond what I already knew. I was on Prince of Wales Island. Alaska. And in case you were wondering: Population 5559.

The driver slammed to a stop. This time I braced myself, thankfully, to avoid body parts colliding with Jeep parts again. One of my captors leaned in and fiddled with a key to the handcuffs, releasing me, leaving the blindfold firmly in place. Before I could reach up myself and pull it off, I was unceremoniously yanked from the back seat. I don't know what I had been expecting, but it wasn't this. This was peace. Quiet. Leaves rustling in the trees and a little further away, the sounds of sea birds and waves gently hitting the beach. Delicious.

"Okay. On three." One of my kidnappers shouted. "1, 2, 3. Open your eyes!" She said this with more glee than I felt a kidnapping actually warranted, especially considering how I reeked of salmon or maybe it was halibut. Either way, not delicious.

"Admit it, Alex. You love it. I mean, who wouldn't?"

Now would be a good time to explain. Olive, aka Kidnapper #1, is my best and newest friend, along with Jackson, aka Kidnapper #2, Olive's best friend since they were five when she informed him that they were going to be best friends forever. Olive is the Big Bang. Jackson happily travels in her gravitational field.

From the minute I had arrived on Prince of Wales Island, and for reasons unknown to me, they took me on as their Project, with me kicking and screaming all the way. Olive calls me enigmatic. Private more accurately describes me. Although, private was clearly viewed as enigmatic by certain parties. And speaking of parties, for the last few weeks, Olive has been badgering me to divulge my birthday, something I have skirted around, obfuscated regarding and generally avoided sharing.

Ultimately, The Strong Force (Olive) met The Impenetrable Will (me) and still, Olive won. She picked a random date, made it my official

Prince of Wales birthday and planned a party. In secret. They think I am turning 21 this year. I was born July 21st, 2003. Which makes me 18 this year, not 21, something no one in Alaska needs to know. I had no idea where the party would be or when, only that Impenetrable Will or not, it was going to happen at some point. Which turned out to be tonight.

As you can see, it took a kidnapping to get me there. Something that was impossible to imagine happening back home in No-One-Knows-How-To-Find-It-or-Plans-On-Going-There, New Jersey.

Getting back to when I was unceremoniously dragged out of the Jeep, Olive ripped off my blindfold. "Please walk," Jackson said. "You know if you don't. . ." He didn't need to finish. Olive would get him to fling me over his shoulder and carry me the rest of the way.

I opened my eyes to find we were standing at the beginning of a winding boardwalk, the Tongass National Forest on our right and Whale Pass on the left. Strings of fairy lights were threaded through the trees giving off an enchanted and mystical feeling to the evening. A fox skittered through the brush, not too far from my muddy boots. The night air was filled with the scent of evergreen, moss and the sea and I breathed it all in.

Olive grabbed my sleeve and pulled me along a boardwalk which ended at the doors to the local community center where a sign announced a birthday party for the island's newest resident. I rubbed my palms on my jeans. How did I manage to get myself into this mess? I had moved to a lighthouse in Alaska for privacy, space, independence and peace. Not parties and kidnappings.

Olive pushed me forward. I took a shaky breath, imagining a

group of Olive's friends would be waiting to crowd in on me, only to find it was much worse. The place was standing room only. Multi-colored lights crisscrossed the entire ceiling. A long wooden table at the end was set up as a bar, now crowded with people getting an early start on their relationship with Vodka and Tonic. My eye traveled to a group of high school kids hanging around the fringe of the action, checking for the perfect storm of unattended drinks and an inattentive bartender. In another corner, a young couple, ducking under cowboy hats, were stealing kisses. A young mom danced through the crowd, her newborn baby swaying in a sling across her chest. One of the local bands was playing a melody Olive later informed me was by Credence, followed by an eye roll and a duh. The room was closing in on me. Still time to run. I backed up and bumped into Jackson. The song ended and now the band was striking up the first bars of Happy Birthday. This is what happens when you lose focus, I reminded myself.

I won't go into the painful-for-me, boring-for-you details of the next hours of well-meaning birthday greetings and the ensuing questions, including everything from blush-worthy details about my first love to why I was beating my head against a brick wall rehabilitating a derelict lighthouse at the end of the Alaska. I expertly avoided the questions, turning the questions back on each interrogator, while dodging cell phone cameras by lifting a glass, turning away or rubbing my eyes, while silently praying no photos ended up on Facebook, Instagram or Snapchat, immortalized for a hundred years.

By now you are probably wondering if I was an escapee from a maximum security prison or maybe from an asylum for the mentally unstable? Close. I grew up in rural New Jersey. I know, you probably didn't think New Jersey had rural areas, but you would be wrong. 42% of Jersey is forested. My family has no TV, internet or other "distractions." We weren't a cult, but at times it felt that way. Olive assures me I am the only person who has never seen a Star Wars movie, watched Oprah or read the Twilight trilogy, foremost among a long list. She assures me this is unequivocally true. I, on the other hand, feel confident that there has to be at least one other person on this planet who has not seen, watched or read any of the above. I am quick to assure her.

She is equally aghast that I am new to popular wisdom that girls should stand strong in the face of opposing forces, particularly those of the "penile variety," a term also new to me. Olive insists that woman should think for ourselves, because "If you obey all the rules, you miss all the fun." And, not to be left out, "Bitches get things done." *

In truth, I was raised by a long line of strong women; however, I can say with absolute certainty that the words "bitches get things done" have never crossed the lips of a single one of them.

Finally, people were more interested in getting food than in me, so Olive, Jackson and I filled plates and sat down to a table covered in white linen. A large white candle flickered next to an icy cold bottle of Growling Bear Winery's Wild Berry Cabernet, ready to toast my supposed 21st. At 22, Jackson could drink a toast. For Olive, 16 going on 39, ginger beer would have to suffice.

* Katherine Hepburn and Tina Fey, in that order, Olive tells me.

I was taking my first bite of food, just starting to relax, when Noah (more later on who Noah is and how very annoying he can be) and his little sister, Willow arrived at our table. When I stood to greet her, Willow threw her arms around my neck. I picked her up to spin her in a circle, fork still in hand, before setting her on her feet and letting her know how happy I was to see her. Noah flashed me a 100 watt smile and my hand tightened around my fork. I felt my toes, mouth and shoulders tighten. I felt trapped. Worse than I had by dozens of well-wishers. Worse than being kidnapped, for heaven's sake.

Resolved to be a big girl and get through this with the grace I had learned at my grandmother's elbow, I nodded and smiled my way through the rest of the meal, concentrating on making sure Willow felt comfortable as we listened intently to Olive's go over all the gory details of how she'd managed the coup—namely by sending out dozens of e-mails and notices about the party without my suspecting a thing and, furthermore, getting me here without bloodshed. Meanwhile, having finished their meals, couples were moving onto a makeshift dance floor, while others drifted out and down the lighted walkway to the water or onto the serene trails that crisscrossed the woods.

I watched as Noah pulled Willow up, both of them laughing as he suddenly tripped and then righted himself again. When their dance ended, he returned Willow to the table, stood over me. Politeness won over and I forced myself to look up. When it dawned on me that he was silently asking for a dance, I held up a hand in a stop gesture.

"I can't dance."

He took my outreached hand and maneuvered me up and out of my chair before I could protest. "It's easy." Walking backwards, he pulled me along the wide plank wood floor.

"It's almost midnight!" Olive shouted.

I jerked at the sound, tripped and landed on Noah's foot.

Of course, he hopped around, moaning, the big baby.

"I warned you," I said and turned away.

He gently pulled me back around. "Take off your shoes."

"Excuse me?"

He crouched down, not waiting for a reply, and began unlacing my sneakers; one and then the other. It was so personal that I couldn't move, like a deer in a pair of headlights. When he finished, he stood and lifted me up, so that now my feet were resting on his, exactly as he'd done with Willow earlier.

I looked over his shoulder to Olive, sending the universal symbol for Help. But I didn't actually know what it was and, anyway, she was busy pouring each of us a glass of our assigned beverage. When she finally finished, she waved us over. Thank you, Olive.

"Let's do a countdown."

"Let's not," Noah said, giving me a look I couldn't decipher.

Ignoring him, Jackson lifted a glass.

"Do you smell salmon?" I asked.

"What?"

"Never mind."

I looked from Jackson to Olive, thinking about how thankful I was for their friendship, even if it did include unwanted parties and terroristic tendencies on their part, grateful that I didn't actually smell like old fish despite soggy pants, accepting the inevitable. Did I mention that Olive always wins? I am sure that I did.

11:57 pm: Olive shoved a glass at me. It felt smooth and cool in my hand. I attempted to relax. Good friends, good food, relative safety, I reminded myself.

11:58: "To Alex." Olive held up her glass.

Noah lifted his glass and squeezed my hand, one he still hadn't returned to me. Friends and neighbors close by gathered, lifting glasses, while dancing couples wandered over to grab glasses and pass them around.

11:59: I watched as a row of beautify Black Forest cuckoo clocks, which hung on the wall above the bar, chimed, slightly out of time and tune.

12 o'clock: The hour struck and simultaneously every fairy light, bar light, chandelier bulb, string light, every single light of every single kind in every part of every room of the community center blew out in one swift, massive explosion of glass.

12:01: Jackson grabbed Olive and pulled her under the table.

Noah did the same with Willow.

I stood, unmoved, my head back, eyes open wide and held up my hands as if to stop what couldn't be stopped. Time slowed. I watched as thousands of pieces of shimmering glass that were suspended above us melted before my eyes, replaced seconds later by a silvery galaxy spreading across the ceiling, ultimately shattering into an ocean of gray-blue drops, until, as if the air could no longer sustain them, they rained softly down upon us. As the first drops touched my lips and evaporated, the room fell into complete and utter darkness.

Except for a figure standing in the door, his face in shadows, the light behind him creating a ghostly halo.

BOOK ONE

CHAPTER ONE

How To Survive a Kidnapping

Kidnapping #1, two months earlier

You're making a mistake!" I shouted for at least the tenth time, repeating the words even as they were lost on the wind. No one heard me, or wanted to, that much was clear.

The boat bounced along the waves between Lumni Island and Prince of Wales Island in southeast Alaska. The wind was biting through my thin jacket, the water spray penetrating so that I was shivering like a dog left out in a winter storm. While trying to keep down my lunch of yogurt and wafer thin apple slices, I held onto the boat railing and watched as the stranger standing in the bow navigated the choppy water. Silent. Firm in his resolve to ignore me.

I closed my eyes, but a strong sense of imminent danger forced them open in time to find the shore coming up close and at the rate we were speeding along, I thought I might have to take my life in my hands and jump in order to get away from this madman. The boat sk–med along the dock and with no time to lose, I made my decision and leaped.

Even I know it's never going to end well when someone shouts, "What in bloody hell are you doing?" followed by "Freaking Cheechako" and "Get her out of the water before she drowns."

The first shout came as I hit the frigid water and sank like a dead weight in the murky water, my jeans and hoodie dragging me under. I struggled to keep from stinking, bobbed up, catching a breath, in time to rescue Harry, the stuffed raccoon I'd had since I was a child. Clutching him to my chest, I sank again and then bobbed back up for the second time. If I didn't get out of the water soon, all the shivering in the world was not going to warm me. How long does it take for hypothermia to set in? I had looked it up before coming to Alaska. A wave pushed me under and I gulped water. I was going to drown on my first week in Alaska.

As I my thoughts bounced between that of a cold grave and a stark prison, something snagged my collar and with a sharp yank I surfaced long enough to spit out a mouth full of water before another wave hit me from the back. Someone shouted to pull the rope tighter. What rope? I caught an angry remark about tourists who didn't know what the bleep, blank and fudge they were doing, as I was hauled up with a grunt and dumped onto a slimy, wooden dock where I landed flat on my back, gasping for air that would not come.

"Can you hear me?" Someone leaned in close, pounding on my back. "Do you know your name?"

I spit water and caught a breath.

"She didn't hit her head, El."

I slowly rolled over, hoping I wouldn't barf all over her boots and was knocked back as a large gallumping animal of the dog variety who flew onto my chest and proceeded to lick my chin and nose and eyelids. I made a sound somewhere between a snore and a snort, turning my face away from the gloppy, intruding tongue.

"She lives!" A voice full of sarcasm and irritation announced.

"Stop being a prick, and make yourself useful, Gab-ree-el." I couldn't help noting something in her voice that said no one else got away with calling him Gabriel. "Blankets. Go. I'm Ellie. Ignore Gabe, he's—?" There was a noise. She turned around and snarled, "Hey! You bunch of hyenas. Hand over the phones."

"Ah, Ellie."

"You, too, Mac. No photos." Fortunately, Ellie appeared to carry weight with the onlookers or my bedraggled hair and soaking-wet rear would by now be plastered all over social media. She pocketed the phones then wrapped both me in the warm blankets someone had dropped beside her.

I stopped shivering. Bad sign or good? My bones began to ache. The giant dog moved from my chest to my side and I found myself looking at the woman who make it look effortless to command blind obedience from a gaggle of Alaska fishermen.

"Can you sit up? Does anything feel broken?"

I shook my head, regretting it instantly.

"Never mind. We have to get you warmed up for real. These blankets aren't cutting it."

I patted the dog mindlessly and looked blankly out over at the water. Before my illustrious dive, I had been camping on Lumni Island, inside the island's defunct and derelict lighthouse. My new home.

Two years of planning on my part and in the course of one day I had traveled 4,500 miles from New Jersey, hoping that no one from home would find me here. Considering my recent abduction and the obvious interest of the locals, I had to wonder if I had made the worst decision of my life in choosing a tiny island off the coast of Prince Wales Island, Alaska where everyone knew everyone.

The dog looked at me with deep, knowing eyes. Maybe he knew something I didn't and would tell me that things weren't as bad as they seemed. I took another peek at the waves as they pushed up against the dock, the dark clouds foreboding, covering the sun.

Of course. It was only appropriate.

CHAPTER TWO

How to Win Friends

Ellie, my rescuer, I found out later, ran the combination cafe, library and post office in town. She has a reputation as Opinionated and Outspoken when she wasn't being In-Your-Face-Don't-Mess-With-Me-Mom. I don't know why, but, me, she treated like a long lost child. Protective. Open. Sweet. From what I'd seen so far, the other residents—all 47 of them—most likely only saw the sunny side of her on Easter and Christmas. The dog was called Sebastian. He'd turned up on the beach one day, no one knew from where. Probably fell off a fishing boat, some say. Kind of like me. He was adopted by a local fisherman and Ellie was dog-sitting for a few days.

Sebastian, determined not to let me out of his sight, followed us to Ellie's rooms behind Darwin's Theory, her coffee house. My lips were still a serious shade of blue, my hair a nest of ripe seaweed, old fish scales and oil. While Ellie was busy stripping off my soaked boots, I wondered if a pair of garden clippers would be necessary to get my crusty jeans off and the gunk out of my hair. But I guess a tourist or two had fallen off the dock before, because she had the routine down to a science: upstairs to fill a tub with warm water, urge me up the stairs, strip and into the water you go. Apparently, with water temperatures around 50 in the summer, frostbite can set in right after hypothermia and warm water, not too hot, was the best remedy.

My boots out of the way, Ellie closed the door to the bathroom behind me, leaving me to my worries. There was no way I was getting back to the lighthouse tonight. The harbor master, Gabe, didn't seem like a good bet for taking me out after dark. Maybe tomorrow. I didn't want to think about it. I pried the sodden jeans off my body, slipped into the tub and lowered my head into the water, At least I had Harry and Sebastian, who was now leaning his head over the tub, slurping sudsy water with abandon.

I must have been crazy to think I could live in a rundown lighthouse off the coast of Alaska. I'd never been further west than New Jersey. I have a healthy respect for the dangers of stingrays, jelly fish and sharks, avoiding them at all costs. And they have those in Alaska. Right? I have no building skills. Practically no skills at all. If you don't count being an artist as a skill. Which doesn't count for a lot when a relic of a building—gorgeous building, albeit—comes with hundred year old plumbing, rotting floors, crumbling cement steps and life-threatening wiring, along with at least a dozen other problems I was sure would surface in the near future.

The bath water was lukewarm by the time Ellie peaked around the door, tossing in two beach towels and an extra large bathrobe. Followed by one half of a pair of slippers. Bunny slippers. Then the other. "Don't worry. Things have a way of looking up," she tossed in as well. Sebastian seemed to nod his agreement as he grabbed a slipper, gumming it quietly.

Hmm. First day in Alaska: abducted from my new home, pissed off the grumpy harbor master, saved from drowning by same. best jeans plastered with muck, dignity—history. An inauspicious start, although maybe Ellie was right. I mean, things couldn't get much worse. But first I had to learn plumbing, electricity, roofing, flooring, masonry and carpentry if I was going to fix up the lighthouse and have a decent place to live.

My plan in coming to Alaska was to stay under the local radar. Not going well, so far. Maybe I could dye my hair. Pierce my nose. Shave my head. Not that it would make any difference. One way or another, if I wasn't really under arrest, this was the new plan. Fix the lighthouse, live in the lighthouse. Become a ghost.

Chapter Three

When Being a Ghost Doesn't Work

Handing over a cup of hot chocolate, Ellie settled me onto a comfy couch, embroidered with flowers and trees in reds, yellows, greens and blues. "Start from the beginning. Where did you come from and what the hell did Edward do?" she commanded, like she would brook no dissent.

Who was Edward? I looked around, stalling for time and hoping she wouldn't get around to asking me why I was here and how I intended to take care of myself. One wall of the room was made up of large windows which looked out over the water, letting in a ton of sunlight and giving an expansive feel to the cozy space. A stone fireplace with a massive mantle lined with seashells and framed photos took up most of another wall.

"Uh, hmm," Ellie coughed, getting my attention.

"I'm Alexandria." Simple. Truthful. Not too much information.

"Oh my God! You're not Alex?"

I nodded.

"We thought. I mean. We were expecting . . ."

A boy. A man? Not a girl weighing in under 120 pounds who was less than 5'4".

"Never mind. You own the lighthouse." Her expression landed somewhere between dumbfounded and flabbergasted. "And now you're supposed to . . ."

"Fix it. Yes." I nodded, as she worked to scrub the look of astonishment off her face.

"Ok, then." She shook her head, but the crinkle between her eyes remained. Puzzled. Confused. "So, why did you jump out of Edward's boat when you were just about at the dock."

"Um." Maybe I could leave out the part about being arrested for suspicion of drug smuggling by the Alaska Coast Guard. "I was camping when his Coast Guard boat—"

"Not Coast Guard. Yet, anyway," Ellie interrupted. "But go on."

Not Coast Guard? "The Coast Guard boat, I mean, the boat landed; the officer came over to my camp and started asking a lot of questions. Apparently, I didn't answer them sufficiently, because he said he was taking me in."

"What the f—? That's—" She jumped up and paced to the window and back several times before giving me a look that told me to continue and not to leave a single thing out.

"He said I was under suspicion of drug smuggling."

Ellie's face was a road map to hell, if there ever was one. Her fists clenched as if she were getting ready to take down a grizzly bear bare-handed. Her body was so rigid I was afraid she might have a stroke or a heart attack.

I shook my head. "It's nothing." In truth, I had no idea what was going on except that it definitely wasn't nothing. If that makes sense. "Don't worry. I'm fine," I assured her.

Her next look read a lot like, "Wait 'til I get my hands on him because I'm going to kill him." I'm guessing Edward had no business being on the island, let alone kidnapping me in the name of the law—which he was not affiliated with and at this rate might never be. Note: I wasn't fine and we both knew it. The problem was, there would be no calming her down until she decided I actually was fine. I leaned back into the couch cushions and closed my eyes.

"So you came along willingly?"

I absolutely would not tell her about how he'd thrown me over his shoulder and hauled me out to the boat with threats of jail if I continued to resist. Meaning, stop kicking and pounding him on the back and biting his arm.

"Absolutely," I lied. PS. I am a terrible liar.

I yawned and moaned a little, rubbing my shoulder. "I'm exhausted, Ellie. Is there some way for me to get back to the island tonight?"

"You're sleeping here tonight." She headed out of the room and called over her shoulder, "And don't think I was born yesterday. This isn't over. Not by a long shot."

I tried not to, but my eyes drifted closed, so tired. So peaceful. So quiet. Until it wasn't.

The front door slammed open with a resounding thwack jolting my eyes open. "Mom. Mom! Where are you? I heard— Oh, hi," she said when she noticed me half-asleep on the couch. "You must be the tourist who fell off Edward's boat. I'm Olive."

What to say? "Um. I'm Alexandria."

"Alex. The Alex?"

"Yes, Olive. The Alex." Ellie came through the kitchen door. "Where have you been?"

Finally something familiar—The Mom Voice—which brought up the unhappy reminder that my own mom must be sick with worry by now.

"And for heaven's sakes, what are you wearing?" Ellie took in a deep breath and sighed.

Olive, tall and as slender as a ballerina, was dressed in a lacy and beribboned, pink dress, poofed out by multiple petticoats, that was partially covered by a fluorescent yellow jacket in a slick fabric fit for an oceanic journey to the South Pole, but was really for fishing, I gathered. Knee-high brown rubber boots completed the ensemble.

"It was Jackson," Olive stated, as if that made any sense. Ellie looked like it did, mumbling something that sounded like, "Hardly," and "Doubtful."

Could this normal-looking family somehow be completely bonkers?

I think I fell back to sleep on that thought, because when I awoke the sun was pouring in through the windows, blinding me. I was on the same couch, covered by a blanket I didn't recognize; Harry was tucked under my arm and Sebastian was stretched out on the floor along the length of the couch. His head perked up when I sat up. A note rested on the coffee table, along with a plate holding two crispy chocolate croissants. "Clothes in the bathroom. New toothbrush on the sink. Come to the cafe when you're ready. PS. I hope you're not gluten-free."

On the bottom of the note was squeezed in, presumably by Olive, "Can't wait for you to meet Jackson? Hurry up! P.S. I don't usually dress as Princess Kate to go fishing. Just so you know I'm not nuts." On the back of the page, she continued. "I was trying on my new prom dress when Jackson came storming in and dragged me off to the dock, shouting something about lights at the lighthouse and a boat. Mystery solved. It's you!!!"

She was heavy on exclamation points.

I rubbed my neck and stretched. If I waited much longer, I had a feeling she would come and find me. Best to meet the situation head on, face the music on my terms. I got up and touched my fingers to my toes, feeling each and every ache and pain from last night's fall and subsequent rescue. I gave Sebastian a rub before neatly folding the blanket and heading for the bathroom with my new best friend following close behind.

"Woof." He tilted his head up toward me. "Woof!"

Which I took to mean, "I'll be waiting for you when you get out," but which turned out to mean, "My turn." Because when I turned on the shower, he jumped in and stood under the spray like he owned the place and this was just another day in the life of Sebastian the dog. Shower, croissant then off to work.

Crazy place, Alaska. I turned the water to hot and stepped in beside him, happy to let the hot, steamy water pound all my fears and worries away.

Chapter Four

How I Came to Own a Lighthouse

My great-grandmother was going to live forever. At least that's what my 6-year-old mind believed. Something I never outgrew. Unhappily, she left me when I was barely 16 and I'm not sure I have ever forgiven her. The events that followed her passing could not be considered normal by any means and yet no one questioned them. I cried every day for weeks until one day my parents brought me with them to a lawyer's office. I remember there was a green marble apple on the lawyer's desk, she had short dark hair that framed her face like a pixie and she wore a business suit that managed to show way more cleavage than my parents would think was appropriate. I remember sitting on a hard chair in the waiting room, the tears threatening to spill out as I stared at that green apple. Long story short, we were ushered her into her office where we learned that great-grandma had left her house in the Pinelands to my parents, as well as a long list of stocks and bonds, but by then I had stopped listening. Until the lawyer asked to speak to me privately. It seems odd now that my parents would have agreed, but they did. The lawyer looked me up and down wordlessly. I stared back at her. If I spoke I knew the tears would flow and some part of me rebelled at the thought of doing do when I was being appraised like a calf at the county fair.

"Your parents are aware of the fact that your great-grandmother left you the house at the shore, her art and art supplies, along with a hefty college fund, which is enough to take you through a PhD at Harvard, should you choose to attend. These are things you are at liberty to discuss with them. However, there is an additional legacy. If you tell anyone in your family about this before you turn 18, the property will revert to a charity named by your great-grandmother. Do you understand?"

Of course I understood. I was almost 16, not 5. Although, I didn't think telling a minor to keep secrets from her parents was a good thing. So I hesitated. You would have, too.

She handed me an envelope that was addressed to me. I recognized my great-grandmother's handwriting at once. As you already guessed, my inheritance was the lighthouse in Alaska. In the letter, she explained that she wasn't leaving it to my grandmother or my mother, because neither of them had "the imagination necessary" to leave New Jersey to go live in a lighthouse. And most importantly, this was to be my "escape plan," if and when I should ever need or want one.

I was too stunned to do more than fold the letter carefully and tuck it into my pocket.

I walked out wondering, why had I ever agreed? I hated secrets.

Chapter Five

How to Be Gracious Under Pressure

You're going to LOVE Alaska!"

I think, by now, you can guess who that was.

The croissants were warm and creamy and delectable. I ate both in quick succession, leaving me yearning for a hot cup of tea or maybe cream-laden coffee. The clothes Ellie left for me included a Batman T-shirt and stretchy yoga pants, along with a pair of neon orange water shoes that were a half size too large, but serviceable. At least I wouldn't be slipping off the dock any time soon.

"There's fishing, of course. And jet skiing. And swimming," Olive enthused. "And movies. Did you know we have a movie theater? Well, not an actual theater. But Sam Gallagher has a big screen in his yard and projects movies on it every Friday night in the summer. And we have—"

"Give her a chance to breath." A young man with a nice smile walked in and gave Olive a quick hug . "I'm Jackson. You're Alex, right?"

Jackson reminded me of the next door neighbor in one of the few movies I'd seen. We didn't have TV at my house. No VCR or DVD player. My dad was a professor of Anthropology. My mom a professor of Sociology. Neither of them saw the point. I didn't remember the actor's name; I probably never knew it. I did remember that the film was a remake of an older one, based on a Shakespearean play, Romeo and Juliet. Shakespeare being something my parents approved of. Jackson reached out his hand and I suppose I shook it, lost in thought. "Welcome to POW."

I got the reference. POW. Prince of Wales. Prisoner of war. A joke. Which didn't seem funny to me. I must have frowned. I did. He was giving me a funny look, his forehead creased, his mouth crooked, like he was trying to figure out a particularly difficult math problem.

"Okay. That's enough, you two," Ellie said. "Here, Alex. I made you some coffee."

I thanked her and lifted the cup to my mouth. Nice and hot. I sipped. The perfect way to avoid questions and questioning looks. Ellie's cafe was a sturdy log structure with a collection of Alaskana lining the walls: photos, fishing poles, a rusty rotor from an airplane. Old spoons, forks and knives hung from the ceiling. A wooden frame filled with fishing hooks sat on the mantle. (I'm told the hooks are removed from various body parts with regularity each year during the annual fishing derby.) The table tops were bright red. The floors, wide, thick planks. In front of the fireplace overstuffed chairs were arranged behind a table holding well-worn books and magazines, along with a chess set. The perfect place to sit back and watch over the sea and boats with a hot cup of whatever suits you.

"Alex, some packages arrived for you while you were sleeping."

I think I mentioned before that Ellie's cafe doubles as the local post office and library, the norm in small towns around Alaska.

"Come on back. I can show you."

We went through a side door to a storage area with a little window in the front, presumably for postal customers. I had shipped ahead some personal items that I knew I would need right away, including my favorite books and a box of old photos. It looked like some of those had arrived as well as others that I had ordered from online suppliers I found via the computers at the college library back in New Jersey: food staples like pasta, rice and beans, extra flashlights and batteries, a camping stove, matches, bottled water, trash bags, a composting toilet and plenty of TP. It's not that I thought I couldn't get those things on Prince of Wales Island, but better safe than sorry.

"I can take you over to the island," Jackson offered, knowing that I had no way to get all these boxes to the island now that I was on the harbor master's naughty list. Even so, I was reluctant to take Jackson up on his offer, because that would leave way too much time for him to ask questions about why I decided to come here in the first place and how I was ever going to take on the lighthouse repairs. All. By. Myself.

"Great!" I heard Ellie say. "Olive. Come and give us a hand."

And . . . it was decided. Jackson and Olive were helping me and I didn't get a say in the matter. Like everything about Ellie, she spoke and people obeyed. Ellie steered a large postal cart toward the boxes and began tossing them in. Jackson, Olive and I followed suite. With the four of us working, we loaded the cart, rolled it to the dock and loaded the boxes onto a medium size vessel named The Guardian. I wondered if this was Jackson's boat or one belonging to his parents, but I stopped myself from asking. Especially since I didn't want him asking questions in return.

Loading the packages onto the boat took no time at all. As we loaded the last box, Ellie came over to me with a woven basket slung over her arm. "This is so you won't go hungry. Olive, go, help her, but be home before dark. And remember, helping doesn't mean you get to interrogate her. Got it?" Then she leaned in and gave me a quick hug and a kiss on one cheek. "Don't be a stranger."

And just like that, we were setting sail, so to speak, off to my tiny island. Thank the heavens.

The lighthouse loomed over us as Jackson guided The Guardian toward land, edging it between the boulders and sharp rocks, the water lapping around us, as we pulled alongside the dock and tied up. I caught Jackson rubbing his forehead and I could almost read his thoughts. How were we going to offload all these boxes without falling through the rotting dock boards and ending up in need of rescue ourselves?

The captain who had dropped me off from Ketchikan the day before had a similar reaction. In the end, he'd dropped anchor away from the dock, hauled an inflatable over the side and sent me on my way. Which is how I'd ended up at the island with only a backpack, Harry the raccoon and a rubber dinghy.

"I'm so sorry," I started, blowing out a sigh. "I wasn't thinking."

Hmm. I would have to buy a boat that could go in as far as the dingy but that was sturdier and could make longer trips. Or order in a load of wood and nails and fix the darn thing. That was all there was to it. "I'll work something out. You go back home. Your mom will be worrying, Olive."

"As if," she snorted as while Jackson disappeared below deck. I wasn't sure why. I rubbed my eyes, then the back of my neck. I knew the dock would hold my weight, because I'd tested it the night before. I wasn't, however, going to let them risk it. Especially not carrying cargo.

Jackson's head appeared through the hatch of the lower deck. "Here, Olive. Grab the end of this."

Up came a long board. Olive took one end and pulled. I came over and looked down at Jackson.

"Don't just stand there with your mouth hanging open," Olive said. "Grab a board."

Altogether we unloaded about fifty 10 foot boards, numerous boxes of deck nails and exactly three long-handled hammers. Apparently, while I'd been sleeping, Ellie, who had heard all about the rotting dock and falling down lighthouse from the captain who had dropped me off, had been plotting and planning. Jackson and Olive were all too happy to help. Help I resisted vociferously. Except Olive threatened to bring her tent and sleeping bag and move in with me after calling in every one of Jackson's Coast Guard recruit buddies to come over and help if I didn't concede. (He'd been accepted to the academy and was leaving in the fall, much to Olive's dismay.) Worse, Olive threatened to tell Ellie that I was being uncooperative, recalcitrant and an over-all pain in the rear if I resisted their help. Blackmail 101.

That having been decided, we got to work. After many sweaty hours of prying, tugging, hammering and hitting assorted fingernails later, miracles of miracles, I had a fully functioning dock.

Was everyone in Alaska this kind?

The view from the dock was so perfect that I had to sigh, releasing all the stress from the last few months. New Jersey has beautiful beaches, but nothing like the solitude and isolation of Lumni Island. Neither Olive or Jackson made a move to leave. My only option was to open the basket Ellie had sent with us. Inside I found a large, yelloow table cloth, which Olive volunteered to spread out on the ground by the beach. I pulled out a jar of olives and thick sandwiches, slabs of coffee cake and sliced veggies. Lastly, there was a large thermos of coffee and several ginger sodas.

"Your mom is . . ." Words failed me. This was so sweet.

"I know," Olive said, holding up two sandwiches. "Roast beef or grilled cheese?"

I pointed to a sandwich that looked like grilled cheese and she handed it over. While I had been researching Alaska, I read that Alaskans eat deer and moose and rabbit and grouse and ptarmigan, so I didn't think this was the time to mention that I am a vegetarian.

Maybe they wouldn't notice.

The day was so beautiful, the lunch so warm and filling, that we all laid back on the blanket and silently watched the clouds move across the sky. Jackson was the first to break the spell. He hopped up—to walk off lunch, he said—but I was sure it was to inspect the lighthouse for needed repairs. He didn't say that was his plan, but it was obvious. He had a small notebook out and was noting the cracked windows, crumbling steps and lack of heat, to name a few of the items on my own to- do list. When he came back out of the lighthouse, I got up and went over to meet him.

He dipped his head and put a hand on the back of his neck. "Alex um . . . ," he started. "I'm not sure . . . uh. I mean . . ."

Olive, who was right behind me by then, interrupted. "You can't live here, is what he's trying to say."

He rubbed the hairs sticking up on top of his head and sighed.

"Spit it out, Jackson. You know it and I know it."

It's not as if it was any of their business. Even so, I stopped myself from snapping at them.

"She's in denial," Olive insisted.

"Why don't you think I can live here?" I asked, trying to be the voice of calm. The voice of reason. Ask questions to understand the other person. Don't lash out. This was something my mother had drilled into me my whole life.

"For one—" Olive started.

"I didn't say she couldn't live here. It's just—"

"It's just that it's a dump!" Olive announced. "Falling down.

Decrepit. Spooky. Probably a drug runner's hideout. Pirates. Bandits . . ."

I turned and walked past her to the large, wooden double doors and walked inside the lighthouse. The lights came on.

"What the heck!" Olive looked around like she'd seen a ghost. "How'd you get electricity?"

"That light wasn't working a few minutes ago," Jackson added.

I shrugged. I had no idea. The electricity had worked just fine last night. The ancient stove in the lighthouse heated up like magic. The soup I'd cooked on it with my limited supplies tasted sublime. After dinner, I'd climbed the stairs to the top and unrolled my sleeping bag, enjoying the warmth of the tiny room, and quickly fell asleep to the sounds of waves meeting the shore. There were still the repairs to the stairs and windows and the lack of furnishings to deal with, but to me it was paradise. Free for the first time in my life. A depth and breath of raw nature surrounding and infusing me with peace. No one to answer to. No rules. Although, I was never one to need rules; I had always followed willingly.

I looked away from Olive in time to see Jackson trip and stumble across the stone floor, landing hard on his elbow. I reached out to catch him, but missed.

"Here, let me—" I started, but Jackson waved me off with his good arm. "I'm fine."

Meanwhile, Olive crossed her arms over her chest. "You're not fine."

"I'm fine," he said, rubbing his sore arm and looking at his feet.

"Fine." Olive said.

"Fine." He replied.

It felt good to laugh.

Being with Jackson and Olive on that first day reminded me of something I never want to forget. Following willingly hasn't worked for me in a very long time and I was done with it.

Starting with this lighthouse. And continuing from here on out.

CHAPTER SIX

How to Live in a Lighthouse

You are probably wondering how someone goes about purchasing a lighthouse, which are traditionally owned and operated by the U. S. Coast Guard. In the year 2000, approximately, the Coast Guard started selling lighthouses that were designated as "no longer critical" to their mission. A process which continues today. I researched it. Some have sold for as high as a million dollars. Others for as low as $15,000.

I count myself fortunate that great-gran was smart enough to find this one and save it for me. In turn, it was my job to literally save it. Even if it takes me a lifetime of work. That was part of the reason I fell in love with it. The lighthouse, deserted and barren, was something tangible to work on while I was also working on the intangible part—finding myself. Not that I could or would share any of this with Olive or Jackson, not even when they gave me questioning looks, clearly wondering what would bring a Jersey girl to a place so far from everything she had ever known.

It was time to stop daydreaming and get back to work. I had boxes to unpack. Although cleaning came first. The worst of the mess included years worth of duck and goose dropping, bird feathers and rodent nuggets. Thankfully, I'd thought to ship some humane mouse traps, just in case.

While I looked over the boxes, frowning and going over my To-Do list in my head, Jackson stepped over to the box marked Tools. "Here. Let me." He pulled out a pocket knife and waved it, waiting for my nod of approval.

"That's okay." I held up a hand, positioning myself between him and the pile of boxes. "I want to clean up before I start on any repairs."

Olive interrupted. "Have you ever worked on a house? Do you even know how to change a light bulb?"

"Olive. Leave it," Jackson said. Softly, though. Like she was right.

She pointed at me and gave me a look. "Check out her fingernails. I bet she never picked up a hammer in her life."

Jackson rubbed his chin and frowned. "If she says she doesn't need help..."

I nodded, because, even though it was clear that I could use the help, I didn't want it. I had packed plenty of how-to books. I also had internet on my new cell phone and had bookmarked dozens of relevant how-to websites. Plus, I had an entire box of duct tape. Duct tape is pretty good for everything. It can fix broken windows and ripped clothing. Keep a motor from falling off a boat. You can build a raft out of duct tape in an emergency. Lunar module repair. It's amazing what a little research can tell you.

"I have everything I need, Olive. But, thank you." I was going for a conciliatory yet firm tone, hoping for the best.

Jackson shrugged. "We'll come back out tomorrow with lunch, if that's okay with you."

I nodded.

Olive gave me a hug. Jackson, awkward, went to pat my arm. His fingertip touched my shoulder and I was jolted with a shock that traveled all the way down to my toes. He gave no indication of feeling it. I shook it off and shrugged. Static electricity. Or maybe a storm was approaching. I waved them off and turned back to the lighthouse. As they walked toward the shore, I couldn't help but hear them arguing.

"What the hell were you thinking, Jack? We can't leave her out here alone. She's going to—"

"I know that. But it's her business."

"Seriously?"

"Besides, if you keep offering to help, it'll only tick her off."

"Then what do we do?"

A shrug in response.

"Well, think fast, stupid, before a shark gets her or she's kidnapped by pirates."

"She already got herself kidnapped." Jackson pulled his hand through his hair and shook his head.

"Not entirely her fault, but yeah, that was unfortunate. Damn over-zealous—," Olive said

"I get it. You can stop now."

They climbed on board and Jackson began untying the ropes that held the boat to the new dock. The engine started up and they slowly pulled out into the open water.

"She's gotta be wondering what the hell she's gotten herself into," Olive said

"She should."

"Why are you being so hard on her?"

"Remember Chris McCandless. Broken down school bus. Alaska wilderness. No experience. Mortal danger. Death. The end."

"Hmm."

"You know I'm right. Let's get out of here. We'll talk with Ellie tonight. Maybe she can come up with an idea on how we keep her from getting herself killed."

"One Alex can't refuse." Olive gave him a shoulder bump.

"You sound like the Godfather. But sure.

My ears were tingling. I thought I heard, "You sound like the Godfather." I wasn't sure whose godfather they were talking about, but it appeared that my island was about to be invaded, by helpful and yet opposing forces. As early as tomorrow. So, while they were plotting to breach the shores of my tiny island, I would have to come up with a completely reasonable explanation as to why I not only didn't want their help, but didn't need it. One they would accept.

I looked up to the sky, hoping for an early star to wish upon.

When I didn't find one, I went ahead and made a wish anyway.

Chapter Seven

Darwin's Theory meets Star Trek

Olive was oddly silent on the trip back to Prince of Wales Island, Jackson couldn't help noticing. He knew she didn't feel comfortable leaving Alex alone at the lighthouse. He didn't either. Still, he recognized in Alex a person who could not be pushed and also realized that pushing would only result in their losing before they were started. Winter was months away, so it wasn't exactly the emergency Olive liked to think. He had plenty of time before he would leave for his first year at the Coast Guard Academy. More than enough to figure something out. Not that any of this was his business.

With the main island fast approaching, he throttled back on the engine until he was close enough to navigate the boat into an open moorage space close to Ellie's store. Head down, he got busy with the process of tossing over the anchor and tying up to the dock. When Olive asked and got her answer that he didn't need her help, she leaped over the side, one-handed, and went racing off down the dock.

"Wait up, Olive," he called after her. She turned, waved and kept right on going. The better to get to Ellie first, he figured, so she could impress upon her the seriousness of why Alex shouldn't be left out there alone because if the sharks didn't get her, the pirates surely would. Well, that could wait. Tying up the skiff could not. He finished the chore, double-checking his knots, stretched to loosen the knots in his shoulders, then rubbed his hands down his jeans, all the while thinking about how life could so quickly go from being set down before him like a well-worn map to something entirely different. An audacious young woman from half a world away shows up on his doorstep, so to speak, and the universe shifts. Maybe it was just one degree. But over time, one degree was enough to change a course completely. Basic Skills and Seamanship 101.

"Jackson, how'd it go?" Ellie wrapped him in an embrace when he entered the cafe, then pushed him back, holding his shoulders at arms length. "Olive says it's a disaster about to happen out there." She nodded in the direction of the tiny island that housed Alex's lighthouse.

They were settled in the family quarters behind the cafe now with Olive sprawled out on the couch, watching the scene unfold. He didn't get a chance to answer Ellie's question before she pressed on. "McCandless bad or the bride in the mud flats bad?"

Both of those scenarios had ended in untimely deaths.

When he didn't answer, she barked, "Stop stalling."

"Well . . . probably not that bad. I mean, it's still summer and she has plenty of supplies."

"Go on."

"She won't freeze. We're right here. And she has a cell phone that works. And it's not like we can force her to leave."

Ellie released him, threw herself onto an over-stuffed lime green loveseat and put her feet up. "Right. Relax. Don't panic until panicking is called for. I need wine."

"You don't drink." Olive and Jackson recited.

"Well, I would need wine if I did drink."

"In other news, she said she's planning on buying a small boat for getting back and forth," Olive informed her.

"OMG. Someone is going to have to save that girl from herself," Ellie moaned. "Jackson, are you up for giving her piloting lessons?" She got up and headed for the coffee pot. "In lieu of wine, coffee will have to do. Do you guys want hot chocolate?"

"Coffee for me. Sit. I'll get it," Jackson replied, already getting the cups from a cabinet. Pouring coffee into each cup gave him a chance to think. How much did he want to get involved? On one hand, if he let Alex fend for herself and something bad happened to her, he would never forgive himself. On the other hand, something strange had happened on the island when they had touched hands. A shock like nothing he'd felt before, ran through his entire body. Not chemistry. Not like a storm approaching. Not even lightning. He couldn't explain it. And he was pretty sure he didn't want to.

Maybe it was exhaustion. Stress, he thought. Nothing unworldly. Forget about it. And definitely don't mention it to anyone.

"Earth to Jackson. That coffee isn't getting any hotter," Ellie complained good-naturedly.

He laughed at himself. Otherworldly. Wow, he'd definitely been watching too much Eureka and Star Trek in late-night movie marathons with his fellow coast guard recruits, as they talked excitedly about their upcoming training and the adventures they would have.

"Don't mind Jackson, Mom. He's been discombobulated ever since Alex hit our shores."

"Leave him alone. We're all discombobulated. A pint-size girl living alone on the water?" She shivered. "It gives me chills just thinking about what could happen. Seriously, Jackson. You're going to have to find a way to get her to take lessons. Tomorrow. Not a day later."

"Maybe we could blackmail her." Obviously, that was Olive.

"What? Like, Alex, if you don't do what we want, we're going to pack you in a trunk and ship you off to a deserted island? Oh. Wait. She's already there." Jackson laughed. Except maybe Olive was serious.

"Ha. Ha. You have any better idea?"

"Not blackmail, that's for sure." Jackson snagged her shirt and gave her a shoulder bump followed by a hug.

Meanwhile, Ellie was squinting. A sure sign she was thinking. "Maybe not an entirely crazy idea, Olive."

Jackson rubbed his eyes and sighed. "Oh, no. Don't tell me you've gone over to the dark side, too, Ellie."

"I wasn't thinking blackmail like, 'You give me your first born or

I tell the feds how you were the one who heisted the Liberty Bell." Jackson waited. Olive leaned in closer. "I was thinking, more like we tell her we need her."

"How's that supposed to—"

"We, as in the community, need her . . ."

"So, in exchange for our labor, she . . ." Jackson trailed off.

"From the supplies that have been arriving for her, it looks like she's an artist." Jackson gave her a look. She took a sip of coffee and shrugged. "I wasn't snooping. Exactly."

Olive chugged the dregs of her hot chocolate and nodded, like a bobble-head doll. "That could work. We need her to, let's see, we need her to help disadvantaged kids. To . . . give them art classes."

"But we can't pay her. The county doesn't have the money," Ellie added.

"Maybe," Jackson said. "But I doubt that orchestrating a big community event is something she'll jump on." He went over to the bank of windows along the south wall of the loft, which looked out over the docks and out to the island.

"Fine," Olive intoned. "I mean, yes, she's might be a bit of a recluse. But she's friendly. Although, she must want peace and quiet if she signed up to live out on the island. And it's obvious that she's not interested in creature comforts especially . . ." Olive mused out loud.

"The key to helping her, is going to be to get to know her," Ellie said.

Jackson had a dozen things he wished he knew about Alex, not the least of which included the obvious, like what was that shock, how was she letting power on the island and what was she escaping from?

Escape. He didn't know where that thought came from. But somehow it resonated. Maybe she was running away from an abusive boyfriend.

"Jackson?" Olive interrupted his thoughts.

He was letting his imagination run away with him.

"Jackson!"

He turned to Olive and Ellie in time to see a large smirk spread across Olive's face. "I got it! We infiltrate the island. We keep showing up. What's she going to do? She's too nice to send us packing. In the meantime, we learn more about her. Then, like mom said, we'll know what type of blackmail will work."

Jackson rolled his eyes and shook his head, as Olive rambled on about how she was going to be Super Spy or Spy Girl and how she was going to get her man. Woman in this case. That she'd find Alex's weak spot and then Alex would have to let them help.

"No," Jackson interrupted. "We have to give her space."

Before Olive could protest, the door slammed open. "Are you guys looking for trouble?" Gabe, the harbor master, and more importantly, Ellie's friend since grade school, stomped into the room. "What would Jake have to say about all this Machiavellian plotting?"

"Uh, oh." Olive headed for the stairs to get out of the line of fire.

"Mind your own business, Gabe. If Jake isn't here, he doesn't get a vote."

"Jake is out trying to make a living. You, on the other hand, Elllie, are here cooking up trouble." He gave her the evil eye. "Like always."

Ellie humphed. "How much trouble can anyone get into on an island the size of a beluga."

"Don't get me started, El."

"Don't get me started," she warned right back.

Jackson took the stairs in twos, following Olive's lead, escaping what he knew was going to be the same old argument: Gabe, defending Jake's career, having given up the safety of the Harbor Master's job in favor of commercial fishing and Ellie shouting right back at him her three favorite phrases: fishing was dangerous, he had a family to think of and what the fuck did he go to Stanford for in the first place anyway.

That was a whole other story. One he had no power over. The situation with Alex was different. Even though Jackson could see that this whole thing was a recipe for disaster, he had no choice. He was going to stick with Olive because that's what friends do.

And in that way, his fate was sealed. Even if he was the last to realize it. Olive met him at the top of the stairs, looking despondent.

"Don't worry, Ollie. You know your mom can hold her own with Gabe."

"That's not what I'm worried about," she sighed, leaning into Jackson.

"Then what?"

"How's your arm? For real." He looked surprised. As if he'd forgotten all about slamming his elbow into a hard stone floor hours earlier. "Fine. But that's not it. What's wrong?"

"You're leaving."

"August. That's ages."

"Not."

"I'll be back weekends."

"Promise?"

He nodded and hooked his pinkie to hers. "Pinkie swear."

Her mouth quirked up on one side. "Okay then. Now. What are we going to do about Alex?"

Chapter Eight

Tony Soprano and Machiavelli

I've got it!" Olive was busy chopping carrots in the cafe's kitchen, while Jackson leaned against the prep station, waiting for her to continue. "We've been going about this the wrong way. She's never going to do our bidding if she doesn't trust us." She splashed water at Jackson, emphasizing her point.

Olive should get that Supergirl outfit, Jackson thought. Or better still, apply for the FBI, CIA or Homeland Security rather than bothering with photography and journalism, her current dream jobs. She was the perfect balance of innocence and deviousness. Add a set of pearls and a glock and she'd be perfect for the job. Jackson on the other hand was knee-deep in guilt over Olive's plotting and campaign of manipulation and she knew it.

"Don't be such a wuss. It's for her own good," Olive noted.

"You look like an angel, but really you're the devil in XTRATUFs," he teased, half meaning it.

"Well, you look all Nick Nolte/Hugh Jackman, but inside you're actually a cupcake. All sweet and gooey. Ooey, gooey, goodness."

He put his palm on her cheek and pushed her away, making ack ack sounds all the while.

Ignoring him, Olive opened her iPad and googled, "How to gain someone's trust" while Jackson, knowing Olive and how if he didn't help, she would come up some truly crazy ideas, came up with his own list.

"Okay. 1. Be honest 2. Be straightforward about what you're going to do and then do it. 3. Be sincere. 4. Don't try to change the other person."

Olive made a barfing sound. "Those will never work! Look," she said, pointing to a website called, amazingly enough, 5 Incredible Psychological Tricks to Get Anyone to Do What You Want.

1. Advance someone's goals to get them to do you a favor.

2. Mimic people's body language to get them to like you.

3. Confuse people to get them to comply with your request.

4. Ask people for favors when they're tired in order to get them to cooperate.

5. Scare people, so they'll have to give you what you need.

I like it."

"We're going to hell." That's all there was to it. If Olive and Ellie had their way. And he was going along for the ride. Out of what? Loyalty? Duty? Devotion? Three words that pretty much meant the same thing. The situation actually called for three different words. Stupid. Dim-witted. And idiotic. Yep. That described him perfectly.

"Jack, you look like your head is about to explode. Go. Sit." Olive pointed to a chair.

If only she knew. Sitting wasn't going to help. A boatload of Aleve wasn't going to help. An alien brain transfer? Nope. It was not going to help. Nothing. Was. Going. To. Help.

"So, here's the deal. You saw how when she got here she didn't want to be photographed? Step One: We keep photographers away from her. And did you notice how she doesn't like to talk about herself? That's 2. We create a cover story for why she needs her space so people will leave her alone. So far so good. Right? It will endear us to her."

Jackson was too dazed to reply. If Tony Soprano and Machiavelli had a baby—

"And you know how Alex knows nothing about surviving in Alaska? Well, I got this one covered, too. I ask you questions about something she really needs to know, making sure she overhears us. Meanwhile, I act all interested, like I don't already know the answers."

If it wasn't so sneaky, it would be funny.

Which made him smile in spite of himself.

CHAPTER NINE

How to Clean a Lighthouse

Before I started on this journey, I learned one thing—you can find anything on Google. Only, apparently, it's not so. There is no Google guidance on how best to clean a lighthouse. In lieu of the aforementioned non-existent advice, I was going to have to go with plain, old-fashioned common sense. Start from the top and work my way down. I carted a broom to the uppermost landing, pulled on a disposable face mask and began sweeping. 201 steps, 8 landings and 6 hours later and I had every turd, feather, clump of seaweed and rotten leaf swept out of the lighthouse and over the rocks toward the churning sea.

My knees refused to move another inch; exhausted, I heaved myself onto a large rock on the beach, set my broom down and allowed the sound of the surf to wash over me. Crashing waves. Sea birds squawking. A small whistle. Hmm. I must have imagined the sound, but there is was again. A whistle. More persistent this time.

I crawled down from the rock and edged into the water. Fog had rolled in and now it was hard to distinguish the sea from land. I followed the sound of the whistle until I saw a dolphin, nosing something forward. I crept deeper into the water so that now the waves were lapping over my knees, in time for a wave to carry a tiny, ball of fur to me.

Nothing in my research had prepared me for this. A gift from a dolphin? Should I pick it up? What if it was poisonous or rabid? Or worse, dead. I heard a mew, no a moan, so soft I wasn't sure if it might have been the wind. Dangerous or not, I couldn't leave it. I lifted the fur ball to my chest to warm it up and there it was again. A shock. Not as strong as before. I ignored it. Because looking up at me, with big brown eyes, too big for such a tiny frame, was the most trusting creature I had ever met. A waterlogged and barely breathing puppy.

I looked back to the place where I had last seen the dolphin, but it was gone. Odd. I had heard of dolphins rescuing drowning people. Never of them saving a drowning puppy. I tucked the puppy into my shirt next to my heart. I had never had a pet before, but I knew I had to keep him warm. "Don't die on me. Please."

I didn't need a book on how to nurse a puppy back to health to know that dehydration was the enemy. My parents had insisted on signing me up for First Aid training on my 10th birthday. I'm not sure what they thought was going to happen. Would I be called on to repair a broken arm when a school mate fell off the swings? Give CPR, heaven forbid, to my mom or dad? My parents had lots of things I was required to do and learn, but I was rarely given explanations. The term, Brook No Dissent, came to mind.

For lack of a baby bottle, I would have to hand feed the puppy. Exhausted or not. In my art supplies was a new airbrush which included a tube and a tank. That would do. I found the appropriate box, sifted through until I found the airbrush then filled it with water. Inside the lighthouse, with the midnight sun shining through the curved window, I sank down to the floor, my back to the wall and squirted small amounts of liquid into her willing mouth. Slowly, over the next few minutes, her breathing evened out, her heart beat became less erratic until she shifted deeper into my chest, snoring softly.

My eye lids fluttered and closed. A creaky noise coming from somewhere I couldn't pinpoint made me open them again. I listened but the sound was not repeated. Old buildings and creaky noises. I couldn't let myself wander down the path of ghosts and goblins that old buildings conjure up. Or let myself think about the sounds of home. The sweet song of ospreys in the spring. A train horn in the distance. The tree branches brushing against my bedroom window.

I fell asleep again and awoke much later with my head tilted at an uncomfortable angle, my shoulder wet with drool, my knees, neck and back creaky and stiff. Whether I could get to a standing position without help was questionable at that point.

Life is strange. For a while I thought I'd never get rid of Jackson and Olive and now I hadn't seen them for almost a week. In that time, I'd disinfected every surface of the lighthouse, dragged my twin memory foam mattress to the top of the lighthouse. Up all 201 steps. By myself. Or, actually, with the help of my new puppy, who refused to be separated from me for more than ten seconds at a time. So it was move the mattress up one landing, retrieve puppy, deposit her on the landing, take a breather, then move the mattress up another landing, followed by puppy. At least I would stay fit.

Definitely the runt of her litter and small by any standard, I decided to call her Peanut. She was healthy now. Eating mashed up fresh fish that I managed to catch myself, along with canned veggies. We ate the same food and were none the worse for the loss of cereal and grilled cheese. Life on our tiny island was good.

I wasn't, however, kidding myself regarding the long-term issues of living on an island. Winter would be coming soon enough and even though no one was going to catch hantavirus, plague or worse, now that the cleanup was complete, the lighthouse was far from ready. I needed to seal cracks, replace windows, shore up some of the rocks by the dock that were threatening to cave in and repair shutters for when a big storm blew in. Oh, and build a fence so that Peanut could roam without wandering off or falling back into the sea, which was now at the top of my To Do list.

A quick search of the internet told me that I would need a post hole digger, which was absolutely necessary for the job. I would also have to order fence posts and a gate. It was hard to admit it, but it was possible that I had been hasty in refusing help.

Maybe.

CHAPTER TEN

Friends and Storms Go Together Like Peanut Butter and Chocolate

The next weather report I heard warned of an imminent storm. Of course. But, no problem. Peanut and I could camp on one of the landings where there were no windows so that if a window anywhere in the lighthouse broke, we wouldn't be showered in bits of glass.

I began hauling blankets, non-perishable food, water, an old ball I found outside in the grass, books, flashlight and pillows to the third floor landing. To look at the sea, you would never think a storm was imminent. The water was clear and smooth and calm. Not a single ripple as far as I could see. I walked outside to the water's edge with Peanut trailing behind, stumbling on rocks and clumps of seaweed. I was learning fast that a fact of life on the island was the steady stream of debris that washes up on the sand. Broken shells. Feathers. Glass floats, smelling of brine and fish, from Japan. I was setting several glass balls aside carefully when a boat horn sounded, low and persistent. I looked up to see Olive waving from the deck of Jackson's boat. She called out as they approached. "Storm's coming!"

I waved them off. Go back, I wordlessly messaged. But they ignored me. Jackson expertly maneuvered the boat alongside the dock and began tying up while Olive came leaping over the side, racing down the dock until she reached me in a blur. "Did you hear me? There's a storm coming. And it's going to be a big one."

"Um, okay?"

"We came to bring you home."

It was only then that she glanced down and caught sight of Peanut. She leaned in to get a closer look and Peanut jumped into her arms, tail wagging like a propeller.

"Where did you come from, you little cupcake?" She rubbed his head and looked over at me questioningly.

"She washed ashore, half drowned. "

Olive looked her over, from tail to nose.

Jackson took that moment to show up. "Who are you, little one?" he directed at the pup, fluffing up the hair on the puppy's head as Olive pressed her into Jackson's arms.

"Meet Peanut," I said. "She washed ashore."

It was Jackson's turn to do an inspection. "I hate to tell you. But Peanut is a he."

I'd never had a pet. I'd never taken a life drawing class. Still, you'd think I could tell the difference between a female and male puppy. But in my own defense, Peanut was incredibly tiny and I hadn't actually done an inspection before deciding that he was a she.

"Oops," Olive said.

I felt blood rush to my face. How embarrassing.

"An easy mistake," Jackson said, to ease the awkwardness.

"Yeah." Olive again. "I once thought a guy at the mall in Ketchikan was a girl. I called him ma'am and I thought I was going to die when he set me straight. And then there was the time when we went to Nordies on a trip to Anchorage and I asked a sales lady when her baby was due. I can't even talk about it."

So maybe it wasn't as bad as all that.

"And if you've never seen a pen—," Olive stopped in her tracks. "I mean. Never mind. Let's forget it. We have to get back before the storm hits."

Looking back at the sea, it was as if one large black cloud had descended like an enormous umbrella. The wind began to roar and the waves picked up, whipping against the rocks. I'd seen storms come in fast in New Jersey, but nothing like this. I could barely hear as Jackson shouted to Olive to come help unload the supplies and for me and Peanut to run for cover before the inevitable downpour.

Peanut was shaking furiously as great streaks of lightning lit the sky. I needed to help Olive and Jackson, but I couldn't leave Peanut. I ran for the cottage, counting the seconds and holding my breath until the two of them came running in after us minutes later.

A quick check told us our cell phones were out. Every one of them, along with the electricity. The storm was so strong now that Jackson could no longer get to the ship-to-shore radio on the boat to let Ellie know we were safe. For the time being, there was nothing to do except light some candles, hope we didn't run out of matches, snuggle under piles of covers and wait. Because no one was getting back to the Prince of Wales Island tonight.

"Do you have any dog biscuits?" Olive asked from under her pile of covers.

I dug into my pocket and handed over a piece of dried fish. "He loves these."

"Speaking of which, he is going to need a new name. How 'bout Jasper? He looks like a Jasper to me. Don't you," she said, nuzzling her nose to his. "What'dya say, Jack?"

Jackson ran a hand along Peanut's bony spine. "Poseidon."

"No. People would end up calling him Poo. Not going to happen. How about Indiana. After Indiana Jones. Because he's so brave and went on a great adventure at sea. Or maybe Gemini? Pancake? Phoenix?"

"Not Phoenix," I said abruptly.

"Okay. Then . . ."

"How about we let Alex decide if she wants to change his name."

I held up both hands in a Don't Fight, Kids kind of way.

"I know," Olive said, not able to let good enough alone. "Juneau."

Actually, it fit. Juneau is the capital of Alaska and he is an Alaska boy.

Jackson looked over at me and he had to be thinking I was going to object, but I surprised them both by saying, "I like it. Juneau it is."

Crowded together on the third floor of the landing while the storm lashed the island actually felt good. I opened a jar of olives and a bag of chips and handed around bottles of sparkling water.

"So . . . how do you like living on the island?" Olive asked over a mouth full of chips.

"Charming," Jackson teased.

"I love it." And I realized it was true. I loved it truly and deeply, like I was meant to be here. "The waves, the sea air, the peace."

"That's all well and good, but—"

"I know. I have a lot to learn."

"Speaking of which," Jackson said. "If you are thinking of buying a boat, you should consider taking a piloting course."

Olive shot him a smile. Like he'd won the battle, but she'd won the war. "No time like the present. It's not like we have anything else to do."

Which meant I got to spend what felt like years listening to Jackson go over Alaska boating law, charts, navigation aids, plotting courses, mariner's compass, converting between true and magnetic north and dead reckoning. And finally, the Seaman's Eye skills for checking that one is on course. If I am remembering correctly. And that was all before he started working on knots. Bowline, square knot, Figure 8, clove hitch, round turn and two half hitches and cleat hitch. The essentials. I admit it. I drifted off a couple of times. Until one of them nudged me awake. Finally I gave up and shook off my sleepiness.

"Where did you learn all of this, Jackson?" I realized I still knew very little about either of them. "Unless you don't want to—"

"Alex, you can ask me anything." He said it with such sincerity, that I felt a twinge of guilt for all the lying I had been doing since I'd arrived in Alaska. "When I was eight, I nearly drowned," he said. "It made me realize that you don't mess around with the ocean. The ocean is amazing, but it can kill you as quick as you can spit."

"Now who's being charming," Olive asked.

"Wouldn't that make you want to stay away from the ocean?" I asked.

"You can choke on a burrito, but you still have to eat. That's how it is with me. The ocean is part of me. Or I'm part of it."

Olive smacked him on the arm. "We're 97% water, so duh."

They continued their sparring, back and forth, as the wind pounded against the lighthouse, making it sway slightly, but me? I let myself drift, with Juneau snoring gently against my chest.

Storm and all, it wasn't a bad way to end the day.

Chapter Eleven

How You Never Know What to Expect

I thought I'd dreamt the storm, because when I awoke the sea was calm, the wind not even a whisper. It was as if the storm had never happened. Olive and Jackson were sprawled out on the floor, snoring. But when I sat up and felt under the covers there was no Juneau. I checked beside Olive. Not there. Getting more worried by the second, I pushed Jackson until he rolled over, but Juneau wasn't there either. I shook Jackson. "Have you seen Juneau?"

Jackson opened one eye. Yawned. "Who?"

"I can't find Juneau!"

He sat up, rubbing his eyes. "Don't panic. He's here somewhere."

I wasn't panicking. My voice had gone up several octaves and my heart was in my throat. I was about to toss my non-existent breakfast. But I was not panicking.

"Did you check upstairs?"

"What's going on?" Olive threw her blankets aside. "I am starving.

Do we have anything to eat?"

"It's Juneau," Jackson said.

"He's missing," I shouted as I took the stairs at a run to the top of the lighthouse.

Jackson went in the other direction. I shouted after him, asking if he'd found any sign of Juneau. No reply.

Olive came up behind me. "We'll find him."

I couldn't breathe. What if, in the storm, a window had blown open and he'd been swept away? What if, out in that terrifying storm all alone, an eagle had gotten him. Or an owl? I couldn't think straight.

"Alex. Stop." Olive wrapped her arms around me. "We'll find him." Jackson called up to us. "I may have found something."

Olive and I raced down the stairs, slippery from where water had seeped in overnight, to the bottom floor where Jackson was pointing to a door to a small wooden structure jutting out from one side of the lighthouse. One I hadn't had time to investigate since it was secured with a rusty lock.

"See that broken part on the bottom. He could have squeezed through there."

Olive lifted her leg into a karate pose. "Let's kick the door in." Jackson grabbed her leg and she went down in a heap. "Ouch."

"What if he's behind the door?" Jackson pulled a knife from his back pocket and began work on the lock. I was counting the seconds until he had the lock popped and was pushing the heavy door open.

"Get a flashlight, Olive."

Olive ran to her stash of supplies and was back in a flash, shining the beam of light through the darkness, all in under a minute.

I peered through the crack in the door. "I don't see him!"

"Hold on." Jackson pushed the door further and stepped through gingerly, pressing a foot on each floor board, to ensure the wooden boards under his feet were solid. The flashlight beam was dim, but inside the room we could see some lone boxes and a stack of wool blankets. A 1942 calendar hung on the wall.

"What the heck?" Jackson yelped as he tripped over something.

"Shesh," Olive said. "Clumsy any?"

"Something tripped me." He crouched down and felt around the floor. His hand hit something. "Here. It's a handle, I think."

Olive came over quickly and hit the spot with the light. "A trap door! Move, let me." She bumped him over and yanked on the handle. It made a sound like warped wood that had been stuck in a frame for a very long time.

Jackson nudged her aside and grabbed the handle with two hands and pulled, then pulled again. It took four or five attempts before the trap door budged. Beneath the door it was dark, but I could make out the top tread of what appeared to be a set of stairs. Who knew how long they had been there or in what condition they were in now. Not that it mattered because Olive didn't care. She brushed past us and leaned into the opening.

"It's not too bad," she said, holding her nose as a cloud of ancient dust and mildew drifted up. "Ack. Ack," she coughed. "I'm fine. Nothing to worry about. Just a little dust."

She twisted around and wiggled into the opening feet first. There was nothing to do but follow. The stairs descended about six or seven feet. The walls were made of packed dirt, supported with wooden cross beams. Above us a single bare bulb flickered although no light switch or pull was noticeable.

Once on solid ground we crept forward single file, as the tunnel was only wide enough for one. Jackson bent since he was too tall to stand up straight without hitting his head on a low beam or collecting who knew how many years worth of spider webs in his hair.

"This is amazing," Olive whispered. If you didn't count the spiders and general creepiness factor. "Where do you think it leads?"

I had been wondering the same thing. We had traveled about twenty-five to fifty feet, if my calculations were correct, scanning for Juneau and finding nothing, before arriving at a second staircase leading back up. This one hadn't fared as well as the first. The walls and floors were rotting in places, with some boards missing altogether. A broken leg or twisted ankle waiting to happen.

Even Olive held back. "What now?"

"Hand me the light." Jackson waved the light around until it landed on a hatch above the stairs. The stairs and hatch were as rotten as the walls and floors, with several steps missing. "Should be easy. You guys stay here."

That command was like a battle cry to Olive. Even I knew that much. Jackson stepped over the worse of the rotting boards, broke through the hatch easily and pulled himself up through the opening. He turned to call to us, but Olive was right behind him, pulling herself up without any help from him, thank you very much.

Long story short, we found ourselves in the abandoned keeper's cottage which was about 50 feet from the lighthouse. On the bright side there wasn't a dead creature in sight. No bags of moldering trash. No pirates, drug caches or a single sign of clandestine groups having held meetings here within the last forty years, I guessed, from the current level of dust and decay.

The cottage was basic and functional. I immediately set about looking for Juneau. Four tiny rooms. A kitchen, dining and living room in one. A bunk room held a twin bed with a carved head and foot board and a damp mattress. A minuscule office hosted a metal desk and swivel chair. A newspaper with the headline, "Alaska becomes the 49th State", was tacked up on the wall. And a powder room. Shower, toilet, sink. No sign of Juneau.

The sound of crashing wood followed by a yelp made me run back into the living room in time to see Jackson leaning through a new hole in the floor. I rushed over to him. The hole was across the room from where we had entered, heaven help us, Olive was gone.

"Olive! Are you hurt?" Jackson shouted down the opening.

"Old ladder. Behind the cottage," I said.

He nodded curtly, handed me the flashlight and rushed out. While he was gone, I tucked the flashlight into my back pocket, dropped into the hole and landed none-too-gracefully on the bottom.

Olive was stretched out on the floor next to me. I put my face to hers. She was breathing steadily. Then I quickly ran my hands over her arms and legs. No protruding bones and she didn't yelp in pain at my touch. I was about to call her name when something brushed up against my side. I desperately hoped it wasn't a rat or something worse. A furry creature climbed onto Olive and started licking her face. "Juneau!" Olive whispered.

Thank goodness.

"Olive. Are you okay? Where does it hurt?"

She gave an almost imperceptible nod. "Ouch. My head."

"As is to be expected."

"I think I'm going to hurt like hell tomorrow."

"So true." I breathed more freely than I had in I don't know how long. Olive was conscious and Juneau was found.

"Where are we?" Olive asked. "One minute I was telling Jackson how clumsy he was and the next, I'm . . . Where am I?"

Initially, I had suspected that we were in a long-forgotten well, but it turned out to be another room. The floor and walls and ceiling were comprised of roughly hewn wood, with a single light bulb above. I reached for the cord and a dim light filled the room to show a row of shelves holding rusty tools, jars of preserves, lanterns, rope and fishing nets. In the opposite corner of the room were stacks of boxes along with a dust-covered trunk of unknown origin.

Spying the old trunk, Olive sat up easily. "Wow. An old sea captain's trunk. We need to investigate."

"Not now," I said as a narrow ladder came down through the opening. "Alex, are you down there? Is Olive okay?"

"She's fine." I turned back to Olive. "The trunk can wait. We need to get you out of here."

"But."

"No buts. We are getting you out of here so we can do a proper check. You may have a concussion. Or a broken scaphoid."

"Or a twisted ankle. A shattered skull. I get it. But, Alex. I'm not going anywhere until you at least check out that door that's behind the chest."

What door?

"I don't see any door. Come on. Let's see if you can stand. Because that ladder is not going to climb itself."

I handed Juneau up to Jackson first, then with him pulling from above and me pushing from below, we got Olive back to the cottage, where she excitedly turned to Jackson. "Jack, you wouldn't believe it. There's a pirate's hideout down there."

He looked over at me, checking to see if it was the concussion talking. I shrugged.

"And a treasure chest. Not to mention there's another secret door. And we all know that when where's one hidden staircase, there must be more!"

I wondered why there would have to be more. But Olive read my mind.

"Think about it. That dock wasn't always here. Smugglers had to have someplace to stash their booty."

It was looking like Olive hadn't suffered any permanent physical damage. Still, Jackson did all of the first responder things you do while Juneau looked on, making sure Jackson didn't leave anything out.

Once Olive was proclaimed "fit for duty", Jackson stood. "We have to get back. Ellie will be worried sick."

Olive nodded with a disappointed look on her face. The hunt for secret tunnels, staircases and treasure would have to wait for another day. And there would be another day, if I knew anything about Olive at all.

"At least Juneau's safe," I said by way of cheering her up. "I can't begin to tell you how much I appreciate your finding him."

Jackson opened the cottage door. I was about to follow when he took off running.

It couldn't be. But it was. A huge chunk of the dock was missing.

Along with Jackson's beloved boat.

CHAPTER TWELVE

Wolf vs Dog

"You should start a blog. Seriously. I don't know the title yet, but think about it. Jersey girl comes to island in Alaska. Adopts a wolf. Loses boat. Finds secret tunnel. Gets stranded on a deserted island. People would eat it up," Olive informed me.

I didn't know how to answer. It was my fault that Jackson's boat was missing, but what was that about a wolf? Or me blogging. I'd come to a remote place in Alaska to get away from, well, everything. But, wait. Wolf?!

Jackson was frowning. I would too in his place. "Olive, you know as well as I do that it's illegal to domesticate a wolf pup in Alaska. Not that Juneau is a wolf. So don't go around saying that. Got it?" He shifted his focus to me. "Ignore her. She's off her meds."

Does anyone ever ignore Olive? She is as persistent as the tides when she wants to be, but even Olive could not change the fact that she and

Jackson were stranded here. At least until cell service returned or someone on the mainland came out to rescue them.

I couldn't do anything about that, but I could start with finding a way to keep Juneau, my perfect little escape artist, safe.

"Whatcha doing?" Olive asked. I jumped. She has a bad habit of sneaking up on people.

I looked out to the sandy beach where broken pallets, dock boards, heavy rope and old bottles had drifted ashore. From the bits and pieces, we had enough raw materials now to cobble together a small play yard for Juneau.

The universe was shining on us by giving us work to keep our minds off the colossal mess we were in. We finished the enclosure quickly and with Juneau inside, proceeded to work on the tunnel stairs and hatch until we were exhausted and starving.

Olive offered to fix a makeshift lunch while Jackson went to organize the left-over beach debris. I was covered in dirt, sweat and graime from head to toe. I wandered into the cottage, taking Juneau with me, to see if there was any chance for warm water today and—miracle of miracles— water came out of the rusty shower head, blissfully clean and warm. I shed my clothes and hopped in. Puppy and all. I let the stream of water wash over us. I scrubbed myself from my toes to the top of my head while Juneau jumped around in the spray joyfully.

Finally and reluctantly, I stepped out of the shower, dried myself quickly, then slipped on my T-shirt and jeans. Juneau shook himself off, raining water on my dry clothes. I didn't care. I felt heavenly. At least until the door to the cottage blasted open.

"Hurry up," Olive shouted. "You're not going to believe what we found!"

Olive was already racing back toward Jackson before I got to the door. I didn't know how much more excitement I could take. I was used to quiet days reading and listening to music, with an equally quiet and contemplative family. Juneau ran ahead, caught up with Olive and leaped into the air in his excitement.

Reminder to all. Not a wolf.

The waves crashed around Olive's ankles as she waved something above her head, jumping around as energetically as Juneau. I moved closer, the wet sand between my toes and the sun in my eyes. It reminded me of laying on the beach under a large multi-colored umbrella at the Jersey shore.

"Earth to Alex." Olive was almost to me. "We found an actual message in an actual bottle."

My heart leapt. When I was a kid, I was obsessed with finding a message in a bottle. I can't even tell you the number of hours I'd scoured the shore in the hopes of finding one. While other kids were building sand castles and sunbathing and collecting shells, I searched for the illusive message in a bottle.

"Did you know that the oldest bottle ever found with a message in it was part of an experiment?"

She rolled her eyes, as in Who Cares.

Which did nothing to deter me. "It was 1906. A marine biologist in England tossed over a thousand bottles with messages into the ocean in order to research ocean currents."

"Fascinating."

"The last bottle that was found from his experiment was at sea for 108 years, 4 months and 18 days. It was found in 2015. A woman vacationing on Amrum Island in Germany found it."

"Forget her. Look at this."

Olive's enthusiasm was contagious. I took the pro-offered bottle. The glass was cloudy and rippled like an old window.

She grabbed it back. "Too slow. Look what I found inside."

She held up a perfectly preserved piece of paper, as old as the bottle. And there was indeed a message. "I can't read it," Olive moaned. "Is it Latin? Greek?"

"Neither." Jackson peered over her shoulder. "It's someone's idea of a joke. That isn't a real language."

I reached out and barely touched a corner of the page, steadying myself, too late. The blood left my head in one large rush. My arms and legs turned to lead. My vision faded. My stomach lurched. The temperature was rising. Then the world started spinning.

Until it didn't.

CHAPTER THIRTEEN

Olive Tells Her Story

It was love at first sight." I put a hand over my heart and sighed. It was so romantic.

"Are you kidding me? They didn't even speak." Jackson

"It was the way they looked at each other. True. Love."

"Olive. Lay back down," Jackson said. "The doc said you have to rest. Your mom too."

"I'm not a baby"

"Whatever."

"If I rest any more I'm going to turn into a pumpkin," I groaned.

"More like a potato. A couch potato. And on what planet does two strangers staring at each other equal love?"

"You wouldn't know love if it came up and bit you," I said. "And they weren't staring. They were looking. It's kismet. Two parts of one soul meeting."

"Oh. Barf."

Ellie came in on "barf." "Olive, lay down right now or I am going to ship Jackson off and you will recuperate in your room," she threatened. "Alone. No company of any kind. Got it?"

"Yeah. Yeah."

Ellie sat down with a book and my argument with Jackson continued, albeit quieter than before.

"I'd say you were crazy, but you have a head injury." Jackson

"You want to make a bet?" Olive

"That you have a head injury?" Jackson

"No. That what we were witnessing was love at first sight. Mom, tell him."

"If it will get you two to stop bickering. Okay. Start from the beginning. How did it go down? I'm listening," Ellie said on a sigh.

"So, Alex fainted. You knew that part."

Ellie nodded, patiently.

"So then Jackson gives me a hard time. Accusing me. 'What did you do to her?'"

"So you know, I didn't do anything. Here's what really happened. Alex tried to read the message in the bottle and then fainted. Know-it-all over there (aka Jackson) rushed in, all bossy like. 'Don't move her. She's in shock.' I rolled my eyes, obviously."

'It was too much hard work on an empty stomach. She's not used to it,' Jackson insisted.

It was obvious to me what was wrong. Stress from nearly losing Juneau. Which makes a lot more sense. No one who comes to fix up a lighthouse on a tiny island in the middle of nowhere is afraid of hard work.

We got her sitting up, but she was acting strange. Right, Jack? I can't explain it. Remote. Making believe nothing happened. I wanted to ask her about it, but a boat horn sounded and yay, Coast Guard to the rescue. Then Jackson waved and shouted. 'Woo hoo. We're saved!'"

"That was you, dork."

"Prove it."

"Okay, you two. I get it. For whatever reason, she fainted. How was she when you left?"

"Fine. But that's not the best part. Don't look at me like that. You know what I mean. After the Coast Guard showed up to rescue us, we were on our way home and they took the long way around, looking for other people stranded by the storm. We were passing Noah's houseboat and that's when it happened. He was out on his deck looking out over the water. She was leaning against the boat railing. They looked right at each other and it was as if lightning passed between them."

"O.M.G. Check her eyes, Ellie. Her head injury must be worse than I thought," Jackson said.

"And then Alex insisted on going back to the island. Said she was fine. Needed to clean up after the storm. We didn't want to."

"The Coast Guard can't just kidnap people, Ollie."

"So, we turned back and dropped her off."

"Jackson. You'd better get going," Ellie interjected. "Find your boat. Olive, you fell down a hole and hit your head, so it's bedtime for you. And what the hell were you doing, anyway? Never mind. Get to bed. Now! We'll talk about this later."

End of story. Except, Jackson can deny it all he wants, but weird things keep happening when Alex is around. Fine. Don't believe me. But then why do the lights go on when she walks into the lighthouse? And why do they go off when she leaves?

When there was no way there could be electricity on the island in the first place.

Chapter Fourteen

Caves, Mysteries and Right Back Where I started

The weather wasn't exactly cold and yet I was chilled straight through my clothes and into my bones, even though I had Juneau tucked into my jacket and he was as warm as a heating pad. Maybe I was coming down with something. Or maybe climbing over slippery rocks and drenched beaches to get to the other side of the island wasn't such a good idea. The beaches were covered in seaweed and shells from the storm. Bits of washed up coral was making walking treacherous and the wind was howling again, knocking me off balance.

Regardless, I had no choice. From my vantage point on the boat, I had noticed what appeared to be an entrance to a cave on the other side of the island. I had to know if there were any places where people could hide since strange things had been happening, including the message in a bottle.

My phone beeped. A text message from Olive. "Mom has me in

bed. I. Am. So. Freaking. Bored. What are you doing?"

Which made me smile. Me? Just looking for boogie men.

"Cleaning up. Nothing interesting happening here."

"Mom took me to the doc. Just a sprain and no permanent brain damage. LOL."

I texted back. "I really sorry you got hurt. What can I do to help?"

"I'm cool. Reading. The Art of War."

It was hard to believe Olive was in high school. She could take over the world if not for being stuck on an island in southeast Alaska.

"I'll call you later." I slipped the phone into my pocket and stopped to consider my options. Should I continue searching the island or turn back and get to work setting up my studio? I was already half way there, so I pushed on. Thinking about the letter all the while. "Come home," it read. Was the letter meant for me or was this an unbelievable coincidence? Did it mean someone knew where I was and, more importantly, would that someone be coming to get me?

I turned the questions over in my mind, but nothing came to me as I continued along the beach to where it narrowed and the waves had cleaned the sand rather than leaving anything behind. A steep, craggy hill loomed above me to my right, close to the water's edge. I continued on past the closest side the hill, expecting to find more of the same topography and instead stumbled into a gaping opening.

A cave. This was what I had come for, but in truth had been hoping

I would not find. I peered inside and took a deep breath, then I nearly jumped out of my skin. Whew. It was only a text message from Olive. I took a calming breath. Keep breathing, I reminded myself. Olive. What was I going to do about her? If I ignored the text, she would keep sending text after text.

"Still bored. What are you doing now?"

If she was going to ask me what I was doing every five minutes, this was going to be a very long day.

I replied. "Exploring a cave." Then deleted it. "Reading. The Count of Monte Cristo."

"It's official. Your life is as boring as mine. Talk to you later. Mom just arrived with soup. She's confiscating my phone. Love you."

Which reminded me of my mother. Every night before I went to bed, she would say, "I love you and I like you."

And still I ran away.

Inside the cave, the walls shone with a soft, blue light. I knew enough science to understand that some life forms can produce light, as well as certain bacteria. But I didn't know they lived in Alaska. The thought of millions of bacteria living on the walls of the cave made me want to run in the opposite direction. Entering any cave is eerie enough without worrying about being assaulted by unknown microorganisms, among other things. As I delved deeper into the cave, I heard something skittering around by my feet and went for my flashlight. It was gone. That was enough for me.

I turned and ran. Back to the beach where my flashlight lay on the rocks, apparently having dropped out of my backpack. I leaned down and palmed it. Something in the air felt different from before. I glanced up. Had that jetty been there before? The one peeking out of the water, encircling the land as far as I could see. Was it low tide?

I sank down onto the sand and let Juneau scamper on the beach. He raced between the rocks and seaweed, trying to catch the waves as they rushed onto the shore, charging them as they receded, leaving a foamy spray behind.

No one would be landing a boat on this side of the island. The jetty would make sure of that. And Juneau would ensure that no one would surprise me in my sleep. I was safe. I repeated it to myself slowly. I was safe.

I unpacked the snacks I had brought. Juneau settled in beside me and gnawed on a treat while I ate a chocolate chip granola bar. Fortified by chocolate, I resolved to finish the job I had started, determined to approach this like a scientist. Systematically. Logically. Analytically. And with an open mind. Not jumping at every sound. Or running away at the first unknown I came across. Keeping these goals in mind, I scooped up Juneau and proceeded, one step at a time. The flashlight helped to keep my fears at bay. No super rats charged me when we ventured into the cave. I moved in deeper. No sleeping bags or food caches were in evidence, hinting at recent squatters. No bare bones. Human or otherwise. Much further in, the cave ceiling rose to fifty feet or so above my head and the path widened until we met a stream of aquamarine water with a path on one side. Where I'd been expecting the cave to get darker, it actually grew lighter and brighter, as light bounced off the water, creating shifting patterns along the cave walls.

I settled myself on the floor of the cave with Juneau beside me and switched off the flashlight. It was mesmerizing. Better than the Atlantic Ocean under a super moon at the Jersey shore, where my family vacationed each year. I wished they could see this.

The next thing I knew, I was waking up. I didn't know what time it was. My phone battery was dead. Juneau snored softly in his sleep. I stretched. My legs and back were stiff enough for me to know that we'd been here for quite some time. I got up, unsteadily and picked Juneau up. He continued to sleep as I slipped him inside my jacket and continued our journey.

We must have walked for twenty minutes or more as the cave grew darker and darker. I was fumbling for the flashlight when I literally ran into a door. There was no rusty lock or hinges on this door. There were plenty of cobwebs, though. Good. It meant no one had used the door for a very long time. I leaned in and pushed. It was a harder task than I had expected. I set Juneau down.

"Juneau, stay."

I leaned into the door with my back and pushed, again and again. Nothing. Hmm. Of course. I pulled. The door shifted an inch. Then, as I pulled harder, it shifted again. Until finally, I managed an opening that was barely wide enough for me to squeeze through sideways, with only a minor scrape or two.

It wasn't what I'd expected. What had I been expecting? I'd plowed into this lighthouse project without much thought as to what I might be getting myself into. So, maybe thinking ahead wasn't in my current wheel house. Meaning I couldn't fault myself for being surprised when I pushed past the door. One thing was certain. Olive would be thrilled.

I was right back where the mystery had started.

In the little room Olive had fallen into earlier today.

CHAPTER FIFTEEN

How To Get Rid Of Unwanted Visitors (Without Feeling Guilty)

I wanted to explore the room, but Juneau was having none of it. He rushed the ladder, punctuated with sharp barks. This was not his I'm Hungry bark. Nor his Let Me Roam the Beach in Privacy Because I've Been Holding It In For Too Long bark. This one was high pitched. A new kind of urgent. Intruder! Intruder! It shouted.

"Alex!" a distant voice called.

I took the ladder steps two at a time with Juneau under one arm, climbed up into the cabin and peered out the door. I didn't recognize the voice, nor the person pulling himself up onto the dock, in one swift, agile move, calling my name as if he knew me. Then he saw me and stopped. I didn't move.

"Olive said—" The wind took the rest of his words. He apparently knew Olive. Which meant he wasn't here on a mission from my family. I let out the breath I was holding.

Another minute, then two, passed.

"I'm Noah," he called out.

Juneau, who had stopped barking, wiggled down abruptly from my arms and rushed the stranger. Noah, if I'd heard him correctly, scooped him up and rubbed Juneau's head with his knuckles, leaning in so their foreheads were touching.

So maybe he was okay.

"What a fine wolf pup, you are," he muttered into Juneau's ear.

Or not.

I rushed over and yanked Juneau from his arms and stood tall. A gladiator preparing to defend her fort. "He is not a wolf. You live in Alaska. You should know that." I glared at him, taking several steps back.

"Actually—" he started.

"Actually," I interrupted, "what are you doing here? I don't remember sending an invitation."

One corner of his mouth turned up.

"And what's that look?" I mean, really. A look that said he knew something I didn't know. Or maybe he was laughing. Not funny.

I continued to glare and the minutes continued to pass with neither of us moving.

"Fine. Suit yourself. You can leave now."

He stayed.

"I mean it. Scoot." I waved a hand at him, shooing him away.

Lightning shot across the sky.

"You're definitely alive."

Duh, as Olive would say.

Dark clouds blew in. Storms came in fast in Alaska. This was the second reminder I had of that fact.

He turned and headed for the dock, laughing. Seriously. Laughing? What the f . . . fruitcake.

He hopped down into his skiff. Another gymnastic move. And pushed away from the dock.

The wind howled his farewell.

First. What the heck was all that about? Secondly, I didn't know what Olive had to do with this, but she was going to regret it. And lastly. I have never spoken to another soul that way in any of the 148,963,200 breaths I've taken in my life.

What had gotten into me? Maybe it was Alaska. A wild place calling for carefree, even careless, behavior. Maybe I was finally emerging from my chrysalis.

I was not going to feel guilty. Noah deserved it. He had no business barging in on me, making a pest of himself, and calling Juneau a WOLF! Now he would likely go back to Prince of Wales Island and tell Olive that I was inhospitable. Rude. A brat.

Oddly enough, I could live with that.

It didn't take long before the text from Olive arrived: "What happened? Noah offered to go out and check on you when I couldn't reach you and you turned on him like a mama bear protecting her cubs. What gives? P.S. I found a skiff for you. Cheap. Good condition. You're going to need it."

I acknowledged that I was going to need something. Possibly to have my head examined, as an old friend of mine used to suggest. But now was not the time to think about missing him. Or anyone else from home for that matter. Yes, I needed an easy to handle vessel so I wouldn't have to depend on Olive or Jackson or anyone else to get to town and back with supplies or to haul trash and laundry. But I wasn't ready to answer her text either. She'd sent someone out to the island. A stranger. To my sanctuary. Refuge. Etc. Etc. She has a big heart, but I was drawing the line. I was not her charity case. She didn't have to rescue me. Which started me thinking. What was it about me that made her think I needed rescuing?

Text from Olive: "I know you're there."

Ignoring her, I got to work on setting up my painting studio. I nudged the easel over a few inches to afford me the best view of the clouds that perched far above the water. I already had an image sketched out in my mind. The view was inspiring, but empty landscapes were never my style. I paint images with quirky characters doing the unexpected: a child bathing a wide-eyed puppy in an antiquated washing machine, an unnaturally tall octogenarian balancing in a canoe while holding an umbrella to catch a breeze that was blowing hard across a pond. My favorite was a heron soaring across the sky with a cherry ice pop dripping onto fields of poppies below. In broad strokes and brilliant colors.

It would be impossible for me not to paint Olive. And Juneau.

Another text from Olive interrupted my reverie. "What do you say to the boat? The seller will take payments. You don't have to come up with any money now. He wants it out of his garage. Like soon!"

Meaning. Stop Ignoring Me.

She continued, "Oh, and I forgot to mention. We're having a work party for the community center tomorrow. Unless you want to be That Person, you need to be there."

What I needed was a dictionary: Alaskan to English. How did a 16- year-old-going-on-17 manage to take control over my life in such a short amount of time? I did understand one thing, though. I had better show up at that work party or the entire island would decide not only was I an inhospitable, rude brat, but a city snob who had moved here to take their lighthouse and who didn't give a fig about giving back to the community. I'd seen the bumper stickers. Tourists stay crunchy - even in milk. Accompanied by a photo of a polar bear. And another one: Cheechakos: They're magically delicious. A cheechako being anyone new to Alaska. You see my point. Fit in or regret it. Fortunately, it appears anyone can fit in. As long as you remember community is everything. That and nature. Don't abuse animals. Don't hunt illegally. Don't snag a fish then act like you caught it legally. (I read a pamphlet.) Don't sit back while the town needs you.

I was buying a boat. And going to a work party.

Woo-hoo. Or is it, Ye ha?

But that was tomorrow. Now, with Juneau tucked into his blankets, I started sketching like I was possessed. A rough hewn boat tossed about on a furious sea. Poseidon's fork pierced through tiny boat's name: The Chinook.

Oh, God. It suddenly occurred to me that I shouldn't have sent Noah back out into an approaching storm. I am such a—. Stop. No time for recriminations. I didn't know how, but I had to find out if Noah was safe.

A text from Olive beeped: "I get it. I'm bossy. Ignore me. But you really don't want to miss out on this boat. In other news: I am picking you up for the work party tomorrow bright and early. In your new boat. PS. Do you have Carhartts? Never mind. I'll find some for you."

I looked up from my phone to find that the storm had subsided. At least now I didn't have to find a surreptitious way to check up on Noah.

Juneau looked up at me, telegraphing a message of his own and I knew what he was thinking. What the heck are Carhartts?

Exactly my question, Juneau. Exactly my question.

Chapter Sixteen

Keep Alaska Weird

Alaska is called the last frontier. I'm not sure why, but it's definitely unique. There are outhouse races, for one. Hard to believe, but true. Ice golf. Oyster slurping. There's also an Ugly Fish Toss. Residents in unique and strange costumes plunge into icy cold water annually for The Polar Plunge. The oddest and most fun event? Frozen turkey bowling. I know all of these things because Olive, having arrived at my door at the crack of dawn, and who hasn't stopped talking since, filled me in on all of the above ways in which Alaskans raise money for charity.

Why all of this was relevant, though, is because Olive feels that between the two of us we can come up with unique and exciting fundraising ideas in order to buy equipment and supplies for the new community center.

I had to wonder how much more unique than frozen turkey bowling one could get, but then again, maybe that's just me.

I had only seen the community center from a distance, but I knew is was reincarnated from a defunct, floating fish-processing barge. For a visual, cross a floating dock with a mini-mall, add a substantial amount of rust, peeling paint, and in this case a leaky roof, and you have a good idea of what the community center currently looks like.

A local processing company donated the barge rather than do the work necessary to pass a stringent annual inspection that was coming up. Since the community center would definitely not be venturing out on the high seas and we had an entire community of volunteers to do the work, it was a perfect solution to address the need for a community center on the island.

"Come on, Alex. We don't have all day," Olive complained loudly.

"What am I going to do about Juneau? I can't leave him here." Good excuse. No one could fault me. You don't leave puppies alone on deserted islands. There had to be a rule about that somewhere in the Alaska handbook.

"He's coming with. Stop stalling."

"He can't." People will say he's a wolf. Not a good plan.

"He can. Stop shaking your head and move it. He can stay at my mom's. Sam will spoil him with dried salmon and fresh blueberries. I already asked."

She should run for office. Manage the women's movement. Take over Google. "Who's Sam?" I wasn't giving in without a fight.

"He helps out at the cafe sometimes. I've known him forever."

It was inevitable. I caved.

She threw a pair of overalls at me. One that matched the ones she was wearing. "Put these on. You're going to need them."

I checked the label. Yep. The elusive and mysterious Carhartts.

I have never purchased a fashion magazine, dressed to fit in or spent a fortune on clothing. But if you've never seen Carhartt overalls, well, even I was afraid to go out in public wearing them. Not only were they an indescribable shade of orange, or maybe yellow, but they were made of an unknown fabric, so stiff that movement became a challenge. I made a mental note to give myself plenty of advance notice should the need for the ladies room arise. I am not vain, but, sorry, I did not want to meet half of Prince of Wales Island wearing what resembled prison wear. In baby shit yellow.

Olive read my thoughts. "Don't worry. Everyone will be wearing them." She patted my back sympathetically. "Or worse."

She didn't mention that mine, being a new pair, would stand out like new cowboy boots in Texas. Not that I had ever been to Texas. I read that somewhere.

My hair pulled back in a ponytail, sporting my brand new Alaska wear, I felt like a little girl playing dress up in daddy's clothes. My plan was to slip them off as soon as Olive wasn't looking. However, it turned out she was right. No one seemed to notice me when we arrived at the dock where the community center was moored. Boisterous music, mixed with laughter, greeted us as we crossed the dock. I was surprised the boat could handle this many people all at once., since I thought it looked like it might collapse under the weight at any moment. Olive, and the rest of the island residents, however, didn't appear to be concerned. Maybe I was being negative. What was a little listing to one side, anyway?

We entered a room that was a good sixty feet in length and thirty feet wide. Heavy canvas tarps, already paint-splattered, were spread across the wooden floor, indicating the work party had started without us. Volunteers were lined up at each wall with long poles sporting paint rollers loaded with paint in a variety of colors. One wall clearly slated to be a cheerful orange. Another lime green.

I recognized Gabe, the harbor master, who looked to be inspecting rivets in the walls and floors. Ellie was at the far end of the room working alongside and speaking in hushed tones to a man I assumed must be Olive's father. Jackson was working on the wall directly in front of us with a group of friends, making good progress on the orange color. I moved in closer.

"Whatcha doing?"

I nearly jumped out of my skin. "Olive!"

"What?"

"You frightened me."

"Well, what were you doing eavesdropping on Creed and Edward?" (Edward of previous kidnapping fame.)

"What?" I feigned innocence to the best of my ability, but lying has never been my strong suit, not having had much practice. Any, in truth.

"You heard me."

I admit, I hesitated. Obfuscate or have to explain what I had been doing?

"I don't have to answer you," I said with a firmness that surprised me.

"You don't have to answer what?" Noah interjected. Where'd he come from?

If I could have screamed, I would have, but that would have been impolite, called undue attention to me and . . . "Nothing," I answered.

"Nothing," Olive repeated, then reconsidered, with a look that bordered on evil. "I was asking what kind of tampons she prefers. Because the ones I use—" Noah left in a flash, blushing from his neck, all the way up to the roots of his hair. "Works every time."

Easy to believe it worked. Hard to believe she'd had the nerve to use the line before. "Really?"

"No. Not really. But hey, it worked."

My stomach growled. The smell of pizza drew my attention from Olive to the one wall not currently covered in wet paint, where a long, white table was set up. As we got closer, I saw that the table was laden with crocks of chili, vegetarian and not, potato salad, onion rings, subs and the aforementioned pizza, next to a full tray of quickly wilting veggies. On the floor beside the table was a deep metal trough filled with ice and soda (Pop in Alaska. Soda in New Jersey). I watched as two workers stopped at the table to get a cold drink before heading back to work. I was tempted to take a veggie sub but hesitated. Could any sub outside of New Jersey be as good as ones from home?

"Skip the subs. Grab a few crab cakes before they disappear." Noah.

"Really," I said. Noncommittal with a bit of a chill.

"You're from the East Coast right? I heard Maryland crab cakes are good, but no one makes them like Ellie."

Was he digging for information?

"Small town. Word travels. Don't look so worried. No one knows about your running away from your arranged marriage," he said.

"Lame," Olive said.

"I need to . . . I'd better . . ."

"Go?" Olive made a hand gesture to Noah that I translated as "Scoot."

"Is everything okay?" She asked me when he had drifted off. "You look green."

I wasn't about to answer that; luckily for me Olive turned and saw something that had her heading across the room toward her mom and dad, zigzagging between open paint cans and paint trays, looking like she was ready to tear someone's head off. Danger personified. I followed her, bumping into more than one person along the way. We didn't get far before their loud voices reached us.

"You promised." Ellie was pacing now. A caged tiger. I pitied Olive's dad, no matter what he'd done to cause her ire.

"It can't be helped." Olive's father stood tall and stiff, a stone fortress, broadcasting his resistance. Worse, indifference.

"If I can't trust you—"

"Things change. You can't expect—"

Jackson drifted over, took her arm and teased, "Trying to get out of work?"

Olive glared at her parents, unmoved by Jackson's attempt to divert her attention.

"Come on," he said, as he guided us to a group of his friends where he formally introduced me.

Olive, however, kept glancing back at her parents, but then must have realized there was something she could actually control. Operating with the precision of a secret service detachment, she steered us away from the group, into another room where we ran across the one person I was hoping I would not have to see again today.

"We meet again," Noah said, clearly amused.

"Original." I had the urge to smack that smile right off of his face. Oh my God. What was happening to me? This man brought out a side of me I had never seen or felt before. I am a person of peace, as boring as that may sound. I don't go around wanting to slap people. Deep breath. Calm ocean breezes. Sandy beaches.

"Alex!"

Count to 110. Resist the dark side.

"Alex?"

Turn. Walk away. Right now.

"Alex!"

"Gotta go." I turned and headed for the ladies room where I ripped off my overalls, then sat in a stall and took a few deep breaths, following my own advice.

Olive found me and leaned under the toilet door. "Are you okay?" she asked.

Turn the tables on your adversary. Was that in The Art of War? "Are you okay, Olive?"

"Same old, same old," she said, making light of her parents fighting in public, even though I suspected she'd been crying.

Then Jackson walked in. What the heck?

"Read the sign!" Olive shouted. "Ladies room."

He crouched down, put his arm around her and held on tight. "They'll work it out. They always do."

"Yeah, I've heard that one before." But she leaned into him anyway. Resting her head on his shoulder. He wrapped both arms around her, holding her like he would protect her from everything bad the world had to throw at her.

It was hard to know what I should do. After all, I was sitting on a toilet. Not exactly a power position. My parents had never raised their voices to each other and were in agreement on all things. It felt odd to learn that not everyone else had that kind of life. That not every family shared the same values and views. I was completely out of touch with her world and the only thing I could do was to be there to listen when she was ready to talk.

Noah came into the ladies room next. I had already folded my Carhartts, tucked them behind the toilet and escaped the stall when he put a hand on my elbow. "Come on. There's nothing we can do here." I followed him into the main hall until we stopped at one of the walls with a space between painters.

"You're gonna get paint all over your new clothes," he noted.

I shrugged in an "these are old" way.

He didn't believe me, apparently, because he hauled his own shirt over his head, and tossed it to me before handing me a clean paint roller.

"Here. Put this on," he said, waiting for me to acquiesce.

I breathed a sign of relief that he had layered up that morning and had another T-shirt on under the one he'd given me. I pulled the garment over my head. It came down to my knees and smelled of Noah. Lemony. Like a crisp breeze.

He nodded and got back to work. I watched as he dipped a roller into a paint laden tray, still thinking about Olive. Noah noticed my watchfulness, but said nothing. He climbed a ladder to paint the high areas, while I kept to the lower ones. We worked for what must have been hours. Up and down, we moved our rollers in silence as we listened to the music that was coming from a radio in the corner, songs I had never heard before.

"Do you like that song?" Noah finally leaned down to ask.

"What?"

"The song. You were dancing."

I absolutely was not dancing. "I was not dancing," I informed him.

"Swaying, then."

Hmm.

"And humming. Well?"

"Well, what?"

"Do you like it? The song? Take Me To Church? Hozier?"

"Yes, I like it. Are you happy?"

He laughed. "Indubitably."

"What is that supposed to mean?"

"Nothing."

Resist. Resist. Resist.

I should leave. A graceful exit was called for. I'd done my share. Worked. Mingled. Played counselor, to the best of my limited ability. Stopped myself from murdering an infuriating, maddening, exasperating, infernal, irritating, bothersome, vexatious human being.

"Don't go down to their level," my mom always said. I could move. There were plenty of other walls to be painted. I turned quickly to leave and, just my luck, my left foot landed in the center of my paint tray. When I pulled it up in a knee-jerk reaction, my right knee buckled causing me to lose my balance. There was no way I could have avoided landing rear end first in Noah's full-to-overflowing paint tray.

I was a vision in lime green.

As I sat pondering my next move, I heard something click. I looked up in time to catch Olive looking much happier than I'd seen her in hours. "This is going to look great in the newsletter," she said, bent over belly laughing.

I should have been happy that she was happy, but enough was enough. I put a hand down on the wet floor, slipping around like a wet seal, fell again and by the time I'd managed to get to my knees, in an attempt to grab her phone and dunk the blasted thing into the nearest paint tray, I had paint everywhere. In my hair, up my nose, on my eyelashes, in my mouth and places you really don't want to know about. Note. Don't scratch when covered with paint. If my aim was to be unobtrusive, and it was, I had failed miserably.

Someone tossed a towel to me. Noah again. Why wouldn't he just go away? Was it his sole purpose in life to torture me? My cheeks were so red, what with the green paint and my red cheeks, I felt like a Christmas lawn ornament.

Noah reached down and pulled me up, not letting go until I was steady. I shook off his hands, but not before I noticed how he smelled like his shirt. All lemony and good. I took that moment to clean off my face and hair as much as possible, not that much was possible, avoiding his eyes.

"You do make an impression," he said as he righted the paint trays and tossed a cascade of paper towels on top to soak up the spilled paint.

There was nothing I could say. Sadly, he was right. There was no disputing the fact.

"Don't worry. People here will love you for being human."

What did he mean by that? Did people think I was different? That I didn't act human?

"Fallible." He said, reading my thoughts, again.

I'm fallible. God knows, I am fallible. Anyone who thinks otherwise, hasn't been paying attention.

"Approachable."

I am approachable as hell! "Are you done?"

He didn't get a chance to answer. I turned away, this time successfully sidestepping the paint trays, and crashed into what felt like a solid brick wall, but was actually a complete stranger.

Could it get any worse? Repeat after me. No. It. Could. Not.

The stranger placed a hand on each of my shoulders, and pushed me back two or three inches, keeping a firm grip on me. In case I flung myself at him again? He was tall enough that I had to tilt my head back to see his face. He smelled like paint and Old Spice, endearing me to him. I used to give my grandfather Old Spice every birthday from the time I was old enough to have enough money to give him a gift that wasn't homemade.

"Hi." Brilliant. Just brilliant.

I noted that paint was now smeared across his flannel shirt and corduroy jeans. That was how close we were.

"I'm Sam," he said. His eyes were gray. The rarest of eye colors.

"I'm Alex."

"I know." His hair curled softly around his ears, brushing his collar.

"Um."

"Welcome."

Don't even think about it. Men are controlled substances, I reminded myself. Not interested.

"You can let me go now," I said. Not in the tone even close to the tone I'd previously used on Noah.

"I brought Juneau. He's in the office."

"Thanks."

"He's a really great wol . . ."

Arrgh! My head was going to explode, I knew it.

"Uh, pup?" he corrected.

"Hey, Sam," Olive sidled up to him and landed a precocious hip bump on him. To me she whispered, "You're drooling."

Not drooling.

Wait a minute. I smelled wine. Something alcoholic. "Have you been drinking?" I hissed in her ear.

That was right before Sam picked her up and spun her around in a big circle, causing her to let out a whoop.

People touch each other a lot here, did you know that? I scrunched my forehead in confusion. I thought she was interested in Jackson.

Noah interrupted my thoughts. "They're not an item."

Unfortunately for Olive, her mom and dad were passing by at the exact moment I made that not-funny-after-all comment about her drinking. Ellie grabbed Olive by her hoodie, fast as a hawk, leaned in and sniffed her breath.

"You've been drinking!" she said. Not a question. Low enough not to advertise the fact to the entire assembly, but telegraphing her anger all the same.

"How? When?" her dad asked, coming up behind Ellie.

"We're leaving. Now," Ellie said and before Olive could say boo, her parents whisked her off of the barge, down the dock toward home, where I could imagine a long, one-sided conversation regarding responsibility, underaged drinking and how she was not going to see the light of day until she was at least thirty-five.

I peeked around. No one was acting as if they'd noticed. Good. I turned to find Noah. Still there.

"Noah, do you think it'll be okay?"

"She'll be barfing into a toilet and wishing she'd never gotten into the adult punch. Otherwise, she'll be fine."

I meant about her parents, but left it there.

"About what you said earlier. Why would it matter to me about Sam and Olive?"

"I thought you would want to know. So you wouldn't worry."

Hmmph. "Worry? Excuse me?! I'm not worried." I pointed at his chest. "And when I want to know something from you I'll—" I stopped myself.

There was no understanding this knee-jerk reaction I had to everything Noah said to me. I stopped myself and sighed. This wasn't getting me anywhere.

"I'm leaving now," I said, pulling myself up to full height, squaring my shoulders and lifting my chin in defiance.

"You're good at that."

Don't answer him.

Wait. How would he know?

Chapter Seventeen

How Olive Always Wins

I didn't expect it, but the work party wasn't all work. Work happened, but so did drinking, impromptu dancing, laughing and a fair amount of sneaking off to avoid work, doing heaven knows what. When I mentioned this to Olive, she'd looked at me like I was an alien, laughed and shook her head.

I have to admit it, I also spent an inordinate amount of time not working, deliberately listening in on the conversations around me. It was to my benefit, after all, to see if anyone was showing too much interest in either Juneau or in me. Along the way, I learned some interesting things. One. Sam helps out in the cafe because he and Ellie are old college friends and because it is a nice break from his real job as an ornithologist, researching eagle habitat in southeast Alaska. Two. I found out that at least three local girls were half in love with Jackson, and by agreement, they all thought he was pretty dreamy. Three. A group of commercial fishermen had laid bets that this "broken down old barge will sink before the paint dries." Four. A couple of scientist types mentioned the sudden appearance of rocky outcroppings around the lighthouse, the very ones I'd seen, and they attributed them to a change in plate tectonics due to a submerged earthquake. Nothing about wolves or escapees from Jersey. At least not within earshot of me. Whew.

A respectable amount of time after Olive was dragged away by her parents, I made my excuses, left the work party and headed for my very own boat and my first solo voyage out to the lighthouse. Even though I had been a passenger many times and had memorized the route, I had a fair amount of trepidation about making it back on my own. Not that I would admit that to anyone. I climbed aboard, careful not to rock the boat, settled Juneau into his life jacket and turned the key to the engine. It started up quickly and quietly and I steered in the direction of the island. The night sky was clear with a path of stars which seemed to be leading the way home. The waves were as calm as falling snow. It felt like the universe was on our side.

Thoughts about the work party, Sam, Olive, the possibility of my secrets being discovered, Noah and everything that had happened throughout the day simply dropped away, replaced by feelings of peace and contentment and stayed with me as we pulled up to the dock, what was left of it, tied off, gathered ourselves up and climbed the steps of the lighthouse, with the moon shining in through the windows, lulling us to sleep.

"Ahoy, there!" Juneau leaped up from the bed, jumping up to the window, just out of his reach, waking me up. "What is it, Junie Bug?"

My eyes felt like they were glued shut. Or maybe I didn't want to open them.

"If you're not dressed, get dressed. I'm on my way up."

Olive!

Big sigh. What was Olive doing here at—I checked the time—7 o'clock in the morning?

"Mayday." She exploded into my bedroom, dropped a rolling suitcase on the floor and tossed a newspaper at my head. "Did you hear about the barge?"

The headline glared at me: New Community Center Sinking!

Scanning the article, I looked over the who, what, when, where and how of it, all that were known at the time of printing. The lead photo showed a long, jagged crack running along the hull of the barge, which was listing to one side more than ever.

It didn't look good.

"It's a disaster," Olive said. "We have to do something."

I knuckled the sleep from my eyes. Juneau wiggled his way into Olive's lap where she'd settled down on the edge of the bed.

"Wake up," she insisted.

Not a morning person. My favorite thing is to paint into the wee hours of the night and then sleep all morning and half the afternoon, given the opportunity.

"I have an idea," she said, more sheepishly than was her norm, making me suspicious and I am not the suspicious sort.

"What do you have in mind?" I asked, though I wasn't at all sure I wanted to know.

"It's brilliant. We hold the community center classes here!"

I pulled my grandmother's quilt over my head and lay back down. No. No. No. That wasn't going to happen.

"I mean, you want to help, don't you?" Olive said, casting puppy dog eyes my way. Actually, I didn't see her puppy dog eyes since I was still under the blanket, but I know what she is like. "Only until they can get it fixed. You're one of us, after all, and you do have all this space," she babbled on. If you can't convince them, confuse them.

Ignore her. But then again, no answer, is an answer. I peeked over the covers, shaking my head. "Sorry, but—"

"You can't say no."

"I'll help in some other way. Name it." Juneau nodded. He didn't want his sanctuary invaded any more than I did.

"Alex—"

"It won't work."

"Well, unless you have any bright ideas, that's our only option."

"Well. I. Will. I will pay for the repairs to the community center."

"You don't have that kind of money."

She couldn't possibly know that I had money to spare.

"We can hold a fundraiser to cover the rest."

"Maybe. But—"

"Olive?" I realized something. "What is that suitcase for?"

"I'm done with all the arguing at home. I moved out."

I was more than a little stunned and speechless.

"And now I'm moving in."

All the synonyms for impossible situation and impossible person ran through my head like my life flashing before my eyes: out of the question, unfeasible, impractical, nonviable, unworkable, unthinkable, unimaginable, inconceivable, absurd, implausible, far-fetched, outrageous, preposterous, ridiculous, absurd, futile, maddening, intolerable, unbearable, unendurable, exasperating, infuriating, irritating. Did I forget any?

"It's going to be so much fun."

Based on the fact that her suitcase weighed practically nothing—I knew this because I was getting ready to haul it back to the dock—Olive didn't actually plan to stay for long. But even a day or two was too long.

I had to distract her. Make her forget about staying here, because staying here was never going to happen.

"Olive," I started, as I reached the bottom floor with her suitcase. Olive, who was following, unusually quiet, lifted the case from my hand and headed for the keeper's cottage. I dogged her steps. "Olive. I noticed a lot of people at the work party wearing shirts with writing on them."

She gave me a look that I'd figured meant she was wondering if I had been locked in a closet for my none too distant youth.

"A few of them said, 'She Persisted,'" I asked, the question implicit in my voice.

"Elizabeth Warren! You have to know her. Senator?"

"And Bernie shirts."

"OMG. They ran for president."

It was working.

"Women's March?"

"Washington, DC. The entire nation. The world! Marching for women's rights!" She shook her head and sighed. "Good thing I showed up. You need me."

Of course, I knew all that. But now she was even more determined to stay. She lifted her suitcase from my now limp hand and marched the rest of the way to the cottage, pushed through the door and tossed the suitcase on the bed. "This will do."

I walked in behind her and the lights came on. Like I was a remote control or something.

"You're like my uncle, only in reverse. He stopped every watch he ever wore. And he could totally blow a computer after using it for a week or so. You're a force of nature."

Freak of nature, was more like it. Weirdo. And worse than that, calling attention to myself.

Maybe I could talk with Ellie about it. No, she had enough on her mind with marital problems and now a runaway teen. Speaking of which,

I would have to call her. The question was, whether I should tell Olive and face her wrath now or not tell her and face her wrath later.

"Olive. I. Um. NeedToCallEllie." I ran the words together, hoping for what?

She waved a hand dismissively at me. "Don't bother. She knows I'm here."

So now I had two problems. One, finding a way to keep the community center classes away from the island. Two, finding a way to keep Olive away from the island.

"Oh." Well, good. Not good. Sigh. "Um, how long . . . ?"

But she was already stretched out on the bed, earbuds firmly planted in her ears, probably listening to motivational tapes on how to take over the world with the complete backing and all encompassing love of mankind.

I had no choice. I had to call Ellie and let her know that Olive hadn't run off to join Cirque de Soleil or signed up for a research expedition headed for the Arctic Sea. On the off chance that Olive hadn't really told her where she was.

I left the cottage contemplating my next move. I was all the way to the boat dock when my cell rang.

"Alex? This is Ellie. I know Olive is there," she said. "Don't worry. I know this isn't your fault. You would never do such a thing to your mother."

Ouch. She didn't know me at all. I had done exactly that to my mother. Only worse. I'd traveled 4,300 miles away in an effort to get away from the plans my mother had for me.

"She can stay."

What? Shaken from my reverie, I opened my mouth to protest.

"She needs a time out while we straighten things out around here."

How long was a time out? "Um, how—"

"A few days at most. That should be enough for her to tire of living without pizza and Pop Tarts."

"Um."

"Don't tell her I called." With that she hung up, immediately followed by a loud crash, simultaneous skreech and subsequent cursing.

I raced in the direction of the scream. Outside. Around the bend. There lay a crumbled figure. Juneau whimpered as I approached. "Olive! What happened? Olive!"

The angle of her leg didn't look at all like it was supposed to. But she was breathing. I knew this because when she saw me, she sighed.

"Don't tell my mom. I'm begging you. Just don't."

Chapter Eighteen

How Eavesdropping and Traumatic Head Injury Work

"I repeat, what happened?" I asked Olive as I checked for broken bones and for signs of a concussion. First Aid wasn't my best subject in high school, but I had passed with a B+. "Do you feel nauseated? Does your head hurt?" I asked, when really I wanted to scream, "How the hell did this happen? I left you on the bed, listening to world domination tapes, so how did you manage to fall out of a window in the lighthouse?" Instead, I asked, "Does it hurt here?" as I was helping her move her leg into a more natural position.

"Yes," she shouted, "you—I mean, it's not too bad. Thanks for helping."

"Are you going to tell me what you were doing?"

"Would you believe suicide by lighthouse?"

"From the second floor?" Bad plan.

"Um. Getting some fresh air?"

"Wouldn't going outside have served that purpose better?"

"Truth? I was doing a new yoga stretch. You lean over a chair, only I didn't have one, so the window ledge seemed suitable."

"Really?"

"No. You're right. I was trying get to a bird's egg that was lodged in one of the stones outside the window and leaned out too far."

I turned away since she apparently had no intention of confessing.

"Fine. I wanted to hear what my mom was saying."

Sigh. Of course, Olive would have heard. She yawned and closed her eyes. Juneau snuggled up next to her.

"She said you could stay. But now it's out of the question." Wow. I sounded like my mother.

"You can't send me back," she said. Her speech was slightly slurred. Concussion? I checked her pupils. They looked fine, but I wasn't taking any chances. "Wake up. You can't go to sleep if you have a concussion."

"I'm okat, I mean, okan, okay. Let me schtay."

"You need an x-ray and possibly an MRI."

"It isn't that bad," she said as she maneuvered herself up, taking a spin and landing in a heap at my feet. By the time Juneau yelped in concern, I had 911 on the line, who promptly informed me they were sending out the Coast Guard for a medical pickup.

My head was beginning to ache. Olive was broken. I should have stayed in New Jersey and faced my problems. If I had, she would be safe at home.

It wasn't easy, but I managed to get her back in bed snuggled under more blankets than she probably needed, with a hot bowl of soup and a dozen cookies I'd procured from the bakery earlier in the week. I couldn't do enough.

She took the babying in stride. "It's not your fault," she said between sips of soup and bites of cookie. "You weren't the one eavesdropping. My mom always says eavesdroppers pay."

"Really?"

"No. But she would have if she'd thought of it. Anyway, the saying goes, 'Eavesdroppers hear things they won't like,' or something like that."

"Oh."

She nearly dropped the soup and I grabbed for it.

Out of nowhere, she asked, "Alex, what do you think about men?"

"Men? As in, men who eavesdrop? Men who fall out of windows?"

She rolled her eyes. "No. Just men. Are they a total waste of time? Career-busters? Liars?"

Where was this coming from? She must have a concussion? I mean, why else would she be dropping soup and asking odd questions about men if not for a traumatic brain injury? Olive's father was none of those things, that I knew of. Yes, it looked like he'd promised to put less emphasis on work. But . . ."

"I mean, can you depend on any of them?"

"What brought this up, Olive? Your dad—"

"He's good. I mean, he's okay. But, it just looks like men put their own needs above everyone else's. What am I talking about? You've never even dated." Pause. "Have you?"

"It's true, I don't have much experience, but the men in my family have always been honorable. My mother and grandmother were involved in family decisions. Not like it was a favor, but like it was written in stone. I think you've been watching too much reality TV."

"My dad works too much. Jackson is leaving. What do they care about me?"

If I didn't know better, I'd say she'd gotten into the Alaskan Ale. Not that I had any on the island.

"And another thing, while we're on the subject of men. Do you think it's okay to have sex with someone when you have no intention of getting seriously involved with that person? I mean, you wouldn't give up pizza just if you become a vegetarian. You wouldn't give up cupcakes just because you become a nun."

Can anyone say concussion! "Um. Maybe we should—"

"I think Noah would be a hot chocolate cupcake with chili pepper frosting if he were a cupcake, don't you."

"Um. No?"

"You'd be an apple pie cupcake. With cream cheese frosting. And I'd be . . ."

"You could never be a cupcake, Olive."

"What? I'm not soft or sweet?"

Do not give away even a twinge of a smile. Not a crinkle of an eye. This much I knew when dealing with Olive.

"You would be an eagle. Loyal and soaring high," I said, which seemed to appease her.

She checked her phone, fumbled it, then started clicking. I wasn't sure what she was searching for until she put it down and announced, "Well, you would be an okapi."

"A reclusive animal related to the giraffe?" I had a wealth of strange information at my disposal. Years of studying instead of partying.

"Enigmatic. Shy. When is your birthday? That could explain everything."

Ignoring her question, I added, "Rarely seen by humans." There was no use arguing.

She returned to her phone. "Noah would be a pachyderm. Steadfast, loyal, empathetic and creative." Then sighed. "I love him." She shook her head. "Wait, not Noah."

Jackson. It was obvious. "So you're an eagle and I'm an okapi?"

"I'd rather be Bat Girl. Righting wrongs. Protecting the vulnerable and downtrodden."

"Superheroes never end up happy."

"How do you know that?" She gave me a look that said she knew I had been raised by wolves and knew nothing about cultural icons.

"Superheroes all seem to lead tragic lives." I ignored her question. There was no reason she had to know that I had sneaked a peak at some worn copies of superhero books on my journey to Alaska. Not that I needed to sneak. That was my upbringing talking. I could read anything I wanted now.

"Fine. But if you were a super hero, what super power would you have? Me, I'd like to fly." She stretched out her arms imitating wings. "I bet you'd pick invisibility."

Invisibility might be useful. But, no.

"Stop stalling, Alex. What would you pick?"

"I would pick contentment. Happiness."

She shook her head in disappointment. "Why would you pick a lame super power like that when you could control the electromagnetic field, lift a planet with a pinky, turn the ocean into a mile high curtain of rain?"

Because. "I never expected to be happy," I said, under my breath.

A horn blast carried out over the water toward shore. There was no chance of Olive having heard me. "The boat's here," I announced with great relief. Men, sex, cupcakes, superpowers. In my family, we didn't talk about men as if they were cupcakes, superpowers as if they were a possibility and definitely not about sex. Maybe that conversation was on my mom's to-do list for some time in the future. Maybe I was glad I wasn't there to hear it.

Olive went back to her phone, cooking up more trouble, no doubt, while I went out to greet the Coast Guard—or Coasties as people around here call them. They moored and came rushing ashore with a stretcher and a large medical bag. It looked like the entire Coast Guard was invading the island. Surely they didn't need 10, no 12, no 16! Coasties to take one girl back to the hospital. Except when I looked closer, I saw that it was most of the guys from the community center party, led by Jackson.

"Where is she?" Jackson called out when he was almost upon me, urgency filling his voice. I pointed to the cottage and he rushed past, followed by a cadre of men on a mission. A sight to behold. I only wish Olive could have seen it. She would consider the accident and a broken whatever it turned out to me was well worth it. Almost as good as a parade.

Before I could finish that last thought, they were rushing her out on a stretcher, Jackson running beside her, holding her hand, repeating words of comfort. The next time I saw her I would have to tell her all about it.

And it was then that I realized that she drew people into her life who were honorable, dedicated and committed to her, even if she didn't see it.

That was her super power.

Chapter Nineteen

Newspaper Headline: Local Lass's Lighthouse Leap

In the Prince of Wales newspaper, local news goes on page one. Alaska news goes on page two. News from everywhere else starts on page three, unless there is a plethora of local and Alaska stories that day and then world news gets pushed back to page four, closely followed by sports, comics and classified ads. The best of today's news included a story on a local cat that found its way onto a bush plane (aka a two-seater aircraft common in Alaska) that was headed for Kotzebue. Fortunately, the cat—Ferdinand—made it home safely and everyone let out a collective sigh. The best classified ad on this day read: Wanted—person of any gender to pick up stinky, holey underwear from the middle of the bathroom floor, because my partner seems to think there is a fleet of fairies that drop in at night to pick up holey, stinky underwear from the middle of the bathroom floor. Work hours: two frigging minutes a day!

On to the news about Olive. The paper reported how she had sprained her ankle badly and may have fractured her scaphoid, a tiny bone in the hand, thanks to me. I already knew from talking with Ellie last night, that a scaphoid break is hard to heal and that Olive could be in a cast up to her elbow for up to four months if she had in fact broken that bone. As fate would have it, the cast was on her right arm and she's right-handed. They would know more next week when she went back for a second set of x-rays.

After the rescue crew had taken Olive away, I spent the evening between calls to Ellie and painting an image of Olive with large eagle wings, flying a course around the top of the lighthouse. She had a key held close on a chain around her neck. Juneau rode stretched out on her back, his ears swept back by the wind. Far below, barely visible, I stood on the beach, looking up at them as they moved through a backdrop of enormous white clouds leaving a trail of ominous darker clouds behind them. Drifting down toward me in the painting were tiny snowflakes, each distinct in size and shape while behind me the ocean howled, threatening to consume me.

I set the paint brush down around 3 a.m. and dropped onto my mattress to wake at 6 a.m. when my phone beeped.

Text from Olive: "I'm feeling no pain, but you're going to have to take over the community center committee for me. Doctor's orders."

A second text followed on the heels of the first: "Don't worry. You won't have to do it alone. Noah is the co-chair."

The universe was conspiring against me. I definitely deserved it.

3rd text from Olive: "My friend, Suki can't do it because she's staying with her grandma in Portland for the summer. And Cassy and Megan are backpacking in Europe with her mom." All friends of Olive's.

All of no help to me.

Text #5 from Olive: "You need to—"

I clicked off my phone. I didn't need to know what new evil plot she was cooking up. Because, obviously, it included me. It was clear what I had to do. Get some sleep, then go to town and deal with Olive face to face. But before that, I needed to come up with my own devious plot to thwart her devious plot. Or plots, as the case may be.

I willed myself to fall back to sleep. It was 9 o'clock when I awoke again, this time by Juneau licking my cheek. He wiggled his tail at me and raced down the lighthouse stairs, directing me to follow. I walked down more slowly, sensing something was different. As I made my way down, I didn't see anything out of place.

Outside, Juneau was pawing the cottage door. I caught up with him and when I opened the door. "Olive's not here, Junie." He jumped on the bed, then went around the room, checking each corner, before sniffing an old wooden dresser. Something shiny under the dresser caught his attention. It was nothing to worry about. Lots of people had been here yesterday. Anyone could have dropped whatever it was that Juneau was pawing with great concentration. He nosed it over to me. A Kennedy silver dollar. Not pirate treasure. Most likely it was a good luck coin that fell from one of the guys' pockets when they were bending, lifting or carrying Olive away.

I slipped it into the top drawer of the dresser, planning on returning it to its rightful owner in the near future. Meanwhile, Juneau nosed another object from under the dresser. A key. What do you do when you find a key? You check nearby locks, knowing the key probably won't fit. But you do it anyway. I went to the door of the cabin first and slipped the key into the opening. It slid in easily. I went to turn it, expecting it to stay in place; however, it turned to the right, as easily as it had fit into the opening. While I was testing the key and finally depositing it in my pocket, Juneau was busy nosing the trapdoor of the tunnel. I went over to see what he was up to and found the latch was askew. I thought I remembered leaving it latched the last time I'd come up from the tunnel. A chill went up my back and I shivered. I reached down and closed the latch with a hard snap. It wasn't that I thought anyone had been sneaking around on the island or in the tunnel, but I had learned not to ignore those times when I felt a twinge of something unexplainable.

Either way, if anyone had been in the tunnel, there was no way they could get up into the cottage now. Satisfied that I'd done all I could, at least for now, I urged Juneau outside, locked the door to the cottage behind us and got ready to go into town to check on Olive.

Getting ready meant packing dog food, a travel kennel and toys for the day, along with Juneau's favorite blanket, one he liked to cuddle up with during his naps. It also meant washing the paint brushes I'd left soaking last night and cleaning up the rest of my painting supplies. After completing those tasks, I stuffed a couple of days worth of garbage into a large plastic bag and tossed it into the boat and took the time to clear the dock of debris that had washed up last night. Juneau watched patiently as I went back inside and looked around for a get-well present for Olive. In the end, I decided on the painting I'd done so quickly the night before. I hadn't depicted Olive as Bat Girl, but she did make an impressive eagle. And I loved how the light played over her and Juneau as they commanded the sky.

"I love it, too," Juneau woofed.

I placed the painting carefully in a box and with that, it was time to leave.

CHAPTER TWENTY

Princess Hell

I found Olive propped up on downy pillows when I arrived at her bedroom door, after having made a turbulent trip across the inlet, with everything she could possibly need to rule her kingdom during her confinement. Laptop, television and of course, cell phone. She wasn't going to starve any time soon, either. On the table beside her was a plate with one jelly filled donut (as evidenced by the red goo oozing from a big bite on one side), a box of Alaska Wild Berry candy and a barely-touched peanut butter and honey sandwich. To add to the festivities, brightly colored helium balloons floated above her bed, with greetings that ran the gamut from Get Well to the not so nice ones: Cry Baby and Wuss. She didn't notice me standing in the doorway immediately as she reached for the donut, dripping jam on her arm, cursing like a New York City dock workers. I must have sucked in my breath. I did. Because she looked up and a huge smile spread across her face. A smile I returned before I found a napkin on the night stand and leaned in to clean the jam from her arm. Which was when she grabbed me in a one-armed hug. "Ouch."

I pushed back from her hug.

"Damn," she said. "What took you so long? They've got me locked up in here like a princess in a tower. Seriously, Mom even makes me call her when I have to go pee. Like I'm two," she complained, rolling her eyes for dramatic effect.

"I am so glad—"

"Stop it. I am so sick of being babied. I. Am. Fine. Get it?"

I hid a smile. Olive is so strong you have to admire her. "Got it," I parroted.

"Good, because we have work to do. And not a lot of time." She shifted in bed and stifled a groan. "What's that?" she asked, pointing behind me.

I pulled out the box I'd been holding behind my back. "It's for you."

"Ooh. Hand it over," she demanded, reaching with her good arm.

She was wrestling with the box when I sensed someone coming up behind me.

Olive went from thrilled to guilty. "I forgot to mention that Noah was on his way over."

"Was?"

"Is."

"Hey," Noah said as he slid by me with a friendly nod and went over to Olive. "She lives!" he joked, making Olive laugh, then cry out in pain, then laugh again.

"Stop. Don't make me laugh."

"Don't go jumping out of lighthouse windows and I won't."

"Leap," I said.

"What?"

"The newspaper said 'leap'; although, actually she—"

"Shush. I'm telling everyone I defeated a band of pirates who were trying to take over the island. You don't want to tarnish my rep."

A small head poked out from behind Noah. "Willow!" Olive skreeched. "OMG!" She tried to get up from the bed and got tangled in the covers, making it impossible. "Get over here. Right this minute!"

The girl, named Willow, apparently, obediently moved closer to Olive's bed.

"I can't believe you're here. I missed you." Olive pulled her onto the bed and held her in a warm hug. "How long are you staying? When did you get here? We are going to have so much fun."

Noah held up a hand. "The rest of the summer. This morning. Not until you're well."

"Party pooper," Olive pouted.

I stood back, taking it all in when Noah pulled up a chair and pushed it toward me. "Sit."

Sit? Like a dog? Juneau, who until then had remained by my side, unsure no doubt if jumping on Olive would be a good thing or bad, leaped into the chair and sat. That solved that problem.

"OMG. Noah, do you see it?" Olive enthused as if she'd just seen Santa coming down her chimney.

He looked over at me, looking for a clue.

"They could be twins."

I was lost.

"Same hair, same heart-shaped face. Same clothing style. Or lack of one."

Noah shook his head, looked at Willow, looked at me and stopped. Clearly thinking she was insane.

"Lots of people . . . coincidence, uh . . . you're . . ."

Noah's words drifted off. Meanwhile, Willow was looking at me and a chill ran up and down my spine. As if we'd met before. Do you believe in past lives? I've never thought about it. Willow kept her straight red hair in a neat pony tail. She wore soft black jeans and an equally soft orange T-shirt. She looked to be somewhere between 10 and 14. She was 12 it turned out.

"Willow meet Alex. She lives in the lighthouse."

Willow hesitated, suggesting to me that she was introverted, the look-before-you-leap type. Unlike Olive. Finally, she looked up at me, meeting my eyes. "You live in the lighthouse?"

I nodded.

"I love lighthouses. I told Noah he should buy it, but he said he had enough to take care of with the houseboat and me each summer." She glanced over at him in a way that told me everything I needed to know. A look that said she couldn't believe he'd given up the opportunity of a lifetime, due to petty practicalities, easily overcome with a little determination and resolve. Something she clearly had.

"And she's an artist," Olive broke in. "She's going to run the fundraiser for the community center with your uncle. And you can help."

"I can?" Willow, barely holding in her excitement, looked to Noah for confirmation.

"Yep. You are now officially the head designer of the art studio," I said.

She took my hand and held it. Our eyes met and my heart did a strange flippy thing. An involuntary smile crossed my face and I noticed my muscles relaxing. A feeling of calm. Rightness. Destiny? Weird.

Even I know that.

Juneau felt something too. When Willow inched closer to his chair, he stretched up and leaned his front paws against her chest. She bent down so their noses were touching.

Damn. I may never let her go.

"I have a great idea," Olive said.

"Another one?" Noah teased.

"We could do a painting of the animal guide of each of the volunteers. Noah you are the pachyderm," Olive said and looked at me.

"Alex agrees."

"Olive, did they give you something for pain," I asked in an attempt to forego what I suspected was about to become another ill-advised, drug induced ramble.

"I see you gals have been talking about me," he said, enjoying my discomfort way too much.

"Loyal and creative," she added. "Alex is an okapi."

"What's an okapi?" Willow asked, scrunching up her forehead.

"You can look it up when we get home."

"Quiet, independent and inscrutable," Olive answered. "And I am Bat Girl. Dadadadadadadadadadadadadadada, Bat Girl!" she sang. "Wait. The present."

"What animal am I?" Willow asked, her face a picture of seriousness. Like something important depended on it.

Noah wrapped an arm around her shoulder and squeezed. "You are a monarch butterfly."

"Hey, aren't we forgetting something?" Olive asked.

"It can wait until later, you should rest," I said, hoping against hope she wouldn't open my gift while Noah was here.

She ignored me and handed the box over to Noah to open. He obliged, gently lifting the painting from its cardboard receptacle. He held it up for Willow to see before handing it to Olive. I lifted Juneau out of his chair as the three of them were scanning the painting and backed up.

I was getting closer to the door when I bumped into someone. I turned to find Ellie carrying a large a bouquet of sweet peas in a glass cylinder, none the worse for the collision. She went over to the night stand, pushed the sandwich plate aside and set the flowers down. "Time to rest," she told Olive.

My excuse to leave. No sneaking necessary.

"Mom. You have to look at this." Olive grabbed Ellie by her sleeve and pulled her closer. That was my cue to quickly make my way down the stairs, out the main part of the cafe and to the dock.

I had one foot in the boat and one on the dock when I heard a strong but melodic voice call out to me. "Alex. Wait."

Willow caught up with me in a few beats, then stood facing me, her arms crossed her arms over her chest, pulling herself up to her full height, which meant she still didn't reach the top of my shoulders.

She aimed a fierce look at me. I returned it with a blank one. I was going for innocent.

"Running away isn't very mature." We stared at each other for I don't know how long. I didn't deny her accusation and finally, she broke the silence.

"Your painting is beautiful."

Could it be possible that I was caught in the event horizon of a black hole, because suddenly it felt that way.

"Maybe I could come to the lighthouse with you one day?"

I had left home and traveled across the country alone. I'd managed to live in a ramshackle building on a deserted island. I had investigated deep, dark tunnels, which contained old bones and possibly dead rats. I could make my own way, going against the most deeply held traditions of my family, prepared to face the ire of said family if they found me. I could do all of these things with steely resolve. But I could not say no to one young girl I barely knew.

I didn't understand why, but I knew I was going to regret what I said next. "Of course."

"Good. Then it's settled."

I sighed. "Wait a sec. Noah has to agree."

"Don't worry about a thing. I got this." She rolled her eyes and smiled. Angelic.

Question: Aren't angels famous for waging fierce battles against evil? And winning?

Answer: Absolutely!

Chapter Twenty-One

Olive's Video Diary

2:00 pm: This totally sucks. I'm stuck in bed, missing any kind of the fun since Mom kicked everyone out all because I "need to rest". With no TV, either. Clearly, if mom and dad wouldn't argue so much, I wouldn't have left in the first place. This is their fault. Oh, rats. I think I hear dad downstairs. I have to make believe I am sleeping now. Zzzzzz.

3:00 pm: Crisis averted. Dad came and went. I am so bored. But at least since I fell out of the window and sprained whatever, mom and dad haven't had one argument. You wanna know what the second best thing about this whole mess is? The great painting Alex gave me. If people understood how talented she is, she'd be famous. I mean it. She'd be mega rich. Then she wouldn't have to live in a falling down lighthouse with sketchy electricity and rusty water and take a boat every time she wants fresh bread or an ice cream cone. And now with her taking over for me on the community center committee, she's going to have to travel back and forth even more. Which also sucks.

Sigh.

Back to the community center, I need to come up with a killer fundraising idea. So far I have:

1. A salmon festival. We rent booths out for a fee, get musicians (to volunteer) and we sell food. Approximate income? $5,000., if we're lucky.

2. Make a calendar of hot local guys. Mostly nude, obviously. I can think of three or four right off the top of my head. Approximate income: depends on the guys who volunteer. Let's say around $6,000.

3. A bake sale. Approximate income: $50. Not even worth it.

4. Wild Woman triathlon? Maybe. We could include a swim, a run, a hike and then the contestants have to jump into a tub of ice cubes at the end. Approx. income: $2,000. Maybe. $3,000. tops.

Doing the math, that doesn't even come close to making the repairs on the barge.

"Olive! Who are you talking to up there?"

Who could I be talking to? She took my phone.

"I was talking to myself. Working on fundraising ideas for the community center," I shouted back.

"How about cleaning out your closet. I'm sure someone on eBay would love all your junk." I think she was kidding. Maybe not. "After you get some rest."

Hmm. An online eBay auction could work. If everyone in town donated one or two things. . . Maybe eBay would let me auction off a few of the hot guys from the calendar . . .

3:30 pm: All right. Done and done. The Salmonfest is scheduled for two weeks from today. Posted on Facebook. Tweeted. Emailed everyone I know to volunteer and/or buy a booth. (My booth is going to be fortune telling.) Arranged for donations of frozen turkeys for frozen turkey bowling. Lined up bands (Noah is our featured performer.) Sent off a letter to the editor letting everyone within a 200 mile radius know about the event. Ouch. My arm is aching from all of the posting, emailing and tweeting. It's going to be so much fun. And $5,000 plus in the community center's bank account ain't bad. Cross your fingers that Alex doesn't hate me, because I started an ebay auction with her painting. Buy it now price? $250,000. Yep. The entire cost of the community center repairs. Obviously, no one will pay that, but it classes up the auction, for one. For two, I priced it seriously high because I really don't want to let it go. Now all I have to do is find a few hundred other items to sell and we'll have it made. Falling asleep now. The pain pills must be kicking in. Hoping Alex doesn't find out about the painting.

Goodnight, diary. Wake me if anything interesting happens.

"Olive, are you awake?"

"Hmm."

"Olive. It's me. Jackson."

"Dreaming."

"I came to see if you're okay."

"Shh. Too loud."

"Olive?"

"Hmm."

"You scared me. No, terrified me. Please don't do anything like this again. Ever."

"Silly."

Someone was sawing under my window. Damn. I was having such a good dream. I rolled over lazily, trying to ignore the noise. Willing it to go away. Bumping into something. Apparently Alex left Juneau for me. What a good friend. I snuggled into him. So soft. I fell back to sleep. Except the sawing didn't stop and finally I couldn't ignore it. Ready to shout out the window that, hey, didn't they know a concussed person was trying to recover in here? I gave Juneau one last snuggle. Wow. I didn't realize how big he was. And warm. I could almost fall back to sleep if it wasn't for the noise under my window. Not under my window. In bed with me. Juneau was snoring like a lumberjack. I gave him a little shove.

"Morning," a sleepy voice came from the other side of my bed.

"What?" I said, rolling over and landed on the floor. "Ouch."

"Oh my God."

"Ow."

Next thing I knew Jackson had me in his arms. He was rubbing my head and saying sorry, over and over and over again. Until my mom walked in.

Busted.

Chapter Twenty-Two

Fortune Telling, Near Death and Tofu

"I'm waiting, Alex." It was clear that it was taking everything Willow had not to tap her toe and pull a face.

"As I mentioned before, you have to talk with Noah." I could recall at least four times that I had told her. Noah was going to be the one who approved or disapproved her having a sleepover at the lighthouse, even though Olive tells me, no one sleeps at these events.

"He says we would be putting you out. That's not true! But he won't listen to me," she said, trying not to pout. So cute, with her arms crossed over her chest. "Why are adults so unreasonable?" her expression telegraphed, loud and clear.

"Well—"

"Willow!" Noah's voice carried over to us on a gust of wind. "I thought you were helping Olive at the fortune telling booth." His face read, Put-Upon-Big-Brother. "I've been looking all over for you."

She checked her shoes.

"I'm not paying you to bother Alex."

"She's not a bother—"

"See? I'm not a bother. She likes me."

Noah tugged on her hoodie. "Not going to work. March," he commanded.

Willow looked over her shoulder at me and silently mouthed, "Help."

I shrugged my shoulders. There was no help for her. Besides, working at the fortune telling booth sounded a lot more fun than selling undercooked burgers. What did they expect anyway? Having a vegetarian cooking meat was asking for trouble, which they realized after one, maybe two, okay three, people bit into very rare burgers, wherein they quickly shifted me over to the face painting booth. However, apparently I was too slow at that.

"It doesn't have to be a masterpiece, Alex," I was informed more than once, before I was shunted off to something they figured no one could mess up. Blowing up helium balloons. Until, that is, I somehow managed to release about twenty balloons into the atmosphere. It must have been nerves. Being surrounded by so many people. One of whom always seemed to be there whenever I turned around.

You know who I'm talking about.

So, no more work for me, Olive decided. Juneau and I were on our own. Which meant we could wander aimlessly, taking in everything the festival had to offer. Or hide out. I hadn't decided which.

"We have to stop meeting like this." Sam came up behind me, leaned down and gave Juneau's fur a ruffle before he landed a soft kiss just shy of my mouth. Startled, I pulled back.

"Too soon?" he asked.

"Too soon for what?"

"Never mind. Where are you two heading?"

The Salmonfest was set up downtown by the dock, with a long row of multi-colored booths filled with everything from handmade ceramic mugs to felted hats, fried halibut and pierogies. We were currently stopped in the middle of the main aisle with a steady stream of people moving past us, like water flowing around rocks in a river bed.

"We're blocking traffic," I said, noticing how we were disrupting the natural choreography of the festival.

With my attention seriously diverted, Juneau took the opportunity to mouth something up from the ground. "Juneau, drop it!" He spit out a half-chewed something. Hot-dog, I think, and I scooped it up with a tissue from my pocket. "Bad dog," I said, affectionately.

"He's hungry. Let's go find something he can eat," Sam suggested, "and where we can get out of this crowd."

An offer that was hard to refuse. The festival was starting to overwhelm me. Too many people, too many odors, too much noise.

He turned and headed to the direction of Ellie's cafe. I followed behind until we reached the back door. The one leading directly into the kitchen. He walked right in as if he owned the place and went up to Ellie, who was at the grill, her hair pulled back in a ponytail, a scarf around her forehead to help with the heat. "Juneau's starving," he offered without preamble.

"Pull up a stool. There isn't an empty seat up front. Lucky me," she aimed at Sam. To Juneau she said, "So, no hotdogs and cotton candy for you, huh, sweetie?"

Joy percolated up from my heart. Love, Juneau and my heart is yours.

Sam opened the refrigerator, pulled out a cooked chicken breast and shredded it before placing it in a bowl for Juneau. I hopped up on a bright red stool at the end of the kitchen counter and after setting Juneau's bowl in front of him, Sam sat beside me.

"Do we need to do something with our hair?" I asked, not wanting to cause trouble for Ellie. In case someone complained about hair in the food.

"As long as you're not cooking, it's all god, I mean good," Ellie answered. "God, I'm tired."

Sam jumped up from his stool and shouldered her aside. "Take a break. What's the next order?"

"I'll help," I offered.

Sam looked at me, questioning. "Can you cook?"

"How hard can it be?" I said, leaving out the part about the raw burgers.

"What have you been eating out there in never-never land?"

Ellie's care packages, actually. Fruit. Raw veggies. Canned this and that. The occasional candy bar.

"Don't bother answering." He held up a hand. "I can guess." He looked me up and down, from my toes to my hairline. Uncomfortable. "You're losing weight."

I wasn't starving, so no big deal, as Olive would say.

While I watched, he dropped breaded shrimp in a vat of oil. Minutes later he took the shrimp out and tossed them into a basket, along with hot fried potatoes and put it in the window for a server to pick it up. Moving on to the next dish. Adding a spice here and there, tasting, flipping, frying, frappeing, whatever you call it, before sliding a dish down to my end of the counter.

"Eat up. I insist."

My mouth started to water. Pavlovian. Disgusting. Drooling.

When I didn't eat immediately, he forked a piece and held it up to my mouth waiting for me to cave.

On the fork was one perfect bite of buttery, spicy omelette made with tofu and packed with fresh vegetables.

"How did you know?" I asked over a mouthfull of omelette.

"That you don't eat meat?"

"Um. Yes."

"Word travels, Doctor Strange."

I rolled my eyes.

"That was the easy part. What people around here can't figure out is how you managed to get power out at the island. Especially power that only seems to come on when you enter a room."

Damn that Olive.

"Not to mention the strange jetties that have cropped up out of nowhere."

My second bite of tofu omelette went down the wrong way and I couldn't get any air. You are probably imagining that it was terrifying. But I can swim a mile without getting winded and hold my breath under water for over a minute. I was trying to cough up the chunk of tofu when Sam came up behind me and pushed his fist under my ribs, fast and hard, and the offending glob popped out of my throat and across the kitchen. I cried out with the newfound breath. The pain in my chest was excruciating, but I was breathing.

"Doc, can you breathe?" Sam was the terrified one. He held me until he was certain my breathing had returned to normal. I didn't care that my cheek was resting on his chest and that I barely knew him. It felt safe and I was afraid if he let go I might fall. Finally, don't ask how long, because I don't know, he released his grip on me, slowly, testing to see if I would be okay, I reasoned.

"Doc, we should have those ribs checked out. I might have cracked a few."

I straightened and, oddly enough, the pain was gone. I pressed on my chest. Nothing. Maybe he'd healed me. What was I thinking? Post choking insanity? Is that a condition?

"I'm really sorry, Doc, but—"

"Why do you keep calling me Doc?"

"It fits. You are the Initially-Perceived-to-be-a-Gap-Girl who can create electricity with a single thought but then heals herself without losing an eyelash in the process. Conclusion, you must be a mad scientist. Like I said, Dr. Strange and her wolf. Good book title. But really, how—"

"How what?"

Noah.

"Gallagher, you can't be in here." Sam tossed Noah a small plastic wrapped package. "At least not without one of these." Which turned out to be a hair net.

Trying hard not to laugh.

"Thanks," Noah replied, unwrapping the hair net and placing it on Juneau's head. Juneau wriggled out of it and began batting it around the kitchen floor.

"What did you do? Put a tracking device on her?"

Noah ignored him, scooped the hair net off of the floor and sat next to me.

"What's going on here? Alex, you look like someone just choked you."

"Almost," Sam added. Traitor.

Noah shot me a questioning look as Juneau hopped up and settled in, so that he was resting half on Noah and half on me.

"Traitor," Sam muttered. "Noah, you need to leave. And Alex, you need to rest. Come on. Olive won't mind if you lay down in her room for a while."

"Why does Alex need to rest?" Noah asked.

"Slight tofu mishap. It's nothing," I told him.

"Juneau, what do you think? See? He agrees. Rest or we're going to the clinic."

"What aren't you two telling me?" Noah insisted.

"Heimlich. He saved me," I told Noah. To Sam I asked, "Did I tell you that you're my hero. Thank you."

"Barf." I'm certain that was Noah, mumbling under his breath.

Tired of waiting for me, Sam picked up Juneau and took my hand. "Come on, Doc. Up."

"Go. Rest," Noah said. "I have to meet up with Willow. I just came by to—never mind. Feel better."

It's more exhausting than you might think, choking. I fell asleep before I had a chance to fully process the fact that people were attributing the odd power surges at the lighthouse and new rock formations to something strange about me. Which, by the way, is nuts. I fell asleep before really coming to grips with the fact that people were talking about me. That realization would come later and hit me like a proverbial brick. For now, I slept. I awoke to an earthquake, that was actually Ellie, shaking me.

"Alex, you can't fall asleep. I don't know what those boys were thinking."

"Mom, that's for a concussion." Olive

"Same difference. They should have taken her to the clinic immediately. Come on, Alex. Time to get up."

When I didn't move, someone asked, "Do you need help?" and before I knew it, I was sitting in a paper gown, in a tiny room, presumably the doctor's office, based on the jar of tongue depressors and the gross posters of intestines, lungs and scary diseases on the walls. I covered my eyes. The posters were everywhere!

As I was fighting back the urge to barf, the doctor, who couldn't have been much older than me, pushed open the door. Luckily my paper dress was closed, my arms wrapped tightly across my chest.

Right behind him was Olive. I was never so happy to see someone. "I'm here as her attorney."

What?

"I mean as her advocate. She may not be in her right mind. She obviously can't sign consent forms." She gave the doctor what we call in New Jersey The Evil Eye, daring her, the doctor, to kick her, Olive, out.

Wow. With Olive watching her every move, she gingerly checked my ribs, stuck a tongue depressor down my throat, asked questions I don't remember and finally said, "Go home. Take two of these for pain and call me in the morning."

"What about x-rays? A CT scan. MRI?" Olive demanded as the doctor headed out the door, giving Olive an indulgent smile.

"Olive, you heard her. I don't have broken ribs." Although it felt like it. "I didn't hit my head. I'm fine," I said, patting her on the shoulder the way my grandmother used to pat me when I had to have a shot at the doctor's office. Which made me really miss her. My grandma, not Olive. I am the worst grand-daughter ever.

"Alex?" I realized Olive was calling me and must have been for a while, because she grabbed my arm and dragged me to the nurse's station. "See, she's loopy. She didn't answer when I called. Something is wrong."

Just to get rid of her, I suspected, the nurse shone a light in my eyes (something the doctor had already done) and confirmed that yes, I was indeed fine and that Olive needed to stop being such a mama bear, because, she repeated, I was fine. End of story.

The waiting room was another story. Ellie, Sam, Noah and Willow were all crammed into a space designed to hold no more than three grown people.

"Doc says she's fine," Olive broadcasted to her audience.

"But I still think a CAT scan is in order.

CHAPTER TWENTY-THREE

The World Turns Upside Down

Willow came over to me and took my hand. Looked me in the eyes before making her own determination of my overall health and well-being. "She's tired, but otherwise, she's fine."

That nobody argued with her assessment, including Olive, was surprising. My face must have broadcast my thoughts, because Noah started to explain.

"Willow is . . ."

I reached for her hand. "Lovely," I concluded.

Hand-in-hand, we were about to exit the office, when a nurse shouted. "Oh my God. It sold! 250,000 freakin' dollars."

I turned, knowing this could not be good.

Willow dropped my hand and rushed over to the nurse. "It's Alex's painting!"

The computer in the nurse's station showed an open eBay page where an image of my painting filled the screen. An inset showed a photo of me, along with my name, as the artist in question.

The fluorescent lights above my head flickered in a ghostly way, buzzing and irritating. Olive, in her drab green hoodie, was hunched over the nurse's left shoulder. Willow had one hand stuck in her hair, the other pointing at the screen. Noah leaned over her, his chin resting on her head. The waiting room chairs, metal and some kind of scratchy fabric, were now empty. A dust ball drifted under the nurse's desk. The walls behind the computer, drab and gray, held a poster of a breaching whale, tacked up with yellow, peeling tape. A red umbrella was propped up in the corner. The temperature in the tiny room was dropping rapidly. Rain began pelting the metal roof of the clinic, at first slowly and then faster and faster.

Olive was so thrilled by her $250,000 sale that she never noticed as Juneau and I quietly slipped away.

I walked to the dock with Juneau tucked inside my jacket. I could taste the salt on the cool sea breeze as I forced my pulse to slow and my breathing to deepen. In that short time, I formulated a plan of sorts. I would go back to the lighthouse while everyone was busy congratulating themselves on the sale of my painting and the subsequent rescue of the community center. I would then pack only what Juneau and I absolutely needed—passport, toothbrush, phone, dog food, cash—and leave.

Find a new place. Be more careful in the future. Don't get so close to people. Don't get found.

I wrangled Juneau into his life jacket, ensuring the clasps were secure, set him down in the skiff, started the engine and set off for the lighthouse, faster than was wise, all the while ruminating over how I'd gotten myself into this mess, blaming myself for ruining everything, over and over, with each minute that passed. Juneau barked and I snapped out of it; the clouds were getting darker, the waves higher. Thunder rolled in. A wave rocked us to the left. Water splashed over the side. Juneau was soaked. I idled the engine, looking for a dry towel.

That was when I heard something, or more accurately, I felt something I couldn't ignore. Juneau felt it too. His ears perked up. He turned toward the back of the boat. I followed his lead, scanning the water for any sign of what was causing my skin to prickle, and then I saw it. In the distance, a small boat was listing to one side. There could have been a person, clinging to the bow, or just as easily not. I couldn't take a chance. Don't panic, I told myself. I hit power on the VHF radio, remembering to turn to channel 16 as Jackson had taught me when he'd installed the radio. I located a dimmer with squelch signs and turned it to maximum, repeating the words burned into my brain from Jackson's training. "Mayday, mayday, mayday. This is The Wanderer, sinking boat, what was the direction? Southeast of Prince of Wales Island? Possible man overboard. Oh, God."

Hours passed, as the waves continued to buffet my own little boat. It crossed my mind that the Coast Guard might be rescuing Juneau and I as well, as I steered toward the now-capsized vessel.

Actually. it was only minutes before the coast guard hailed me back, calmly asking for my position, the number of people endangered and if they had life vests. I could see now that it was a dinghy. Terror is an insane thing. Either it stops you in your tracks or it forces you to charge into action. I stuttered through the information, then gunned the engine. Juneau was barking like I'd never seen him do before. There, clinging to the side of the boat, half-way in the water was a tiny figure. Red hair and, oh, God, was it Willow? A horn blasted and I jumped, veering off course. My radio blared. The coast guard was hailing me again. "Stand down, Wanderer. We are on approach."

I idled the engine back, willing Willow to be safe, and watched as the coast guard went into action with military precision and speed. One tossed a life preserver overboard. It went wide of the boat. I couldn't tell if Willow was conscious. Meanwhile, the storm raged as two Coasties, ones I thought I recognized, in full ocean survival gear, climbed over the side of the Coast Guard cutter. They jumped into the water, one after the other, and as efficient as sharks, began making their way over to Willow's side, slicing through the waves. The first one reached her, but she slipped from his grip and slid under the water. Someone shrieked. Oh, God, it was me. The second man arrived in time to catch her before she was lost under a huge wave.

I slammed my eyes shut. The wind froze my cheeks. Icy water spray clung to my eyelashes, nose and ears. The boat rocked to the point where I had to lean over the side to avoid barfing all over myself. A clap of thunder hit so loud, I nearly tipped overboard. Juneau barked and bit my pants, holding onto me. A wave hit; I got a mouthful of salty water and choked it up. Eyes still closed, I willed the lightning to move on, the waves to calm, the rain to clear, the wind to settle. Every fiber of my being concentrated on undoing what I had done. Because if I hadn't stormed off in a such a huff, Willow might never have felt the need to follow me. If she had never followed me, into a storm no less, she would not have wound up in the sea, fighting for her life. Wind settle, I demanded. Lightning stop. Sea, be at peace.

Voices. Shouting. It brought me back. I opened my eyes. The Coasties were sending a signal of some sort. Improbably, my cell rang. I couldn't be bothered to answer. I watched as a Coastie, still in the water, hooked a winch to Willow's life vest and hauled her out of the water like a fish on a line. He gave a thumbs up and I sank to the flooded floor of my boat, my clothes soaked through to my underwear, shivering and shaking, my teeth clenched enough to break a tooth, with Juneau plastered to my side.

I don't know how long it was before a smaller coast guard vessel came up along side us and pulled us aboard. Someone wrapped me in a heavy blanket. I waved him way. "I'm fine. Take care of Juneau," I managed to say as I stared out in nothingness. My phone rang again. Olive's picture filled the screen. I let it ring. It was then that I noticed that the wind had died down, the waves had calmed and there were no longer any sign of rain or lightning.

A text message alert chimed. "Willow is okay," it read. Followed by, "It's not your fault."

Not true. It was always going to be my fault. And I would never forgive myself.

CHAPTER TWENTY-FOUR

Prince of Wales, The Daily News
Rescue at Sea

Early this morning, the Coast Guard bravely navigated the stormy waters of the Gulf of Alaska to perform a harrowing rescue in ten foot waves, lightening and thunder. A minor, here for the summer, had taken her uncle's skiff out shortly before the unexpected storm swept in. The Coast Guard reports that a mayday call from a nearby vessel, in all likelihood, saved the child's life. Local meteorologists are reporting they were stunned by the ferocity of the storm and lack of any warning.

www.PrinceOfWales.com

"Glad to see everyone made it home safely. That was a hel-a-storm like I've never seen before."

"Not for nothing, but why was Willow out in it anyway?"

"I heard she was chasing after Alex."

"Speaking of Alex. Electricity. Rock outcroppings. And now a major storm?"

"Electricity is weird. The earth surfaces moves up and down about two feet a day. There may be life on Enceladus. That's one of Saturn's moons, geniuses. Strange things happen every day. Get a life." Olive

Chapter Twenty-Five

Best Friends Forever

"Alex?" Olive was chewing on her pinkie, worrying a cuticle. "We're friends, right?" What an innocent question that would be in the real world. But this was Olive's world, as I have come to think of it, so the question sent chills shivering down my back, like someone walking over my grave.

"What I mean is, I know you pretty well now."

She looked to me for approval. A nod. Anything. So I nodded, falling into the trap.

"Why don't you ever talk about your family?"

If I were ten, about now I'd be sticking my tongue out and saying, "Because it's none of your business." The grown-up thing was to ignore her.

"Fine. Let's start small. What's your birthday?"

We were at Noah's houseboat, perched on the sides of Willow's bed, enjoying the gently rocking of the house. My heart was in my throat when we approached Noah's home by water. There is no land access. His houseboat was actually more of a floating cabin, with a deep, wide plank porch. The railings consisted of thick logs strung together with the kind of rope one would find on an ocean going ship. Along one side of the houseboat there was a separate float covered with every sort of blooming flower to be found in the area: peony (Paeonia), delphinium (Delphinium D. elatum), globeflower (Trollius), columbine (Aquilegia), Alaska wild iris (Iris setosa) and Asiatic Lily (Lilium), to name a few. I had learned the names from my grandfather who could grow a cactus in Antarctica. Well, almost. There was a small but flourishing greenhouse on one end of the float, and when I peeked inside, I found Spinacia oleracea (spinach), Chicorium intybus (radicchio), Brassica oleracea (broccoli), Cucurbita maxima (winter squash) and Solanum lycopersicum (tomato), that I could see before Olive pulled me away.

Beside the front door hung two ancient looking lanterns. One red. One green. The door itself was a double door of six inch thick wood carved with figures from the sea. I noted a manatee, starfish, a killer whale and a lemon shark before Olive tugged on my hoodie again. Time to go inside. I was stalling because I didn't want to face Noah and we both knew it.

The plank flooring from the deck continued inside and I later learned it had been salvaged from of an old fishing vessel from the early 1900s by the original houseboat owner. On one end of the room was a well-worn baby grand piano along a bank of windows that stretched from floor to ceiling, giving a panoramic view of the forest beyond Noah's home. A galley kitchen sat to the left with a pass-through window that gave me a glimpse of a smaller but efficient space.

Olive pulled me behind her and into Willow's bedroom where Willow was laying back on her pillow reading a Harry Potter book. Juneau took this opportunity to jump on her, pushing the book aside. "Pet me," he woofed.

Back to Olive's question. I do not celebrate my birthday. We, I mean, my family, do celebrate birthdays, but the particular birthday I have coming up is one I was avoiding. This birthday I turn 18. Not the 21 everyone here thinks I will be. Back home, becoming 18 means marriage in my family. Marriage to a man who they had selected for me, probably before I was even born. Outdated? Old fashioned? Ridiculous? I don't have much experience with how partnering happens in other families. Do most young girls in this world get to choose a husband? It seems that way to me now. But my family is steeped in old traditions with no noticeable inclination to change. Every member of my family, going back hundreds of years has married in this way and there hasn't been a single divorce. Ever.

I was the odd one out. Somewhere along the way, I started seeing a future for myself that did not include marriage. At all. Not that there's anything wrong with marriage per se. It's lovely to be surrounded by a warm, welcoming family. It's comforting to know they will be there for you no matter what. It is reassuring that they will never harm you, carelessly or by design. That is our family code.

Even for all this, I wanted more. Selfish. That's what they would have said had I told them. Immature. Another word I could have expected.

Foolhardy.

Knowing all this, I left to find my own way.

"Earth to Alex!" Olive chucked something at my head. I reached over to pick up a stuffed dragon, one with shimmering green wings and a red tongue, from the floor and absentmindedly handed it to Willow.

"Birthday? Cake? Candles. Balloons? You do know what a birthday is, right?" Olive teased.

"July 28th," I blurted out without thinking. I should have come up with an alternative date. What possessed me to tell the truth, I cannot explain. "But I don't celebrate."

"Too old. I get it. But, hey, then you can drink," Olive said, putting out a hand to high five me. I worked not to roll my eyes, something I had picked up in Alaska. Eye rolling was considered the ultimate in rudeness in my family.

"I don't—"

"I get it. You're saying you want the party to be small. Just friends and family."

Definitely not family. And no party. Was she having trouble with her hearing?

"It's not really on the 28th," I ad-libbed. "I was kidding. It's actually December 25th. I don't celebrate because it's on Christmas. That's a big enough holiday without adding my birthday to it."

"That stinks! I was really hoping for a double party."

"Willow, when is your birthday?" I asked, hoping to shift the focus away from where this conversation was heading.

"Her birthday is July 21st," Noah answered, sneaking up on me. I jumped, then ducked my head, avoiding Noah, or at least trying to avoid him. I can't become invisible, though now I wish that was my super power. He was balancing a plate with a hot dog in one hand and had a drink in the other.

Juneau leaped off the bed, going from 0 to 60 in one second, snagged the hot dog on his first try and downed it as quickly. I mumbled an apology. Juneau had never done anything close to that before. Usually, he is a perfect gentleman. And worse, after he'd done the deed, he jumped right back on the bed and snuggled up to Willow, as if he hadn't stolen her lunch and embarrassed me to the point where I was pretty sure my cheeks would never lose their bright red color.

Olive was snorting with laughter and I couldn't bear to look at Noah; but knowing him as I was beginning to, he was definitely laughing, too.

"I don't want a big party or any presents for my birthday," Willow said, ignoring the dog-ate-hot-dog fiasco. "But . . ."

"Uh, oh," Noah said. "I have a bad feeling about this."

As for me, I was staring at Willow's Wonder Woman poster as if it held the key to longevity.

"What?" Willow asked, her face the picture of innocence.

"What are you up to?" Noah asked on a sigh.

"I want to have a sleep-over at the lighthouse."

"Milking it for all it's worth, aren't you?"

"Alex already said it's okay if you say so and all I'm asking is that you agree. For my birthday." She gave him a puppy-dog look. I was glad it wasn't aimed at me.

The wheels in his head were turning, noticeably. He wasn't going to let her stay with me. I was an accident waiting to happen, as evidenced by Olive falling out of a window and Willow capsizing and nearly drowning.

Olive chimed in with a brilliant suggestion. (I am learning sarcasm out here in the real world.) "Noah can spend the night as well. Then no one has to worry." Olive, pure evil, smiled at me. "It'll be amazeballs."

And so, while I stood mute and unmovable, like an ancient redwood tree, it was all arranged. Noah and Willow were spending the night with me at the lighthouse. This weekend.

Shoot me now.

Another one of Olive's favorite expressions.

Chapter Twenty-Six

Sleepless in Alaska

On the day I left home, I made pancakes. I came downstairs in my pajamas and went to the kitchen. I pulled out great-grandma's recipe box from the shelf above the kitchen sink and opened it to the page for ginger flapjacks, then proceeded to gather the ingredients into our old baby blue mixer: butter, flour, leavening, milk, eggs, red pepper and ginger. I turned the stove on, placed a pan on top and put in a liberal mount of oil, by rote, something I had done a hundred times before in exactly the same manner.

The sun was streaming in through the kitchen windows and I rubbed sleep from my eyes as I mixed the batter into a creamy froth. Mom and dad had already left for work. No one would be home for hours.

One, two, three, I flipped the pancakes onto a plate, poured honey on the side and ate. Mindful of the fact that this was the day I had been planning for over a year.

As part of the plan, I had my college acceptance letters from Rutgers and Stanford ready to show my parents at dinner that night. They would think I was postponing the inevitable by going to college. Either way, I would be leaving for good. I had my argument prepared so there was no way they could say no.

I spent the day being a model daughter, cleaning, cooking, gardening, oiling squeaky doors, taking out the trash, organizing the garden shed and even ridding the basement of spiders and their webs. Dinner—baked salmon, garden fresh salad and roasted asparagus—was ready and on the table when they walked in the door at their normal time, 5:30 on the dot. My dad came in first, shedding his jacket and dumping his backpack on the floor. Mom followed, smiling. Content and happy. Nothing unusual there, until Mom turned and my eyes followed her to the place where Phoenix stood behind her filling the doorway. Phoenix, the one person I had been avoiding successfully for weeks. I had blocked his texts and calls and went so far as to change my email address. Somehow he hadn't gotten the message because here he was.

"We have a surprise for you, Alexandria" my mom said, sounding delighted in a way one might be upon winning the lottery. "Phoenix and his parents just returned from their trip to Naples." She said all this while shepherding them into the house, taking their jackets and guiding them into the living room, where they all sat.

My mother was too polite to say anything like "stop standing there with your mouth hanging open," but it would have been appropriate, because I was standing there with my mouth hanging open. I made the conscious effort to close my mouth.

"Alexandria, you've grown," Phoenix's mom exclaimed, something all adults seem to say to children when they can't think of anything else.

"Into a lovely young woman," Phoenix's dad added.

They weren't even seated before Phoenix's mom pulled a carefully wrapped package from her over-size purse. "We found some lovely lace in Rome to show you."

I must have given her a quizzical look because, she added, "For your wedding dress. I think I mentioned before, we've reserved St. Patrick's cathedral for the big day. And the boathouse in central park. We left the minister to you, as you requested," she told my mother.

Cathedrals, boathouses, ministers! I felt woozy. My heart was exploding. I placed a hand on my chest and tried to breath. "Excuse me," I mumbled as I rushed off to the kitchen where the salmon and asparagus were steadily growing cold and the salad was wilting. I sank down into a red kitchen chair and put my head on the table, praying for it to stop pounding. My head, not the table. Seconds later, a shadow crept up on me, covering the table in darkness.

"Alexandria." Phoenix. He didn't ask for an explanation. Maybe he was as nervous, even terrified, about this arrangement as I was. Most of my life, I'd paid little attention to the idea. Something would change before the time arrived, I felt, even as I plotted and planned out options, in case I was mistaken. But now, reality was wearing an embroidered Valentino dress with Tamara Mellon heels and sitting in my living room.

I lifted my head, stood to my full height, put on a good face and turned. "We'd better join them," I said, and marched out of the kitchen and into the living room. The good daughter, I listened to a monotonous stream of information regarding wedding flowers, wedding wear, wedding music, wedding gifts, wedding photography, etc, all the while thinking of ways to kill myself: head in the oven, accidentally-on-purpose falling from a cliff, ingesting cleaning products (not the herbal kind my mother buys), skydiving without a parachute, swimming with sharks, mixing medicines, staring into the eclipse (no, that one causes blindness, not death), sunburning myself to death—too slow. Regardless, I believe you get the point. The list went on and on, until finally our (my) unwanted guests left, Phoenix with a chaste kiss on my cheek, his parents with quick hugs.

My parents headed off to bed, the food left, congealed and uneaten on the kitchen table.

Me? I wasn't hungry. I was truly, deeply and madly frightened. Some time after midnight, I slipped out the back door of the only home I had known, found the backpack I had hidden in the garden shed months before, intended for use only if all else failed, and left, eyes forward, resolve in place, without looking back, the future firmly ahead of me.

On the day I left home, I ate pancakes. Other than that, nothing else went as planned.

Chapter Twenty-Seven

Prince of Wales Times

The community center is saved!

In an event that has everyone on POW amazed, a painting by Alexandria Aerowyn, and gifted to the community center in order to help with repairs, has sold on eBay for a whopping $250,000. And in case you're thinking somebody is spoofing us, you would be wrong. The check arrived today. Work begins tomorrow.

And in other news, we have an update on the daring rescue at sea of Willow Gallagher. In the tradition of lighthouse keepers everywhere, it was Prince of Wale's own lighthouse keeper, Alex, who saved the life of long-time Prince of Wales resident's niece. On the day of the rescue, Alex found herself caught in an unexpected storm, only to find that Willow was in a small boat not far behind her.

Quick thinking and persistence paid off when Alex called the coast guard and headed for Willow's vessel. Fortunately for everyone involved, the coast guard arrived before Alex had a chance to throw herself over the side of her boat in an attempt to rescue Willow, leaving the coast guard with only one person to rescue.

She may be from Outside, but Alex is Alaskan through and through.

God. They made it sound like I had done something great. I didn't. I didn't save Willow and I hadn't sold the painting. I simply gave it to Olive as a gift and she did the rest. I was actually afraid to go into town now.

However, since coming to Alaska, I have learned the difference between standing still and facing my fears. Noah and Willow were spending the night at the lighthouse tomorrow and I had a long list of things to accomplish before then. No time to wallow.

Whale's Pass is the smallest community on Prince of Wales Island, with roughly 47 full time residents. Craig, the largest town, boasts 1,231. I was headed into Craig today to prepare for the upcoming sleep-over, with a supply list long enough to host a minor dignitary.

I love most things about Prince of Wales. Today was no different. Being on the water reminded me of home by the Jersey shore with its boardwalks and retinue of small, locally owned and operated shops, except here the shops have a certain rustic, old west feel that is warm and somehow comforting. My first stop was Donna's Coffee for coffee, obviously. Ellie does straight up, percolated coffee, no frills. Olive swore it wouldn't be disloyal to stop into Donna's for a triple mocha and a Twinkie, another thing Ellie is certain no one's heart needs and that she refuses to stock.

I found the Twinkie aisle right away; Twinkies in hand, I was heading for the coffee counter, relishing my anonymity, when a woman rushed over to me and gushed: "You're Alex!"

I shook my head and went to turn, but she caught my sleeve. "No, you are. Everyone, Alex is here." As if I was a celebrity.

"Um," I stuttered, but she didn't let me finish before she whipped her phone out, put one arm around me and aimed it at the two of us. "Smile."

People were starting to stare.

"Everyone heard what you did and we can't thank you enough."

I wasn't sure if she was talking about my non-rescue of Willow or my non-donation of the painting. I held up the hand with the Twinkie in it to stop her and she took that opportunity to back me into a corner.

"Take the Twinkie. It's on me." I was shaking my head like a broken bobble-head doll. "This is my place. You need coffee with that. Harve, get this lady some coffee. Make it a triple mocha."

"Um."

"Harve. A triple mocha and hurry. She doesn't have all day."

I tried to push a handful of bills at her, but she acted as if I had called her dearly departed cat a nasty name. "Don't insult me. It's the least we can do, isn't it, Harve?"

Before I knew it, she'd ushered me outside and sat me down at a table. She plopped down in the chair opposite mine and it was only after I had eaten every bite of the Twinkie and finished every drop of my triple mocha that she let me venture beyond her deck. Then and only then did she wave me off, but not before offering me an open invitation to free coffee and Twinkies any time I wanted, in perpetuity, and I'd best remember it.

Olive was going to be so jealous.

After coffee, my To-Do list involved going to the grocery store for all of the must-have food items Olive assured me a 12-year-old would want, then to the sporting goods store for sleeping bags and tents followed by the general store for a few games. I double-checked my list after I escaped from the coffee shop and meandered down the boardwalk, checking out window displays until I reached the North Beach General Store, where I was hoping I could obtain the sporting goods and games in one stop. Sadly, Mr. Bradley, the owner, was in the store and he recognized me.

"Well, if it isn't Alexandria Aerowyn." He practically bowed. "What can I do for you today?"

"I'm having a—"

"Slumber party. Yes, we heard. You'll be needing sleeping bags and tents I hear and some games for Willow," he said over his shoulder as he steered me down an aisle lined with bicycles, baseball bats, water jugs and more.

"Um."

He gathered up an armload of supplies, rambling on about how this one would stand up to the winds out at the lighthouse and how that game was one his grandson swore by; and without input from me, he had the entire mountain of supplies up at the cash register as I trailed behind helplessly.

People in the store were once again staring. I mean, I would.

I went to pull out my wallet and he pushed my hand away. "I wouldn't dream of taking your money," he insisted as he shoved my supplies into oversized carryalls.

"But—"

"Consider it my donation to the community center."

"Uh—"

"What you did? Well, there are no words." He looked to be on the verge of tears, but I was probably wrong about that.

I didn't know what to do. I couldn't accept such an expensive gift, especially for having done nothing. But he was already pushing me out the door.

I turned to say something, although I wasn't sure what. But he was back inside already and I couldn't just stand there with people gaping at me. I turned back the way I'd come. Willow was going to have to do without Fruit Loops and Lucky Charms. I had to get out of here before someone gave me the keys to the city and a new Mercedes.

Of course, it had to have been Olive who was behind the story that would not die. I hadn't saved Willow and yet everyone on Prince of Wales seemed to think differently. As evidenced by the growing number of gifts I kept receiving, which, besides the coffee, Twinkies and sporting goods, included: a hand-knit qiviut scarf (made from the hair of a musk ox) so I would be warm this winter—an implicit Alaska style welcome—dried salmon, a toy for Juneau, a box of Wild Berry chocolates and a bottle of champagne. I don't drink—although recent events had me rethinking that decision.

I really wished I hadn't come to town. But Willow has been talking about it for days, sending me text messages and emoji's. I suspect she was at home right this minute packing as if she was leaving for a winter in Antarctica, even though I had suggested she bring essentials only: toothbrush, favorite stuffed toy, book, pajamas and her favorite blanket. On my end, I managed to procure a frisbee from Ellie and a box of contraband Fruit Loops from Olive. Oh, and marshmallows for the campfire. As for emotional preparedness, I was a mess. So much so that I was considering inviting Olive. And Jackson. Maybe Sam as well. And Ellie. The more the merrier, a great wall of people between me and Noah. That's what I needed.

Unfortunately, Olive was busy, although she couldn't seem to remember doing what. Jackson had a night scheduled with friends. I didn't know where to find Sam. Ellie had a cafe to run. Where was everyone when I needed them? That's what I was wondering. On the bright side, I loved the idea of spending time with Willow, even though being with her sometimes made me miss my own family, knowing that I had stuck a figurative knife in their hearts by doing the one thing they might never be able to forgive me for.

One day I hope to reconcile this whole mess, but in the meantime, every night, before I go to bed, I keep asking myself if it is ever acceptable to harm someone else in order to save yourself? So far the answer is no, and yet, I did it. Am still doing it. How will I ever make it up to them?

My gran always said there is good and bad in each of us and that the solution to every problem in life is to shine a light on the good. She added that every act of goodness, no matter how small, adds to the universe of goodness that surrounds us, which is everything.

I wish gran were here. She would know what to do.

Chapter Twenty-Eight

Olive's Sleepover rules :

1. Get some rest the night before, since no one actually sleeps at a sleepover. (Because if you do, you might wake up with a mustache painted on your face with indelible marker.)

2. Stock up on eye shadow, blush, lipstick and nail colors, because makeovers are an essential ingredient of a successful sleepover.

3. Be prepared to have all your dirty laundry aired, because no subject is off limits and generally boys are the main topic of conversation. Which is unlikely as Noah will be there, meaning there will be no "dirty laundry" and "no boy talk."

4. Don't pick your nose or scratch anywhere you wouldn't want it to be seen online, tormenting you for the rest of your days. (I had other, more important reasons for not wanting photos of me on Facebook; therefore, I would definitely be having a talk with Noah regarding a no-iPhone policy.)

There was more, but I crumbled the list into a ball and threw it on the recycle pile. Willow is an old soul who loves the sea and wildlife and I could imagine her perfectly happy tossing a ball to Juneau and toasting marshmallows over the fire before laying on the sand and watching the stars come out at night. The very thought made the rhythm of my heart calm and my breathing slow.

I don't know if I mentioned it, but the day Willow was rescued, I decided to stay and face the consequences of my actions, whatever they may be. There was no way I was leaving her.

Preparations done, I went to the water's edge as Noah and Willow sailed toward the island. When I say "sailed" I am not romanticizing their arrival. Their boat announced itself with two large white sails that seemed to arrive before the rest of the boat. The sailboat was made of wood worn to a smooth patina and looked like one you would take around the world if you were adventurous. They docked and Willow hopped out first, dragging an overnight bag behind her as Noah tied the boat up and set about lowering the sails. Juneau rushed over, greeting her by repeatedly jumping in her face, tugging on her bag and dancing around her feet, alternately tripping her and dragging her forward. I'd never seen him this happy. It's like he knew she was staying.

I took a deep breath. The tents were up and staked to the ground. The campfire was blazing. I'd set out the sleeping bags and camp chairs and had a bag of marshmallows at the ready, in case Willow wanted to get down to the business of burning them right away. Dinner was warming in the oven. Did I forget anything?

Juneau snatched a frisbee from the ground and offered it to

Willow and off they went, tossing it back and forth, racing up and down the beach, barking and howling like the happiest creatures on earth. I stood and watched, letting their happiness flow over me.

"The simple things are often the best," Noah said, coming up behind me and making me jump. How he always managed to do that was beyond me. And why did my plans to avoid him always go awry? Not to mention, why do I feel such a strong need to avoid him? Besides the fact that he brings out the grumpy in me. Usually. Today I felt more peaceful than I had in days.

"Willow brings that out in people."

I gave him the universal face for What Are You Talking About?"

"She has a way of calming people, animals, you name it."

"It's a gift."

"And a curse."

I knew what he meant. Every good thing has a potential down side.

The frisbee landed at his feet and he tossed it back to Willow. "So, Miss Aerowyn—

"The fire needs tending." I excused myself to get more kindling and another log and concentrated on fussing with a fire that did not need tending, until it was higher and hotter and Willow and Juneau rushed over.

"Marshmallows!" Willow shouted. Juneau woofed his agreement.

"Get some sticks and we'll toast 'em," Noah said. "That is, if Alex is okay with it."

I nodded agreement as Willow tore into the bag of marshmallows.

"Marshmallows before dinner! This is the greatest!" Juneau leapt into the air in agreement. Maybe he didn't know it, but he wasn't getting any marshmallows today, or any day.

There must be a knack to roasting marshmallows, because my first one dripped into the fire, causing sparks to ignite and shoot up like fireworks. My second try morphed into a charred lump, something Santa might save for the stockings of bad little boys and girls. On my third attempt, Willow reached over and took the stick from my hand. "Here, let me." Hers turned out perfectly, although I didn't have the heart to tell her how much I seriously disliked toasted marshmallows. They're gooey and sticky and taste like burnt sugar. I tossed the rest of mine in the fire and went for a package of organic, vegan and gluten free sausages. I pierced the sausages with sticks and handed one each to Noah and Willow.

"Enough marshmallows for today, I think." I dug out several foil-wrapped potatoes that I had buried in the fire earlier. Hopefully, they had cooked all the way through. Olive insisted they would. I had backup food as well. Ellie had made up a picnic basket, having no faith in my culinary skills, one I was happy to accept, just in case. In the end, it came in handy. I burnt more than one sausage and Willow, though she was polite about it, didn't actually like vegan sausages. When I checked the potatoes and found they were raw, I gave in and pulled out the basket.

I passed on the fried chicken, but the apple pie was delicious. Noah took a bite of pie and sighed. For some reason I could not fathom, Ellie had told me that the way to a man's heart was through his stomach.

"Ellie made it," I said. I didn't want to be making my way to any man's heart right now. For one, it would never work. My family would see to that.

He nodded, with a full mouth.

"Ellie makes the best pies. She's going to teach me," Willow said.

She polished off two pieces of fried chicken, some potato salad and was half way through her second piece of pie before I had finished choking down my burnt veggie sausage. She must be growing.

"Growth spurt," Noah said. Was mind-reading his super power?

I tossed a rawhide bone to Juneau and he took off with it into one of the tents. I guess that was in case one of us decided we were also craving a rawhide treat.

When Willow finished with her food and politely helped clean up the paper plates and utensils, she asked, "Alex, can I go exploring in the lighthouse?"

Noah looked over at me and I nodded. "But stay away from the windows," I said. "And hold onto the hand rails when you're taking the stairs." I didn't want any more accidents.

"Okay, Mom." She raced away with Juneau on her heels.

"She means you are babying her."

"I'm simply being careful."

"Mom."

"Fine."

"It's not an insult. You care about her and don't want her to get hurt. I get that," he said. "She does, too."

"Okay." I wasn't being very gracious. You don't have to tell me.

"Nice weather we're having."

"It's beautiful."

"It won't be long before we'll be pulling out the insulated underwear and snow boots."

"Insulated . . ."

"The things you wear under your clothes, so you don't freeze to death."

"Oh."

"God, Alex, you're never going to survive out here in the winter." He sounded angry. Not that my survival was any of his business.

"Says you."

"Says anyone with an ounce of sense in their heads." He shook his head.

Blood was rushing to my head; my stomach felt like I'd swallowed a rock and my fists were clenched. I was about to say something I would regret. I knew it.

"Alex!!!" Willow came crashing into us. Look what I found. She was holding the bottle. "And there's something inside!"

All the blood that had previously rushed to my heart, dropped to my feet. Noah noticed the color leave my face and my efforts to avoid going down in a dead faint and reached out for me.

"Willow! That does not belong to us. You need to put it back."

"But—"

"Now."

"Noah," she pleaded.

"You can put it back now or you can get in the boat and we'll head home. Which is it going to be?"

"Fine. But Alex doesn't mind," she said as she stomped off.

If Juneau could have stomped, I think he would have. In solidarity.

"I'm sorry about that," Noah said.

I was making myself find my breath, forcing my heart to stop beating out of my chest. "It's nothing. I must be coming down with something."

"She's 12. It comes with the territory," he explained.

"So, about the weather," I said, making it clear that any discussion of the bottle or about me, for that matter, was officially closed.

The evening progressed with no further drama. We played a game of Stratego until the campfire started dying out. Noah got up, stretching as he did so. "I'm getting old."

It had never occurred to me to wonder about his age. He was lean and fit. I didn't see any creases or lines around his eyes, but they did crinkle when he smiled.

He went over to the pile of kindling and logs that I had collected earlier and gathered up an armload. When he returned, he tossed pieces on the fire and pushed them around with a stick until he was satisfied. The fire roared.

"Alex?" Willow was laid back on a sleeping bag, looking up at the stars, just as I had predicted. "What superpower would you not want to have?"

That question was one I would not have predicted. She continued, "I wouldn't want to be invisible."

I could think of a time or two when that power could come in handy.

"Everything you eat would show in your stomach. Which would be pretty gross. And then it would get all mushed up and travel through your intestines and then it would go down to—"

"We get your point," Noah interrupted.

"Gross. I also would not want to be able to fly."

Hmm. Flying seemed like a pretty great superpower to have.

"Military radar might think I was a UFO and shoot me down. You know. In a country with a crazy dictator."

"A crazy dictator, huh?" Noah said, looking like he was thinking that a normal country might shoot a UFO down.

"I also wouldn't want to be Elasti-Girl. I mean, what if I got mad in class, one day, lost control and whacked some teacher all the way to Saturn? Right?"

I wasn't sure how to ask, so I came right out with it. "Is anyone giving you reasons to get angry in class?" That she answered right away, without having to think about it, relieved my concerns about a bullying or otherwise abusive teachers.

"No, but you never know. I might one day, when I'm a teenager and my hormones are all over the place."

Noah and I exchanged looks. One that communicated affection for Willow, shared knowledge that she is an old soul and something else I couldn't put my finger on.

"Anything else," I asked.

"Well, Magneto. For obvious reasons."

I crunched my face up giving her the look that says I don't know what you are talking about. You know the one.

"He can put a quarter through someone's head. No one should have that kind of power."

"Very true." I could think of lots of other powers people shouldn't have, like controlling electricity, rock formations and the weather, but didn't mention any of those.

"What about you guys?" she asked.

Noah answered first. "I wouldn't want to be Superman."

"What? Why not? He can scale tall buildings in a single bound. That's pretty cool. And, he has x-ray vision, so you always know who's at the door before you answer it. "

"Although the door thing is pretty cool, the tights don't work for me. I'm more of a Batman kinda guy. Gotta love the cape," he teased. I hope.

"Your turn, Alex." Noah wasn't going to let me off the hook. I almost stuck my tongue out, but then remembered that, one, it was rude and two, tongues aren't as attractive as some people seem to believe.

"Ok. I wouldn't want to have the power . . ." I stalled.

"To," Noah prodded.

"Give me a minute."

"I know, Alex. You wouldn't want the power to read minds."

My eyebrows shot up, Noah's, too.

"Duh. She likes to think the best of people, so why go looking for trouble? She's not nosey and she doesn't care what people think of her."

"What did I tell you about saying 'duh'?" Noah said, but he was laughing so hard, I'm not sure she heard.

I didn't have to ask why it was so funny, because it was true. I do like to think the best of people. I'm not nosey, and three, I don't care what he thinks of me.

I truly don't.

In order to avoid any and all unnecessary conversation with Noah I had a week's worth of activities planned for this overnight event. Next on the list was a vintage Wonder Woman movie. I stretched a white sheet against the lighthouse and aimed a portable projector, purchased for this occasion. Willow and Juneau settled in against a large rock, tucked into one sleeping bag, watching intently. I didn't know dogs watched TV, or in this case a movie, but they were both transfixed.

It was really interesting. I'd never seen a superhero movie before and was almost as absorbed as Willow. As the movie drew to a close, I noticed Willow was nodding off and then jerking awake, then nodding off again. The movie credits rolled and a good fifteen minutes of music did the trick. She was truly asleep. I went for Juneau while Noah lifted Willow, sleeping bag and all and placed her gently in her tent. When he was done tucking her in, he came out and sat by the fire.

I carefully pulled down the sheet and folded it into a perfect square. I gathered up the half full bag of marshmallows and yawned. "I think I'll go to bed now, too. It's been a long day."

"Stay," Noah asked.

Knowing it would be rude to decline, I still didn't answer.

"Please."

I sat. The fire was still going strong, thanks to Noah adding wood throughout the movie. The flames were mesmerizing. Noah sat next to me. For a while we didn't talk. It finally occurred to me that if I didn't say something he might start asking awkward questions.

"What brought you to Alaska, Noah?" I asked, before realizing it was a bad start, because the next logical question from him would be about why I came to Alaska. I didn't give him a chance to answer. "Did you travel much before that?"

"I went to college in Italy. I loved it there, but Alaska called to me. Don't ask me why."

College meant he had to be at least 21, plus his years in Alaska, so maybe 25 or 26. "Did you study music?"

"I studied philosophy and computer wizardry, otherwise known as programming." He laughed, "My parents insisted I have a backup plan."

"Maybe you could teach a programming class at the community center."

"I was thinking about it. Speaking of the community center, the work is almost done. Olive is on a tear to get the classes lined up. You know she's going to talk you into something, so you might as well volunteer for the class you want or she'll have you teaching Hot Yoga or something equally painful."

"Too late. She has me signed up for Painting 101."

"You'll be good at that. I love your work."

Note, awkward silence ensues.

"Alex. I know you were thinking about leaving. I won't ask why, but it would crush Willow. Not that I'm trying to guilt you into staying. I just thought you should know."

When I didn't answer, he continued. "You're probably wondering why I have Willow with me this summer?"

The thought had crossed my mind.

"My older sister travels a lot for her job, so I stepped in to help. I get Willow for school vacations and then I spend a few months in Jersey in the winter."

Jersey! We may have crossed paths, at the shore, at the grocery store, stuck in traffic. It was odd.

"Willow has been asking to stay here with me, so right now we're in negotiations about it. Alex?"

"Hmm."

"I want to thank you."

"Don't be silly. A few marshmallows and that was it," I answered, deflecting his gratitude.

"Not for this, although I appreciate it. Willow was thrilled when you said yes to a sleepover. I meant thank you for saving her. When I thought she was gone, I—"

"Noah, stop. It was my fault she was out on the water alone in the first place. I am the one who should be thanking you, for not hating me."

He shook his head and reached for my hand. "So, what? You knew she was following you?"

"Well, no, but—"

"So, you knew a storm was approaching when even the Coast Guard thought it would be clear seas that day?"

"No."

"Okay, then, you knew she was going to end up in the water fighting for her . . . I don't even want to say it."

"Of course not, but if I hadn't huffed off, she wouldn't have followed me."

"And you have control over the universe and 12-year-old girls. Is that it?"

I crossed my arms over my chest. If he was going to be like that, what could I say?

"Anyway, I wanted to thank you and Willow had an idea." He handed me a package. "Open it."

We stared at each other for several minutes. I lost. I tore the wrapping paper off slowly and opened a small white box. Inside, resting on a bed of cotton, was a bracelet with a row of tiny charms. I felt my face getting bright red; I kept my head down as I fingered each charm. There was a lighthouse with a rotating light on top. Next was a paintbrush, then a heart charm that opened. Inside was a photo of Willow and Noah, arm-in-arm, laughing. The other charms included a howling dog, to represent Juneau, an okapi, to represent me, a totem pole with an eagle spreading its wings and lastly, a miniature 8-ball charm.

"Willow picked the charms. Hence, the 8-ball."

"Hence."

I was joking, but it was perfect. So perfect that tears rushed down my face even though I tried to keep them in. I never cry like that. I don't know what came over me. I covered my mouth and mumbled, "I can't accept this."

It was too much.

Noah leaned in to brush a tear from my cheek. I couldn't seem to breathe. He was so close that if I moved inches to my left, our lips would touch. I held my breath, unsure. The silence was overwhelming. I sensed he was about to do something that could change things forever, and I knew I didn't have forever. Not here. Not with him.

I was about to tell him that when Willow, rubbing the sleep from her eyes, came stumbling out of her tent toward us.

"Alex! Noah! Alex!"

Noah hopped up, went over to her and lifted her into his arms.

"I had a dream."

"A bad dream?"

She shook her head. "Juneau and I were living on the houseboat."

I avoided Noah's eyes.

"Alex?" Willow whispered.

"Hmm."

"Juneau wants to know if we can sleep in your tent tonight."

Willow the dog whisperer.

I looked over at Noah with a silent question.

"Fine by me," he said.

Willow gave me puppy dog eyes for good measure. I shook the tiny 8-ball on my charm bracelet.

Willow leaned over my shoulder and shouted. "The 8-ball says yes!"

And so, there you have it.

The 8-ball said yes.

Chapter Twenty-Nine

The Blueberry Festival

I would have agreed, with or without the 8-Ball, which I am pretty sure she had rigged somehow. Don't look at me that way. She may be 12 but, like Olive, she has a Machiavellian streak. Not really. The real reason I agreed was because I no longer appear to be capable of declining any request made by Willow.

Morning arrived slowly the next day. Stretching and yawning, we ate breakfast over a renewed campfire. After breakfast and packing and hugs from Willow, they set sail, waving goodbye from the water as they headed back to their houseboat. Juneau sat on the end of the dock, head drooping at their departure. All in all, I have to admit: the overnight went much better than I had expected.

Still. I was never, ever going to do that again.

I sat on the beach for long after they had disappeared from view. I don't know how long I would have stayed that way if Juneau hadn't nudged my shoulder with his nose. I scratched his head absent-mindedly. He kept nudging, however. Okay, Juneau, what is it? He was holding the message bottle between his paws. The writing seemed to glow eerily from within the bottle. I didn't know what it all meant, but I'd had enough of it. I grabbed the bottle, stood and went to the end of the dock where I tossed it with all my strength back into the sea. There.

Done. No more cryptic messages. No more mysteries. I gave Juneau a reproachful look, as if he was responsible for I don't know what. He ducked his head. Which meant that now I felt bad. I turned and headed for the lighthouse in search of a treat to make my apologies, all the while thinking about my next painting, which brought my thoughts back to who had purchased my painting and how that going to ruin everything. I shook my head of the negative thought. I would go to the top of the lighthouse and the sea breezes and the stunning view would soothe me. I would stop thinking about things I couldn't control.

Which felt like just about everything.

My foot hit the first step when Juneau started barking. He rarely barks. He races after seabirds without barking. He greets dogs and cats and squirrels and, just about everything, without barking.

"Juneau!"

I recognized that voice.

Willow came racing down the dock and hit the beach, running at top speed until she leaped into my arms, legs around my waist, holding tight.

"We're going to the Blueberry Festival!"

Noah, I could see was tailing far behind, tying up the boat for the second time.

"And guess what?"

Um. "What?"

"We came to get you," she squealed. She actually squealed.

By this time, Noah was standing behind Willow, hands on her shoulders, looking decided sheepish.

I tried to hide my amusement at his discomfort. "What's this I hear about someone taking me somewhere?"

"You have to come. We can't leave you here! All alone!" Willow insisted.

Apparently speaking in exclamation points was her new modus operandi.

Noah leaned into her ear. "What did we say in the boat?"

Willow sighed. "If you want to. But you want to. I know you do. It'll be great!"

I raised my eyebrows in a question. Noah answered. "It's in Ketchikan. Willow heard it on the radio going over and now . . . ," he trailed off.

Willow wiggled down from my arms. "And Noah can play. They have stages and oh, jugglers, and tents with all kinds of cool things people make, all by themselves. They have blueberry pie, blueberry muffins, blueberry tacos." She wrinkled her nose. "I don't like the tacos so much, but blueberry ice cream is my fave."

"And you just heard about this today?" I asked. Surely everyone in the area would know about a festival happening in their own backyard.

"Well," Willow said.

"Well," Noah said.

Suspicious.

Noah broke first. "We knew, but Willow was willing to skip it so she could have her sleepover. On the way home, when we heard it on the radio . . ."

"I see."

"I figured we could kill two—"

"Don't say it, Noah. That's not very nice. We love birds."

And how did I come into this?

"Since we were going, Willow thought . . ."

"Shame on you, Noah. You said—"

"We thought. Is that better? We thought you might enjoy it. That is if you don't have other plans."

Like a fly in a spider's web, I was becoming more and more entangled in the Prince of Wales community. My feet were sticky and my power to resist fading fast.

Willow was tapping her feet. "We don't have all day. If you don't hurry, we're going to miss everything!"

"Fine. I'll get Juneau settled and be ready in a sec."

"No need. Dogs are allowed!" Willow practically leaped into the air. "He can come!"

Noah nodded. "Critters of every variety are welcome."

My first Blueberry Festival.

Hold the blueberry tacos, please.

Chapter Thirty

Blueberry Subterfuge and Blue Barf

If the organizers could have managed it, I was certain it would have been raining blueberries. There were blueberry balloons. Dogs in blueberry costumes. Blueberry sunglasses. Bands singing ballads about blueberries. Blueberry pie with blueberry ice cream. I couldn't stop smiling. It was silly and overwhelming, but in a good way.

Willow tugged on my hand, dragging me forward. As soon as I saw the table lined with blueberry pies and a sign pronouncing the pie eating contest, I dug in my heels, stopping her short. "No."

She gave me a wounded look.

"No." I folded my arms over my chest and gave her my best I Mean It look.

"Noahhh . . ."

"No means no," he replied.

Good.

"Fine. I'll do it all by myself," she pouted. "Juneau, come on. You can be my cheerleader."

She got on line for the contest. Noah and I exchanged looks. OMG, as Olive would say. Willow was the most wonderful creature and the most trying one at the same time. Noah put an arm around my shoulders and navigated me to the chairs set out for the audience. I didn't shrug off his arm and may have leaned in a bit before we sank into our seats to watch usually sane people shove pies into their mouths at an alarming speed.

The bell went off and blueberries were flying. It wasn't long before the first person wretched up globs of blueberry pie and conceded the contest. I had to cover my mouth to keep from laughing. I shouldn't be laughing at someone's discomfort, should I? But it was so much fun. Another contestant bit the dust, blueberry juice dripping from his face, he looked like he was going to be the next to barf. Six to go and Willow was holding her own among the younger contestants, who were separated from the rest, being smart, not smashing pie all over her face, not choking herself, not a single drop of blueberry juice staining her clothing, but spooning in small bites like a robot. It was fascinating.

"She's going to be so sick later."

I must have said it out loud because Noah bumped my shoulder with his.

"She's a pro at this. Besides the younger ones only get one small pie."

A bell rang and a shout went up. The youth contest had ended. Willow was standing on the stage grinning with bright blue lips and teeth. The contest moderator handed her a pie-shaped trophy along with an oversized stuffed blueberry while congratulating her on winning the junior division. She came racing down the steps of the stage.

"Hungry?" I asked as she rushed us.

Noah snorted. He did. Although he'll deny it.

Basking in the glow of Willow's win, it suddenly occurred to me, we hadn't run into anyone else from Prince of Wales. As we walked along in our little group, passing brightly colored booths I wondered aloud, "Where is everyone? Olive. Jackson. Didn't they want to come?"

Noah steered us into a booth selling artisanal breads and assorted pastries. He purchased a braided bread, pulled off a chunk and handed it to me. It was warm and crusty and smelled heavenly.

"Noah?"

"The weather wasn't supposed to be good today. Besides, the fair is all week. Plenty of time."

Okay.

The sun shone down from a bright blue sky as we went from booth to booth. Music filled my heart as we danced into the evening, Juneau, too, to zydeco, folk and even oldies until we were all happily exhausted. In the end, though, it turned out my prediction was correct. Because, even though Willow had finished off "only one small pie", eventually her stomach rebelled, the blueberry pie caught up with her, and, how to say it—we missed the last ferry back to the island.

Luckily Noah had a friend with a vacation cabin nearby, so we had a place to stay until the next ferry. Shortly after we arrived at the cabin, Noah gave Willow peppermint tea, then sent her off to bed. I took the couch. Noah stretched out in front of the fireplace, next to Juneau. I fell asleep as soon as I pulled the covers up to my chin. I don't know how long Juneau and Noah sat up warming themselves by the fire. When I opened my eyes again, it was past noon. The next day!

"Good morning, sleepyhead."

Willow was perched on the edge of the couch, half sitting on my feet. I smiled at her, rubbing the sleep from my eyes. "How are you feeling?"

"Like I could eat a bear."

I laughed. What do they say about children being resilient?

"How about a cup of tea and some toast?" Noah said as he came out of the tiny kitchen carrying a tray with what most likely held tea and toast.

"Yuck."

"No more pie for you, young lady."

"It was the dancing. You don't exercise on a full stomach. Science 101," she informed him. "You're the adult. You didn't know that?"

I covered a laugh by coughing into my napkin.

Noah rolled his eyes as he set the tray on the coffee table in front of me. There was tea, toast, yes, and a whole lot more. A bowl of blueberries. Of course. Sugar topped blueberry muffins. Fresh bread. Butter. Bacon. Eggs. Hot coffee. It was like Easter Sunday at a church potluck. I reached for a cup of coffee, adding milk and honey and took a bite of a muffin. It muffin was warm and sweet and extremely satisfying. The coffee was hot and I realized I never wanted to get up. The fire was roaring. Noah must have gotten up early to stoke the flames. Juneau even had a treat, which he was gnawing on in front of the fireplace. I leaned back and sighed. I could stay here forever looking out the large picture windows, watching the birds in the bird feeder and the clouds as they drifted by.

Noah read my mind. "The next ferry isn't until five. We have all day."

Willow had other ideas. 1. Go back for Day 2 of the Blueberry Festival. 2. Go kayaking. 3. Play Stratego and Clue. 4. Noah stopped her at four, citing the fact that the guest decides. I wish I had my paints with me, or a sketchbook at least. I already had a plethora of Blueberry Festival images in my head aching to get out.

"Alex, can we—," Willow started, but Noah stopped her. "No whining, pleading or manipulating. Alex decides. And to make it fair, we are eliminating options one through three."

"What?!" Willow stomped her foot. "That's not fair!"

"Who ate too much pie?"

"Hmmph."

"I think quiet time is in order. There are books in the bedroom. Go. Read."

I felt terrible and relieved all at the same time. Did it make me a terrible person if I didn't want to play board games or go kayaking or return to the noise and chaos of the Blueberry Festival? It was good for a day, but there is something about a cabin in the woods that is so quiet that all you can hear are the birds.

I sipped my coffee and nibbled on my muffin. Noah sat on the opposite end of the sofa with his feet propped up on the coffee table, reading. So peaceful. I got up to find my own book, decided on a thick book about Alexander Hamilton, and settled in for a day with no demands. The best part? Noah didn't feel the need to talk or find excuses to disrupt the peace. When I did finally get up to check on Willow, I found her and Juneau snuggled together, sharing dreams.

When the alarm on Noah's phone rang, I was shocked to see it was nearly 4:00 p.m. We quickly gathered up stray cups and dishes and did an overall cabin cleaning, after which Noah woke Willow. We took Juneau out for a quick walk and were set to go. Reluctantly, on my part. It would be nice to get home and work on my Blueberry Festival paintings, but still . . .

The ferry ride brought us back to reality and our lives on Prince of Wales Island. From there, we all boarded Noah's boat and headed toward the lighthouse. We each seemed to feel like something was ending. Willow was unusually quiet. I closed my eyes and relaxed into the waves until finally we pulled up to my dock. I opened them to see our little vessel was surrounded by other boats moored at the dock and that the beach was crowded with about ten, no fifteen, people from Prince of Wales, including Olive, Jackson, Ellie and Sam. I shook my head and took a step back. Noah took my hand and helped me out of the boat and onto the dock, then lifted Willow onto the dock as well. "Surprise!" she shouted.

Oh, no. I turned to go back, but Noah put a hand my shoulders and turned me back around.

"What the—?"

"Be nice," Noah said.

"What?"

"They did this for you."

"Why? I don't understand."

Willow tugged on my hand. "Come on. Everyone is waiting!!!"

Olive came crashing down the dock. "Surprised?"

"Surprised" did not begin to cover it. I was confused. Anxious. Petrified. What had they done?"

"What did you do?" I leveled at Olive, then Noah.

"You're gonna love it," Olive said.

Jackson arrived on cue. "This was all Olive," with a look that said, "Don't blame me."

"Come on, before the dock collapses from all our weight," Noah said as he steered us to the shore where I was enveloped in a group hug from hell. At least from an introvert's point of view. Everyone was shouting thanks and wait until you see and more I couldn't hear.

"Enough already," Olive demanded. "Let's show her."

Power of invisibility, come to me. Or flight. I'd take either.

As Olive pulled me from one place to another, it hit me. Noah had tricked me. Had Willow's stomach ache been real? Was that really a friend's cabin? How long had they been planning this? I didn't have time to process it all because Olive was pointing out the freshly painted lighthouse keeper's cottage, which turned out to be the least of the work they had accomplished. The old furniture was gone and in its place was a brand new bed, dresser and desk. In one corner, a state of the art wood cook stove was sending off blasts of heat. The lighthouse itself hadn't escaped their attention, either. I not only had heat there, as well, but two cords of seasoned wood, chopped and stacked neatly outside. Planters with brightly color flowers now ran along the path between the lighthouse and the cottage. That was Willow's idea.

I didn't know what to say. I didn't deserve it, but no one was letting me voice that opinion. I thanked each person individually, but no one was accepting my thanks, insisting they could never repay me.

"Time to eat, people!" Olive announced as she dragged me over to a steaming grill and picnic table that hadn't been there before. "Because I'm friggin' starving."

Close your eyes and imagine floating away on a warm cloud in a starry night and you will know how I felt later that evening. I was sitting by the campfire, staring into the flames when Sam sank down beside me and handed me a plate of chocolate cake, a fork and an icy glass that smelled like lemons and oranges. I took a bite, followed by a sip of the drink. Yum. The chocolate was decadent with rich cream filling. The drink was fruity and tangy. The conversation around the campfire swirled around me as I ate a second piece of cake and downed a second frosty glass of juice. We talked about nothing and everything. What we said didn't matter as much as being together, appreciating the gentle breeze off the water and the sense of community.

As the sun sank lower in the sky, people started drifting away from the fire, toward the dock, their boats and home. Finally, nature called. I went to get up, but my knees had a hard time remembering how. I made it up at last, leaning on Sam's shoulder and stumbled on stiff legs toward the cottage, muttering, "I'm getting old," as Noah had done just yesterday, clutching my half-filled cup in one hand and balancing myself with the other. My head felt light. I was almost to door when the world started spinning. I sank to my knees, catching myself before I fell flat on my face. My stomach was in my throat. The lighthouse had taken on a floaty look. I glanced over at the fire, which also looked floaty. For a second I thought I was going to toss my cookies right then and there. I dropped the cup, closed my eyes and sank down against the cottage, my head back, eyes closed.

"Alex?" Noah was calling my name. I wanted to look up at him, but looking up would mean moving my head and moving my head felt like it would tip the scales toward that vomiting moment.

He crouched down in front of me and put a hand on my forehead.

"What's happened, Alex?"

"I. Um. I." I tried to answer, and was horrified to find I had tipped over onto my side. I needed rest. I would be fine with a little rest. Come back later, after I've rested.

"Alex?" Olive's voice drifted over my prone body. Go away, I prayed. No luck. "What happened? Is she all right?"

"She's drunk!"

"That's ridiculous."

He pointed to the spilled liquid beside me, dipped a finger into the puddle and touched it to his tongue. "Who gave her this?"

"Alex?" Now is was Sam's voice bombarding my poor brain. Please, please, please. I tried to turn, to get up. Nothing was working properly. What had happened to me? Sudden onset of the flu?

"What did you give her, Sam?" Noah asked, poking a finger at Sam's chest.

(I found out all of this much later. Olive was only too happy to fill me in.)

"Punch. I gave her punch."

"The spiked punch or the real punch?"

"Um . . ." He hesitated much longer than Noah was happy with.

"Are you stupid? She's never had a drink in her life. Not to mention that she's not legal."

"Yeah, not to mention," Olive said.

Noah cursed under his breath. "How many did she have?"

"Three," I mumbled, but I'm sure he didn't hear me over the litany of invectives he was busy spewing.

"Well, she can't stay out here alone," Noah finally announced to no one in particular. "Come on, Sleeping Beauty," He hoisted me up and over his shoulder, completely ignoring Sam, who offered to stay and watch over me, and Olive who also offered to stay and watch over me.

It was a miracle I didn't barf all over his shirt.

Lucky him, I thought, before I passed out cold.

Chapter Thirty-One

HANGOVER

/haNG over/

noun

A severe headache or other aftereffects caused by drinking an excess of alcohol.

I looked it up.

It failed to mention the nausea and overwhelming urge to vomit, how even the smallest ray of light feels like blazing swords slashing through every fiber of my brain, irritability, and last but not least, how even the smallest sound is a nuclear explosion.

Multiplied by infinity.

Oh, and did I mention that sitting up was akin to climbing Mt. McKinley?

As Willow would say, duh! How could I not have known this? Why hadn't my mother warned me about drinking punch at parties? Never mind. I know why. I never went to parties.

My cell phone buzzed, setting off a fresh wave of nausea along with the desire to dig a hole and climb in. I ignored it. Aspirin. If I could only get off this couch, I could go in search of the magic elixir that would make all this pain go away. I pushed the covers aside and they landed in a heap on the floor. So far, so good. My pain level was only a 9. So maybe I was moving like a snake at 30 below, like a 108 year old, like a redwood. If you don't succeed and all that. This time I was determined I would get off this couch. Better to rip the bandage off fast. One. Two. Three. OMG. But I was sitting. Yay. Until I fell forward, my head landing on Noah's open laptop. The screen came alive. Ouch. I extricated my head from the computer and leaned my elbows on my knees so that I was eye level with the screen. eBay. Hmm. I wasn't being nosy. Exactly. What was Noah searching for on eBay? I hit the enter button. So sue me. (Not Olive. That's a Jersey saying.) Wait. That could not be right. What. The. F—.

"Good morning, Sunshine." I looked up too fast. Noah was coming out of the bathroom door, a beach towel wrapped around his torso, covering most of the important parts. I looked away quickly. Mistake. I pointed to the computer screen. He had the decency to look guilty.

I don't know how long we stared at each other, him in his towel, dripping onto the old oak floor, me frozen in place, trying not to move, in case it looked like my eyes were drifting down. Not that there was anything to see, except for a fluffy Hello Kitty beach towel. I wasn't going to take even the slightest chance that if my eyes did move that Noah would catch it and misinterpret the entire situation, causing me more embarrassment than I think I could bare. I mean, bear. No. Wait.

BARE

ber/

adjective

1. a person not clothed or covered. "He was bare from the waist up."

synonyms: naked, unclothed, undressed, uncovered, in the nude, stark naked.

Not that one.

BEAR

/ber/

verb

1. carry.

synonyms: bring, transport, move, convey, take, fetch, deliver

2.support.

"I cannot bear it."

synonyms: support, hold up, prop up

"Noah! What did we discuss about you using my Hello Kitty towel?" Willow definitely surprised him, because he jumped.

I can't say if his towel slipped. I was not looking. His face, however, turned red; he turned and was back in the bathroom. Presumably to put on more appropriate attire.

Willow shouted through the bathroom door. "It's never good manners to greet a guest wearing a bath towel," she said like she was reciting a line from an etiquette book. Although, I kind of doubt that the towel and guest situation would have made its way into such a tome, frankly.

Noah came back, rubbing his hair with the Hello Kitty towel.

"We need to talk," I said.

"Willow, did you have your shower?" he asked.

"I was gonna. But someone had my towel."

He snapped it at her. "Well, I don't have it now. Scoot."

After Willow reluctantly hit the bathroom and we heard the shower turn on, Noah turned back to me. "Do you mean, explain how the electricity mysteriously works at the lighthouse? Or do you mean explain how your headache is suddenly gone? Or should I explain how you can make a storm stop in its tracks?"

I turned to the window. "I don't know what you're talking about. I was talking about how you bought my painting. I was also talking about how you tricked me into staying overnight so that Olive could have her way with the lighthouse." I turned back. "Was Willow even sick?"

"It looks like we're at an impasse." He crossed his arms over his chest. I followed suite and glared. But then I realized something. Noah had brought the painting. Not some outsider. Not some family member looking for me. Not a friend of the family who could tell my family, who could then track me down. I was safe. I leaped up and grabbed him up into a hug.

It was slightly awkward, because Willow came out of the bathroom, wrapped in the aforementioned Hello Kitty towel.

"You guys are crazy. You know that, right?"

"Wasn't someone saying something about towels and company?" Noah asked.

"Well, that rule is in the toilet now, isn't it?"

I burst out laughing, covered my mouth with a fist, but I couldn't help myself.

"Willow, Alex isn't feeling well. Can you please put the kettle on for some tea?"

"Olive said you got drunk. That's why you came home with us."

Out of the mouths of babes.

"Willow!"

"Sorrrrry."

To show she really meant it, Willow went into mom mode, insisting I lay down and put my feet up and did I want a warm towel for my head and what kind of tea did I want and on and on. I didn't tell her that Noah had been right. For some reason I was feeling great. The pain was gone, the nausea too. I no longer felt the need to close the shades and not come out until the bears rose in spring. And what was Noah talking about? The electricity works because the electric company shoots it through underground cables, just like they do to every house on the island. The storm stopped because storms have a way of doing that. And I felt better, because I have the constitution of an elephant. Subject closed. But then something occurred to me. "Willow? When did you talk with Olive?"

She looked guilty. Head down. Avoiding our eyes.

"Willow! What did you do this time?"

Willow gave him a look that screamed: Insulted. Affronted. Wronged.

"Don't give me that look. What did you do?"

"Nothing. I told her not to come."

"Olive is coming over?"

"I told her not to."

"And you didn't say anything?"

"She wanted to stop Sam."

"Sam's coming, too?" Noah didn't wait for an answer. He pulled out his cell phone and started tapping. His phone chimed.

"What?" I asked.

"Looks like they're both on their way."

"Oh." I was at a loss for words. Willow escaped to her room while Noah was looking like he was trying not to hit something.

"Let's look on the bright side," I said.

"Which is."

I didn't get a chance to answer before a boat scraped against the large rubber bumpers on the side of the deck.

"Stay here," Noah directed.

"What am I? A dog?" I said. Not that he heard, because he was gone. I peeked out the front door.

"Don't bother to tie up, Sam. You're leaving."

Sam ignored him, tied up and leaped from his boat to the deck. Olive was right on his tail. She pulled up in front of his boat, tied up and jumped on the side of the deck as well.

The hairs on my arms tingled. I could feel trouble coming. I went out onto the deck and stood next to Noah. He couldn't knock Sam senseless with me right there, could he?

"Move aside, Noah. I came to see if Alex is all right."

"Right. After you got her drunk."

Olive jumped into the fray, standing between the two. "Sam. I am warning you. Go. Home. Now," she said, then whispered something next to his ear. Possibly threatening to publish all his naked baby pictures online or something equally abhorrent.

I was expecting Sam to fluff her off, but when he saw me nod and mouth that I was okay, he hopped back into his boat and just like that he left. It's amazing how fast Alaskans can hop in and out of boats without falling in.

"Everyone. Inside!" Noah said.

"What did you say?" I asked.

"Yeah. That means you, too."

Without thinking, I reached out, put my hand on his chest and pushed. A huge splash followed. I looked over the edge of the deck to see Noah bobbing up and down in the water. I kicked off my shoes and jumped in after him, determined to rescue him. Once in the frigid water, I grabbed his neck as I had been taught years ago in a water safety class. We both went under.

He popped up, bringing me with him. "What the hell are you trying to do?" he got in before I managed to drag him down again. "Kill me?" He was back up, pulling me to the deck stairs. He got purchase on the bottom step then and yanked me up behind him, until we were both on the deck, totally drenched.

I swear I heard him muttering, "Crazy. Insane. One hole short of a donut."

Willow appeared with big towels and tossed one to each of us.

As Noah towel dried his hair for the second time today, still mumbling to himself, Willow stated the obvious. "It was her evil twin. But, Noah?"

"Hmm?"

"Do you want to know what else old men do? They talk to themselves." She continued without encouragement from me or Olive, although Olive was enjoying this immensely. "And they groan when they get off the sofa. That's two. You don't want to act like an old man, do you?"

"No!" His look was a cross between miffed and insulted.

"Three. They get cranky and crabby over every little thing."

"I am not cranky or crabby."

"Okay, so that's a yes."

Noah turned and walked away. "We're officially banning the internet for you, young lady."

"Four. Call girls young lady."

Olive bent over laughing. After she finally managed to stop, then start again, then stop again, she hopped back in her boat and pushed off.

"Olive," I called after her. "Wait. Wait for me."

Her boat receded into the distance. Willow bumped into me taking my hand. "Women."

I'm not sure how long we stood that way. I know the sun started to set and my stomach was grumbling.

"So I guess we're not going to talk about it." We were on the boat. Noah and Willow were taking me and Juneau back home. "Giving me the silent treatment?"

I shook my head. "No. Of course not. I was thinking, that's all." The lighthouse came into view. It was such a beautiful sight. I don't think I'd ever been this happy to see anything.

"Just so you know," Noah said, "the subject is not closed."

The subject was so closed. He just didn't know it yet.

"About the painting . . ." I started.

"Hey, I was only—"

"Thank you."

"Thank you?"

"I don't know how you did it, but thank you."

"Don't worry. He's raking it in," Willow said. "He doesn't tell anyone, but he created the Vampire Dating App. Oh, and the Naked Baking with Friends App, and the Hairy—"

"Willow!"

Naked baking? Vampire dating? Life is crazy. People are crazy.

"That was a family secret."

"Alex is family. Once you save someone's life that makes you family."

"Actually, an ancient Chinese belief says that when you save someone's life, you become responsible for that person for the rest of their life," Noah said.

"Cool. Right, Noah?"

Noah rolled his eyes. "Yep. Way cool."

CHAPTER THIRTY-TWO

Maybe Everything Will Be Alright

One day I was pushing a completely innocent man into the sea (not completely innocent), the next I found myself blindfolded, stuffed into the back seat of a Jeep—one reeking of rotting fish and damp seaweed—being driven over bumpy, unpaved roads for what felt like hours, but which was actually not more than a few minutes, after which I was half dragged, half pushed along a winding dirt trail to an unknown and secret location. There was only one thing I was fairly certain of: I was still on Prince of Wales Island. Still Population 5559.

With my eyes covered for the trip, it felt like we had been traveling in circles and I had completely lost my bearings.

"Okay. On three. 1, 2, 3, open your eyes!" Olive shouted at me with more glee than I felt the occasion warranted, considering that the seat of my pants was uncomfortably damp from sitting on wet seaweed and that I now smelled strongly of salmon or halibut or who knew what.

I was currently half past grouchy because at one point we'd hit a bump and my head had slammed against the door of the Jeep. Jackson, Olive's co-conspirator, had swerved and wham. Head meet Door.

I decided. I was putting my foot down. Except, Jackson elbowed me, gently, "Walk. Unless you want to do this the hard way." The hard way being flung over his shoulder and carried the rest of the way. I opened my eyes to find we were standing at the beginning of a winding boardwalk, one I recognized immediately, the Tongass National Forest on our right and Whale Pass on the left. Strings of fairy lights were threaded through the trees giving off a mystical feeling to the evening. A fox skittered through the brush, not too far from my muddy boots. The night air smelled of evergreen, moss and the sea and I breathed it all in. I really must have gotten turned around on the drive, because we were back where we'd started, at the dock and the floating community center.

"Admit it. You love it," Olive said. "Because who wouldn't?"

I should have known . Olive has been a bit obsessed with finding out my birthday ever since I arrived in Alaska. Something I resisted telling her as if my life depended on it. In a way it might. Ultimately, here's what happened when The Strong Forces (Olive and Jackson) met The Impenetrable Will (me). They picked a date, made it my official Prince of Wales birthday and planned the party that, Impenetrable Will or not, was bound to happen. Which turned out to be tonight.

Apparently, not only a party, but a Kidnapping Birthday Party. Something that would never have happened back home in New Jersey.

We approached the end of the brand new ramp to the community center and I rubbed my palms on my jeans. The fairy lights continued past the entrance. Multi-colored lights crisscrossed the ceiling. I noticed the freshly installed wide plank flooring and the vibrant colors of the walls. I took a shaky breath, as Olive pushed me forward, only to find it was worse than I imagined. The center was packed. At one end of the room, a long wooden portable bar was crowded with a small crowd getting an early start on their relationship with Vodka and Tonic. In one corner, a group of high school kids was hanging out around the fringe of the action, checking for the perfect storm of unattended drinks and an inattentive bartender. A young mom danced through the crowd, her newborn baby asleep in a sling across her chest. At the other end of the room, I thought I saw Anna and her husband deep in conversation. I hoped they were working things out. The center of the room held dozens of round tables covered with white cloths and decorated with candles.

Some would call it romantic.

It was not.

No one had noticed me and yet it felt like the room was closing in. Still time to run. I backed up and bumped into Jackson. The song that was playing ended and now the band was striking up the first bars of Happy Birthday. This is what happens when you lose concentration, Alexandria, I reminded myself. As the crowd sang, slightly off-key, I spied Sam. It looked like he was making his way over to me. Good news. A young woman with purple black cropped hair rushed in, linked her arm through his and pulled him off course. Out of the blue, one of the local fishermen stormed over, scooped me up and spun me around before setting me down and moving on. Willow took his place and began dancing around me, radiating joy in a pink and purple tutu and yellow rubber boots. With an alligator print.

Eventually, the birthday song ended and Olive steered me in the direction of the make-your-own-dinner table. There were all the fixings for make-your-own pizza, make-your-own tacos and even make-your-own sundaes. Yum. Balancing my plate, I happily headed for the table Willow had commandeered. I was not so thrilled when Noah squeezed in next to me, too close for comfort, and me, feeling like a convicted felon on the boat over to Alcatraz.

While we ate, some people I knew, and others I didn't, stopped at the table to wish me well, tease me about growing old and even dropping off a present of two: a coupon for a freshly caught halibut from a local fisher, an offer to babysit Juneau the next time I went into the city (meaning Ketchikan, presumably) and more. I tried to be as graceful as possible even as I wished I could disappear.

When Sam sidled up to our table, my entire body clenched, waiting for a confrontation with Noah. Instead, Sam held a hand out to Willow. "Dance, princess?" She jumped up and took off with Sam, her tutu fluttering around her. I watched as the two did their own version of a swing dance mentally preparing myself for the inevitable toast to my supposed 21st. Some of the diners were now finishing their meals, while others were still dancing to slow songs on the makeshift dance floor. A few drifted off, down the lighted walkway along the water's edge or into the serene woods. Jackson and Olive moved to the dance floor as if by unspoken agreement. I sat there awkwardly trying not to look at Noah. He stood and reached out a hand to me.

I made myself look up, then held up a hand in a stop gesture. "I can't dance."

Noah took my hand and pulled me up. "It's easy." Walking backwards he pulled me along the dance floor.

"Don't go far. It's almost midnight!" Olive warned.

I tried to follow, but two steps in I stepped on Noah's foot and yanked my hand away.

"Yeow. Ah. Ah. Ouch."

"Exaggerating any?"

He caught my hand again and pulled me back around. "Take off your shoes."

"Take off my shoes?"

When I didn't comply, he crouched down and removed one shoe and then the other. I stood there like a petrified tree, stunned. Shoes safely tucked under the table, he stood and lifted me so that now my feet were resting on his, like a dad and a child, moving with the music.

My heart felt like a subway train barreling along wobbly tracks, my blood rushed to my face, betraying me, as he pulled me closer. I closed my eyes and allowed the music to rush over me. Only for a second. I look over to Olive silently sending her signal to help.

"Let's do a countdown," she announced as she poured each of us a glass of our assigned beverage. For Olive, being 17 going on 39, ginger beer would have to suffice.

"Let's not," Noah whispered.

11:57   I held the glass Olive shoved into my hand. I attempted to relax. Good friends, good food, relative safety. Maybe everything would be all right.

11:58   "To Alex." Olive held up her glass. Noah lifted his glass and reached out for my hand.

"To Alex," people around the room echoed, grabbing glasses of their own.

11:59   I looked up as a Black Forest cuckoo clock chimed, slightly out of time and tune.

12:00   The clock chimes and every fairy light, every bar light, every chandelier bulb, every string light, every single light of every kind in the every part of every room of the community center blew out in one swift, massive explosion.

12:01   Jackson grabbed Olive to pull her under the table. Noah followed suite with Willow.

I leaned my head back, closed my eyes and held my hands up as if to stop what couldn't be stopped—like a shooting star.

Time slowed as 1,000s of pieces of broken glass melted before my eyes, replaced seconds later by a mesmerizing cloud that spread across the ceiling, ultimately shattering into an ocean of shimmering, gray-blue drops. And as if the air could no longer hold them, they rained softly down upon us.

As the first drops touched my eyelids, the room fell silent. Except for a figure standing in the door, his face shrouded in darkness, the light behind him creating a ghostly halo. All eyes were on him.

"Alexandria."

"Phoenix."

"Ali. It's time to come home."

Chapter Thirty-Three

STUNNED

st●nd/

verb

To knock unconscious or into a dazed or semiconscious state.

To astonish or shock someone so that they are temporarily unable to react.

To make one wish they had the power of invisibility or high-speed flight or the power to transport instantly across time and space.

Chapter Thirty-Four

The Past Becomes Present

Phoenix took a step forward. The glass I was holding shattered as it hit the ground by my feet. Willow pushed her way in front of me, holding out her arms, facing a man she didn't know a thing about. She only knew that she would protect me come what may.

"You leave Alex alone. Right now!"

Noah stepped in front of her.

Suddenly all eyes in the room were on us. Phoenix made the tiniest of bows and stepped back into the door frame, wordlessly turned and disappeared down the gangplank into the night.

"Glad that's over," someone in the crowd said.

It was far from over, I knew.

Willow was tugging on my sleeve. I looked down. "My hero."

Noah was done being Mr. Nice Guy. "What the heck is going

on, Alex?" he asked as people slowly moved away, whispering about faulty circuit breakers and strangers.

"Did you see the rain?" Or was it just me?

Olive came up on my other side. "What rain? Are you all right?"

I nodded as Noah pulled me away. "Alex and I have to talk," he said, like he would brook no dissent.

Willow followed. "Who was that man?" she asked.

"Go sit with Olive and Jackson, Willow."

"No way. You're not being very nice."

"Willow. I mean it!"

"I mean it, too. I'm 12, not 3. Anything you have to say to Alex, you can say to me."

"You're grounded until Christmas if you don't move it. Now."

Arms firmly crossed over her chest. "Fine. Alex will tell me anyway," she said.

But before she huffed off, she pulled me down and whispered, "You're not going crazy. I saw the rain, too."

Chapter Thirty-Five

Freedom beats Guilt. Or Is It The Other Way Around?

I felt like a pickup truck had run right across my chest. Phoenix would be back. That much was clear. After Willow reluctantly left the area, I expected an interrogation from Noah; however, he surprised me. "You look pale. Let me get you something to drink." He pointed to a chair as if to say "Sit" or "Stay," but clearly thought better of it.

I wasn't sure if I had the energy to run again. And keep running. And have Phoenix find me again. And I wasn't sure I wanted to leave my new friends. Sitting there alone, I thought of Willow. So brave and strong, standing in front of me like a superhero, ready to save the day. Standing up to Noah, too, unafraid. It might be time to tell my friends the truth.

Noah reappeared and placed a warm cup of cocoa in my hand.

"That was Phoenix."

Noah nodded.

"I'm supposed to marry him." How was that for the truth? Get it out there. Fast. Like pulling off the proverbial bandage.

Noah's eyebrows shot up. "That's a relief. I thought maybe you'd robbed a bank and were on the run from the Feds."

"You thought—"

"Joke."

"Oh."

"So, you weren't expecting him?"

"Hoping that . . ."

"He wouldn't find you. Did he hit you, Alex?" he asked, his hands clenched into fists, his mouth tight.

"It's not like that."

"I'd like to believe you, but that's what they all say."

How to explain? I wasn't sure where to start. "In my family," I began, "there is a long tradition of arranged marriages." There, I'd said it. "Phoenix and I were promised to each other when we were children. It is an unbreakable contract."

"Alex. It's 2021. We live in American. No one can force you to marry someone."

FORCE

fôrs/ noun

1. strength or energy as an attribute of physical action or movement.

2. an influence tending to change the motion of a body or produce motion or stress in a stationary body. The magnitude of such an influence is often calculated by multiplying the mass of the body by its acceleration.

3. a person or thing regarded as exerting power or influence.

As you can see, force doesn't always involve physical strength.

"You don't understand. I can't defy my family's wishes."

"The hell you can't. You already did, in case you haven't noticed."

"Do you celebrate Thanksgiving? Do you share Christmas traditions? Do you show up for Sunday dinner?"

"That's completely different and you know it. Or you wouldn't be here, 4,000 miles from home."

I sighed.

"Well, you can't go back. I'll make it clear to him, if he's stupid enough to come back."

He never left.

Olive saved me by barging in with a drink in her hand. "Never fear, Olive's here!"

Noah and I stared at each other, unblinking. A show down of sorts.

"Seriously, Alex, who was that creep?" Olive asked. "Okay. Admittedly, 6'4", gorgeous black hair down to his well-toned ass, muscular, but not muscle-bound. Um, still a creep."

I burst out laughing, this side of hysteria.

Noah filled her in. "The short answer. Arranged marriage. He thinks that means something here in Alaska."

"O.M.G. You have got to be kidding me. What is this? The dark ages? You're not going to do it, are you? Of course, you're not. This explains a whole lot. Like why you came to Alaska, for one. Okay. We have to get rid of him. I know. Food poisoning. Or better still, we can drop him off on an iceberg and leave him there. No wait. We have to keep him here."

"What?" Noah's eyebrows shot up.

"No. Seriously. If he stays, we can work our wily ways on him so he'll give up on Alex voluntarily. Plus, we don't want to go to jail. Win win."

"And how do you intend to do that," Noah was crazy enough to ask.

"Manipulation, of course. Skullduggery. Hypnotism, if necessary. And as a last resort, siccing every single girl within a 100 mile radius on him. You know. Whatever it takes."

I believe I saw Noah look up to heaven.

"First. You refuse to leave with him. Then we get him working at the community center, which is when the manipulation and skullduggery will begin. Leave it to me. He'll be on the first flight back home before you know it, telling mommy and daddy it wasn't meant to be."

"I admire your confidence, Olive." That was all I could say.

"I gotta go get Jackson. He'll have some good ideas, too."

Noah and I sat quietly for a while, each thinking our own thoughts.

"Alex. I. I don't want you to leave. I want you to know that—"

I couldn't let him continue. "It's not your decision to make."

Subject closed.

Chapter Thirty-Six

The Wicked Witch and The Good Prince

And as in any good fairy tale, the wicked witch devises her evil plot to destroy the good prince. Except in this case, the wicked witch was Olive and the good prince was Phoenix. Neither of the two all good or all bad, actually. Phoenix was being honorable in fulfilling the promise made by his family. Olive was being honorable in following the code of Alaska: stand up for your friend in the face of any and all odds.

Seeing Phoenix opened up a wound that had only recently started to heal. I missed my family and wished with all my heart that I could have found a way to work things out so that everyone was happy. A child's fantasy. I can see that now.

"Snap out of it," Olive said as she shoved a handful of chips into her mouth, downed half a ginger beer, then followed it up by a loud burp. "Ah, that's good."

We were sharing lunch at the community center, going over the upcoming class schedule and supply order forms. No one had seen Phoenix for days. Juneau was nipping at Olive's heels, inviting her to get up and play. She patted his head and scratched under his chin, a consolation prize.

"He's gone. He saw the odds and hightailed it out of here. Smart boy."

"Why thank you, Olive." Phoenix. Say his name and he appears.

"You," Olive said.

Juneau rushed over to him, ears perked up, tongue hanging out. Phoenix crouched down and gave him a good rub.

"Traitor," I said, under my breath.

"I've been enlisted to help. What can I do?"

Who had enlisted his help? If he was being truthful. Which he always is.

It definitely wasn't Noah who had asked him. Possibly Jackson or Sam?

"Ellie asked me to come over. She said you could use a hand."

"Only if you don't plan on dragging Alex out of here by her hair. Because in that case, you can—"

He gave her a smile that could melt snow and, like a snowflake, I swear she melted a little. "I am your faithful servant."

Olive whispered to me. "Was he born in the middle ages?"

I whispered back. "Stop it. What are we going to do?"

"I told you. Manipulation and Skullduggery."

How that translated into action, I couldn't begin to imagine.

"Leave it to me," she whispered before taking Phoenix by the arm and dragging him to the pottery studio. "We need the clay mixed for the classes tomorrow. Think you're up for that?"

I could almost read her thoughts. Lifting 100 lb. bags of clay all day and he would be too tired to toss me over his shoulder and take me anywhere.

The next day, as it turned out, Phoenix was also occupied all day, thanks to Olive, suspended over the side of the community center, scraping the hull, while Jackson came after him and applied the primer. While Phoenix was busy trying not to fall into the water below, I was in town helping Willow with an "emergency" of "epic proportions," which turned out to be making a pair of pajamas for Noah for Christmas.

When I mentioned that Christmas was months away, Willow gave me a look that let me know how much I didn't understand about planning, organization, Christmas traditions and long-range coordination, etc.

We were at a tiny fabric story which doubled as an art supply and craft shop. Not to mention, they sold bait. "Alex, do you think Noah would want the fabric with the snowmen or the alligators? Or, maybe the cupcakes. I like the cupcakes."

Noah had been kind enough to drop us off while he ran to the post office and library. "Well, I like the alligators. Not that I'm saying a guy can't have cupcake pajamas."

"Because they can."

"Obviously. But alligators are my favorite."

"That settles it. Alligators it is."

We selected matching thread and found the perfect pattern, paid and were outside waiting for Noah before he could see our purchases.

"You gals ready?" Noah came up between us and wrapped an arm around each of us. When no one objects, he said, "Then let's go. Apparently you two have more trouble to cook up at home."

Juneau woofed and we headed back to his houseboat, Willow delighted that we were pulling one over on him. When we arrived, she spirited me and Juneau into her bedroom where she had a vintage sewing machine set up on a table in the corner. Willow got to work right away, figuring out which pattern pieces we needed, laying them on the floor and cutting them out. Before long, she had the pattern pieces pinned to the fabric. I couldn't believe it. Juneau watched, an amazed look on his face. "You've done this before, I gather." So, no monumental emergency. So, no need for me at all.

"Once or twice."

I was about to reply when Noah opened the door a crack and held a cup of something through the opening.

"Get out! Don't come in!" Willow hollered. Juneau jumped up on the door in solidarity.

Noah's eyes were closed. It went straight to my heart how he honored her wishes. "I thought Alex would like something to drink. Are either of you hungry? I'm making lasagna."

"Lasagna! I love lasagna!" Willow said.

"Okay, I'm leaving now. I didn't see any state secrets, so you're safe. I'll call you when the food is ready."

Willow finished sewing two pieces of fabric together, stopped the machine and cut the thread. "Noah. He's a keeper," she said.

The next day Phoenix was once again busy, this time waiting tables at Ellie's cafe. Oddly enough the entire wait staff, including backups and part-timers, had called in sick. Phoenix had stopped in for a cup of coffee and just like that Ellie hijacked his day. While Phoenix was making large quantities of coffee and learning how to flip fried eggs without breaking the yolk, I was busy with Olive, preparing for my painting class while she worked on her pottery classes. On the fourth day since my birthday party, Phoenix was busy replacing boards on the dock at the harbor. Gabe had heard about how Phoenix had built a vacation cabin for his family and quickly conscripted him to help out at the dock.

I was beginning to notice a pattern here.

While Phoenix was exercising his carpentry skills, I had my first class, teaching painting to a group of 1st graders. Willow had volunteered to be my studio assistant and had mixed paints and put them in cups. She'd set up each work station with paint brushes, paint and paper and arranged easels around the room, while I organized two still life arrangements in the center of the room, one with stuffed animals and Legos, the other with action figures and matchbox cars. We had barely finished getting the room ready when a bunch of kids rushed in, parents close behind. The energy in the air was electric. Willow led the kids to the hooks on the wall where they could each select an apron while I talked with several parents about pick up times and handed out schedules for the next classes. Juneau, of course, had his own apron, with a dog bone that Willow had painted on it.

When the kids were all at their easels, I walked around greeting each one. I reached the last easel and sitting there, brush in hand, in an apron that was far too small and far too pink, was Noah.

"Uh, Noah? This is a children's class. You knew that, right?"

"I am a child at heart."

I shook my head.

"You can't refuse me an opportunity to learn from a master. Can you?"

"We're painting legos."

"I'm flexible."

So you see? Part of the town was keeping Phoenix busy and the rest were watching over me. I smiled.

"What are you smiling about?"

"You. That's what. Okay, class. Let's begin. Who knows what happens when you mix yellow with blue?"

Juneau raised his paw.

Chapter Thirty-Seven

Enlighten Me

T hat went well," Willow said as the last of the children happily filed out of the community center with their wobbly paintings in hand.

"I agree. And thank you for all your help. I couldn't have done it without you."

Willow crossed to where Noah was putting away his paints and gave his painting a once over. "So, Noah, maybe painting isn't your thing."

"Willow!"

"Alex, it's cruel to tell someone they're good at something when they have absolutely no talent whatsoever."

"Ouch."

I came over to have a look. I covered my face with my hands and turned around. How could anyone make Legos and stuffed animals look like a gorilla eating a VW camper van? In a snow storm.

"What is it, Noah? A platypus jumping over a hippopotamus?" Olive jumped into the conversation. "Oh, wait. It's a tsunami lifting a house. Like in the Wizard of Oz. But what are those—"

"Okay. I get your point. Give up before someone gets hurt. Come on, Willow. Let's go home. Alex, I'm locking the door. Don't let anyone in."

As if that would matter. It was inevitable that Phoenix would catch up with me. The only unknown was where and when.

After Noah and Willow left, I received an urgent call from the police department. It turns out Phoenix was in jail and I was his one phone call.

The local jail was little more than a cabin with a desk, two chairs, a sink, frig and a fold out bed in one corner. The sheriff was all of 25 years old. When I arrived, Phoenix was stretched out across the bed reading a tattered copy of The Alaska Magazine. Sheriff Joe was ignoring him, filling out paperwork between gulps of coffee.

"Hey, Alex. How's the community center going?"

"Fine, Joe. How's the prisoner?"

"Behaving himself."

I went over to Phoenix, sat on the bed and handed him a small box I'd procured on my way over.

He took the box and opened the lid.

"A cake?"

"With a file inside."

Sheriff Joe asked, "Can I have a piece?"

"Sure." Phoenix handed over the box.

Joe pulled a butter knife from his desk drawer, took three semi-clean plates from the cabinet above the sink and cut the cake. I did the honors, handing out the plates.

The cake box was down to crumbs in a matter of minutes. "So, Joe, what's the charge?"

"Jaywalking. Found him on main crossing against the light."

"Really?"

"Hey. He could have been killed."

"Olive put you up to this, didn't she?"

"I am offended, Alex. You know I would never—"

"Never mind. What's his bail?"

Fast forward to the courthouse bright and early the next day. There was no court reporter to call out the name of the defendant, in this case Phoenix. There were no lawyers.

"Let's make this fast. Young man," the judge said. "Jaywalking is a serious offense."

"Yes, sir."

"You could've been killed. But seeing as you have no priors, I am sentencing you to a month in jail, with the sentence commuted due to your community service in town this week. However, if you are not out of town within 24 hours, your sentence will be reinstated. Are we clear?"

How Olive managed to pull this off, I wasn't sure, but it had manipulation and skullduggery written all over it. She should write a how-to book.

"Yes, sir."

"Now get out of here before I change my mind."

"Nice town," Phoenix said when we were clear of the courtroom and there was no chance of the judge hearing him.

"I guess you ought to go and pack."

It was for the best, I reminded myself.

"You're making a grave mistake, Alexandria."

"I'm beginning to think bailing you out was a grave mistake. Go pack, Phoenix."

He went one way and I went the other. I headed for the community center to clear my mind of Phoenix and family and mistakes of all kinds. It was late when I returned to the lighthouse. The ride over was calm and meditative. I docked and started the walk to the lighthouse purposefully emptying my mind of any disturbing thoughts.

I came around a corner to find there was a fire roaring in the fire pit. Phoenix stepped out from the side of the cottage.

I jumped and screamed simultaneously. "OMG. OMG. I can't breath. Are you trying to give me a heart attack?"

"You never used to be so skittish, Alexandria." He touched my shoulder and a sensation of calm washed over me.

"What are you doing here?"

"I couldn't leave without seeing you."

"I don't see a boat. How did you get here?"

"Does it matter?"

Seeing as how he had no ride back to the mainland and seeing how a big part of me actually did want to see him, I grudgingly made an offer. "You can stay in the keeper's cottage for tonight. But unless you want the judge to drag you back into court, you should leave tomorrow."

"I took the liberty of starting a fire."

"So I see."

"I brought marshmallows and veggie hot dogs."

"You're kidding me?"

"Do you remember the bonfire we had in Surf City? I think you were 14?" Phoenix asked, reminding me of how great I'd had it growing up in New Jersey.

"You were 16."

"You had a mad crush on me."

"Ha. That would be you."

He laughed. "Hardly. You were jail bait," he said as he opened a package of marshmallows with his teeth, stuck two of them on sticks and handed them to me. I worked on toasting them while he broke open the first package of veggie hot dogs, forked a couple and stuck them into the fire.

"What, no drinks?" I teased.

"Oh ye of little faith."

He opened a cooler I hadn't noticed before and took out a bottle and two glasses. He popped the top on the sparkling cider, mango, my favorite, and poured us each a glass.

Watching him, I remembered the young man I actually did have a wild crush on, so bad that seeing him back then often made my guts turn to mush and my heart melt like the marshmallows I was holding in front of me.

Until. Until my mother had The Talk with me. Not the one about the birds and the bees. I'd discovered that one at the library—photos included. When I say The Talk, I mean the one about how our families had agreed that Phoenix and I would be married when I turned 18.

It wasn't that the idea of trying out every one of the birds and the bees positions with Phoenix wasn't high on my To Do Before I Die list. The problem was, not at 18. Not before I'd done anything. Starting with seeing the world outside of New Jersey.

"I remember you lost the top of your bathing suit in the ocean earlier that day," Phoenix said.

My cheeks were on fire. I covered my face with my glass as best I could and took a sip.

"I'm sorry. Your teenage self is hating me right now."

I handed him the marshmallow sticks and reached for a crispy veggie dog.

"Ouch. Hot. Sh . . ." I blew on it and tried again, realizing that, between the jail and the community center, I hadn't eaten a thing all day. "Um. That's good." I snarfed the rest down in a decidedly unladylike fashion and reached for another.

"How many of these did you bring?"

Phoenix laughed, spitting out a chunk of half-chewed hot dog.

"Charming."

"You bring out the best in me."

I took a deep breath and let it out in a sigh. It would be so easy to be with Phoenix. We have history. I have loved him for most of my life. He knows me. My family approves, obviously.

"I've loved you ever since that day," he said.

"What day? Oh."

"When you realized you'd lost your top, you dove back in, rescued it, put it back on and marched out of the ocean and up the beach like you were Cleopatra charming snakes."

"I was dying inside."

"Bravery isn't the lack of fear—"

"It's being afraid and doing what you need to do anyway."

"Exactly. I still love you, Ali."

He hadn't called me Ali since we were kids, not until this week, but I wasn't going to admit my feelings to him.

"And I believe you love me, too."

"Phoenix."

"I get it. It's too soon. You want your freedom." I couldn't speak. "I have something to tell you. Your parents would have if . . . anyway, I convinced them I should be the one to come and tell you."

"I can't." It was too much.

He moved close, so that our shoulders here touching. He ran him fingers across the hands I had clenched in my lap. Our heads touched and we sat breathing in harmony, breath matching breath.

"Phoenix." "Ali." We said the words together, our lips so close I could feel his breath. It was so easy. So right. He kissed me. Softly, and then again. I wrapped my arms around him and he leaned closer; the kiss became stronger, more urgent, like I was falling off a cliff.

He was the one who pushed away first.

"We can't. Not under I tell you."

"You have to understand, Phoenix. I can't go home."

His eyes were so intense, I could hardly pull myself away from them, but I did.

"It's not a choice, Allie."

"This is 2021. We live in the United State of America," I said, parroting Noah.

"There's so much you don't understand."

"Then enlighten me." I said it quickly, like a smart ass, as if there was nothing he could tell me that would have any effect on my decision.

"This isn't about just you and me."

"Our parents will survive."

"Maybe. Probably," he hesitated.

"But what?"

"Have you been experiencing anything strange lately? Powers you don't understand?"

"Of course not."

"Lights turning on when you walk into a room? Natural elements rising up to protect you?"

"Don't be ridiculous."

"The other night, when you turned 18, you saw the rain and lights. Don't deny it."

"There are reasonable explanations for everything. Anyway, what are you saying? That it's magic?"

"It's more than that."

I reached over and touched my hand to his forehead. "Do you have a fever? Because you're acting crazy."

Phoenix sighed and turned his back to me.

"How do you think I found you?"

"I don't know. The painting sold on eBay. You saw it."

"Wrong. We've known where you were this entire time. "

I stood up, ready to what? Run?

"Haven't you every felt that we're different. Our families. All the strange customs, the arranged marriages, the fact that we don't have a choice."

Was this related to the odd message in the bottle. It couldn't be. Or maybe it had to be. I was sure of it now. A message from them to me. Alexandria, come home now.

"Don't be ridiculous, Phoenix. I'm not a prize from a Cracker Jack box."

He stood and put his arms around me, trapping me. He stared down at me, clearly torn, but determined. He leaned in and kissed my neck. Delicious. "They told me to make you."

"Go ahead," I said, so angry that I dared him to be a monster that I knew he couldn't be. I grew up with him. He was a good soul. Final answer. No.

He backed away and let out a breath. "I would never."

We both stood there breathing heavily. Not moving.

"Let's sit." He steered me to back to the fire. I sat, waiting for him to continue. "Like I said, this isn't about us. It is about the survival of humanity."

My look radiated something that translated into "Oh. My. God. Have you been reading Doctor Who?"

"Don't. This is about reparation for a great wrong once done that can never be undone and which can never be forgiven."

"I don't know what you're talking about."

"We didn't grow up in some strange cult."

"Some would disagree."

"Please don't say anything until I've finished. Okay?"

He wasn't going away until I heard him out, that was for sure. "Fine. Okay."

"I know this is impossible to believe, but here goes. Millions of years ago, our people destroyed most of life on a neighboring planet, through a combination of hubris and ignorance. That planet was destroying itself slowly through unending wars and damage to the environment, which was no excuse."

Our people? "I see." In truth, I didn't.

"You don't. We destroyed an entire civilization, Ali." He sighed, as if he was bearing the weight of history. "After much internal debate, in reparation, we agreed to bring the remaining population here, along with a small group of our people who volunteered to stay here as guardians. To ensure that it would never happen again."

"I see."

"Which is why we have arranged marriages. We must each assume our role as guardians by marrying another guardian."

"Okay." Don't say "You're crazy", I reminded myself. That never helps.

"Now that you are 18, you have come into your full powers and you are expected to assume your role."

I put my head on my knees. This was insanity. I stayed that way for some time before looking up at him. "Prove it. Prove everything you're saying is true."

That he didn't look upset surprised me. "Alexandria. Try to hear what I am thinking."

"That's—"

"Easy. Close your eyes, quiet your mind and listen." I did as he asked. You do not mess with crazy people.

"I am not stubborn. I am not being childish. And it's not very nice of you to say that."

"I didn't say it."

"Oh, God. Oh, God. I'm crazy, too."

"You are one of the most important people on this planet."

Impossible. Unthinkable. Unimaginable. Inconceivable. Absurd. Preposterous. Incomprehensible—

"Alex."

"We're guardians."

"If we don't fulfill our purpose, the earth will likely fall into the same trap again. The planet will ultimately become unlivable, irreparably harming all future generations."

"But, how do we do that? Run for office? Develop drought resistant crops? Find a new form of energy? I'm an artist, not a politician or a scientist."

I was thinking about the lights going on without any electrical service, the rocks growing up around the island, the seas calming when Willow's life was in danger, the exploding lights on my birthday. It felt like I was caught up in a tornado and I had lost all sense of direction.

He took a small box from his pocket and handed it to me. I turned the box over in my hands, not wanting to open it and wanting to open it in equal parts. The shape of the box was not right for a ring, which was a relief. It was shaped more like a rectangle, worn from time and handling. "Don't wait too long, Alexandria. We must return before the first snow."

Knowing Phoenix as I did, he wasn't acting like what Olive would call a drama queen. But the first snow was far away. At least in the East. In Alaska, it could snow in September, which was right around the corner. Phoenix said that my family had known where I was all along. I should have asked him how. The box was heavy in my hand and somehow smelled like home; I opened it to find a pendant handcrafted of burnished gold with a deep orange carnelian stone. Judging from the design, it had to be at least a hundred years old if not more. The stone was oval with a fantastical griffin carved into the surface I remembered that the griffin represented courage and boldness. Carnelian symbolizes protection, endurance, leadership and courage.

I ran a finger over the chain and lifted it from its container. I started to slip the pendant over my head, but stopped. Whatever this was about, I didn't want to believe it.

The thought of facing Phoenix tomorrow with my decision to stay in Alaska made my stomach tumble and my head ache. I prayed I wouldn't vomit when the time came. No, I would tell him I was staying and if he refused to accept my decision gracefully, I would stand up tall and repeat my new mantra.

"You have no power over me."

Chapter Thirty-Eight

Sweet Dreams

I had the most delicious dream. In my dream the sun floated through my bedroom windows, filling the room and warming me and I opened my eyes to find Phoenix sleeping on the floor beside my bed. He was lying on his side, snoring softly, one arm under his head, one knee sticking out of the covers, with Juneau stretched out in a Superman position along his side. The best part? In his sleep he had reached up and was holding my hand as I slept. I felt tears in my eyes it was so sweet.

I awoke from the dream to actually find Phoenix holding my hand as he slept on the floor and Juneau right where I knew he would be. I must have moved because Juneau opened one eye, looked at me, closed his eye and sighed, making no further attempt to move. I watched as Phoenix smiled in his sleep, waking up slowly, never releasing my hand, as he stretched his toes, breathing deeply, the day opening for him.

He opened his eyes then, caught me staring and smiled at me, like it was Christmas morning. He sat up, jostling Juneau. "Scoot over," he said as he sat on my bed. When I complied, he laid down next to me, where we stayed, side by side, looking up at the ceiling, holding hands, silently. Juneau jumped up and spread out across both of us, like a benediction.

"We can't do this," I said, finally. I was certain he knew what I meant. Not this. But a future of us.

He closed his eyes again. I felt warmth where his shoulder touched my shoulder, where his hip touched my hip, where his thigh and knee touched my thigh and my knee. Where his toes curled around mine.

I gave up. Why fight it? At least for now, I lied to myself.

I think I fell back to sleep. When I woke up again, it was as if Phoenix and Juneau had not moved an inch. As if in a whisper I heard Phoenix. "I don't see how I can ever leave you."

I turned to him to find he was dreaming. I took a deep breath and released it. I imagined balloons, labeled with all my worries, drifting out of the window, up into the clouds and away. Mom. Dad. Family responsibility. Each written on imaginary balloons. Olive. Noah. Jackson. Ellie. The community center. Willow. Phoenix. Each deserved a balloon for various reasons. I got as far as Ellie when Phoenix opened his eyes.

"Balloons?"

"How did you—"

"That crinkle you get between your eyes when you're worried."

Phoenix and I had sat on the beach many nights releasing imaginery balloons together when we were growing up.

"It's like nothing has changed," he said.

"And everything."

CHAPTER THIRTY-NINE

How To Let Go When All You Want To Do Is To Hold On

Phoenix stood at the end of the dock, the sea and a brilliant blue sky a perfect backdrop. I felt a sense of deep loss. He was leaving. The only connection between me and home. He looked up and started toward me. We boarded my small boat without a word and crossed to the island, arriving on Prince of Wales as if in a dream, where Noah and Willow were waiting for us. Crossed fingers his departure would be drama-free.

I fingered the box in my pocket. We climbed up onto the dock and I handed it to him. At first I thought he would refuse, but he took it wordlessly.

"Phoenix. Have a safe trip." Noah was going for polite. Good. Willow came to my side and held my hand. Moral support I could use.

"Thank you for being nice to Alex," Willow said.

Phoenix smiled down at her. "It was never a question."

I looked out over the water and saw that the ferry was getting closer to town. Phoenix saw it too. He opened the box and removed the pendant. He placed it over my head before I could object.

The pendant touched my skin and I felt my blood turn blue and my breath become liquid. I felt the movement of the earth, all 67,000 miles per hour of it, 137 miles per second. I heard the conversations of the birds and those of the bears out in the woods. Past, present and future held no distinction for me. I closed my eyes and felt the universe expanding, unfathomable, unlimited.

"Alex."

I was . . .

"Alex."

Magical.

"Alex!"

Someone was shaking me.

I knew it then. I was leaving.

Phoenix stood as still as me. Our eyes met and there was no need to say the words.

Willow hugged me. "Alex. You're leaving." A statement not a question.

Olive arrived on Willow's pronouncement. "What is she talking about?"

"I have to, Olive. I have to resolve things. With my family."

Olive went to grab me, to knock some sense into me, force me to see reason; I stepped back and went straight into the water with a loud splash. How fitting.

I was shaking hard, the first signs of hypothermia, by the time Ellie shoved me into a warm shower at her home. I let the water pour over me until it ran cold. I reached for a robe she had tossed on the floor, put it on, stepped out of the shower and jumped a foot when I found Willow sitting on the toilet seat. I barely had a chance to catch my breath when she handed a pair of pajamas to me.

"You're leaving," Willow said. Disappointment meet Frustration.

"I'm sorry."

"Don't be. It's the right thing to do."

"Willow, how did you become so wise?"

"Noah says family comes first."

I looked at the pajamas. Alligators. Amazing and fierce. "That's very true." Pajamas made for those not afraid of anything. "They're perfect."

"Alex? Don't forget about us."

I grabbed her up into a hug. She fit perfectly. I didn't think I could ever let go. "I could never."

I removed the pendant from my neck and placed it over Willow's head. If she had a reaction, I didn't see one. Maybe the magic was gone. "Will you take care of this for me?"

Willow held the pendant away from her body, inspecting every little detail.

"A griffin."

"Like you. Strong and brave. And, Willow, will you help Olive take care of Juneau, too?"

She nodded, solemnly. "I will," she said, with earnest eyes. "Promise."

Chapter forty

PROMISE

/präm•s/

noun

a declaration or assurance that one will do a particular thing or that a particular thing will happen.

My promise to Willow was, I would deal with whatever was waiting for me at home and as soon as it was humanly possible, I would return.

BOOK TWO

Chapter 41

Dear Diary:

This has been a strange and bizarre year.

     1. Found out my parents were serious about an arranged a marriage for me. (Actually, I already knew it.)

     2. Secretly bought a lighthouse in Alaska.

     3. Ran away to above lighthouse in Alaska.

     4. Met a guy who brings out The Hulk in me, and his niece who brings out the Mama Bear in me.

     5. Realized I could create electricity, among other things.

     6. Rescued the above 12-year-old girl by calming an angry sea, no less.

     7. Am possibly an alien—not of the Canadian variety.

     8. The above man of the above arranged marriage showed up to bring me home.

     9. Left Alaska with the man of the above arranged marriage.

10. Landed back in New Jersey and now I am currently choking down twelve assorted wedding cake samples.

If I had a diary, which I don't, that is how it would have read.

Since arriving back home in New Jersey, even considering all the odd things that had happened in Alaska, I have come to believe that everything Phoenix told me was crazy. I didn't save Willow. I didn't create electricity. I actually did become The Hulk with Noah. But I wasn't in charge of saving the universe. I absolutely was not.

"What do you think of the chocolate cherry delight?" the gum chewing server, who was listening to an iPod that was tucked into her apron pocket, asked. Her hair was pulled up in a silky, blonde ponytail, sparkly earrings swung from her ears. She sashayed over to us and bent to touch Phoenix on the shoulder in a too familiar way as she spoke, exposing him to an impressive view of her perky breasts, which he didn't take notice of. Thank God for him!

Not because I am the jealous type.

After all, I have no claim on him.

Phoenix gave her a look I recognized as the one he uses in formal situations. Polite. Cool. Not overly friendly, but not unfriendly, either. "Can you have the cake ready in time for the wedding?" The fact that he was subtly reminding her of his engaged status and that flaunting her boobs (right in front of me!) was not going to fly with him, endeared him to me more than I can tell you.

She, on the other hand, didn't even blink. It's not over until it's over, her cheery smile relayed.

By this time, you may have noticed: Phoenix and I are engaged.

I opened my mouth to yawn (cake tasting isn't nearly as exciting as one might think) and almost choked on a mouthful of too dry strawberry vanilla cake with hints of ginger that Bakery Barbie had stuffed in my mouth. The better to chat up Phoenix, the suspicious side of me concluded. Olive had definitely rubbed off on me, because I didn't feel guilty for thinking it.

It's not like I'd said it out loud.

Phoenix leaned closer to me and licked a bit of frosting from my lip. It worked. Our favorite server stomped off into the nether regions of the bakery, never to be seen by us again. Phoenix stifled a laugh, I thought, but maybe not.

Ten more cakes lined the long, narrow table in the extremely pink presentation area of the bakery. I doubt I had ever seen so much pink in my entire life. Pink walls, pink showcases, spoons, forks and knives with ceramic pink handles, pink platters, pink frosted cupcakes with pink sprinkles, a vase of pink tulips, pink—.

"Alexandria?" Phoenix looped his fingers between mine. His warmth spread through my body, making this cake-tasting fiasco almost bearable.

When I first returned from Alaska, I was ready to be hit with endless supplies of recrimination and motherly disappointment. None came. It was the wedding that was the magic elixir. I had returned to fulfill my familial and universal duties, if you were to believe my parents: marry, mate and procreate. That, apparently, was enough. Let bygones be bygones and all that.

Which is why I was currently eating more cake than any one person had a reasonable expectation of eating in one day. Or lifetime. Blghh. Don't vomit.

At this point, it felt like this last bite of half-masticated sugary concoction had a life of its own.

Phoenix held up a hand in the universal stop signal. "I think that's enough."

Me, too. I discreetly spit the offensive glob into a napkin.

"Let's get out of here." Phoenix latched onto my elbow and steered me out of the shop and into the sunshine. I lifted my face to the sky and closed my eyes. It was orange and yellow and pale green behind my eyelids, like being at the beach.

"Let's hit the beach." He read my mind.

Wait a minute

"Alex, you're looking at me funny."

"What am I thinking?" I was envisioning a giant pink cupcake swallowing the Atlantic City boardwalk.

He didn't hesitate. "I have no earthly idea."

So, good to know.

"It takes a lot of energy to read minds. Besides, I wouldn't invade your privacy that way."

Phoenix sometimes gets a crinkle between his soft gray eyes, like now. He doesn't realize how this drives girls mad. I've seen girls melting all over the place time and time again, when he does this.

I am immune, I lied to myself.

"What were you thinking?" he asked.

"I was thinking that we have an appointment at—"

"Ah, yes. We wouldn't want to ditch the illustrious wedding planner, would we?" He was teasing. It sounded like he would love to ditch the illustrious wedding planner.

Who was this man? Blowing off a parent-orchestrated meeting? Bending the rules?

All of this wedding planning was a nightmare, but I had made a deal with the devil, in order to give myself time. Let me explain. My parents are convinced of everything Phoenix told me about being responsible for the earth's survival. Furthermore, my parents believe that the power of the guardians is diminishing, which makes Phoenix's and my roles all the more important to the ultimate survival of the earth, which is apparently teetering on the brink of destruction.

I am convinced that if that is true, then it is my job to find a way to change all that. Which is how the wedding plans came to be. I agreed to everything they wanted, as long as the wedding was at least six months away, claiming I wanted a Christmas wedding, in turn leaving me time to solve the problem or to make my parents come to their ever loving senses.

In the meantime, let someone else eat cake. I was done.

This may surprise you, but Alaska and New Jersey are not all that different. Seriously.

They are both wild and quirky. On a clear night at the Jersey shore, you can look up to see 250 billion stars that are 100 billion light years away, and yet they feel close enough to reach out and touch. In the dead of winter, in Alaska, look up into the night sky and if you are lucky, you will be mesmerized by a dazzling display of undulating northern lights.

New Jersey has a state dinosaur: the hadrosaurus.

Alaska has the most pilots per capita in the US.

New Jersey had the first drive-in movie theater.

Alaska's flag was designed by a 13-year-old.

New Jersey has the most diners in the US.

Alaska has frozen turkey bowling and outhouse races.

As I was saying. Wild and quirky.

I love New Jersey, but I miss Alaska.

CHAPTER 42

Alaska: Plans A, B, C and D

Olive was fuming. Alex was gone, the lighthouse was empty and everyone was acting strange. Willow was putting on a brave face. Noah was trying way too hard to cheer her up. Jackson was treating Olive like she was going to break at any moment.

Enough already.

Alex hadn't wanted to leave, of that she was certain. Something had happened to make her change her mind. If Olive could figure that out, she might be able to fix everything. Besides, she missed her. Everything on Prince of Wales Island was more interesting with Alex around. She'd single-handedly saved the community center and now she wasn't even here to enjoy the fruits of her labor. Which meant, she wasn't here to teach all the classes Olive had scheduled her for and now Olive had to find someone else to take them on.

Olive was sitting at her desk in her closet-sized office in the community center, working and re-working the schedule, while trying to magically make more teachers appear out of thin air, when she heard a guitar strumming an old Eric Clapton song. A sad one. She checked the time: 1:00 pm. Two hours until Noah's instrument-making class was scheduled to begin. Damn. The last thing she needed now was to hear his overly cheery voice acting as if there wasn't a big hole in the universe.

Willow peeked her head around the door frame to the office but didn't speak.

"Hi, Willow. How you holding up?" No way was she going to do the fake cheery thing everyone else was doing.

Willow came in and plopped into the big swivel chair beside Olive's desk.

"We have to get Alex back."

"I agree. What do you suggest?"

Willow swung her backpack off her shoulder and pulled out a notebook.

"I've been thinking about it." She ruffled through the pages until she came to a page with a turned down corner. "My mom always says that if you want something, you have to plan your attack. My mom says to make sure you have a Plan B, C and D, because Plan A doesn't always work."

"She did, huh?"

"Um huh."

"So, what's Plan A?" Olive was willing to listen to any and all ideas. Because the ones she'd come up were crap.

"1. We remind her of how much we miss her. 2. We let her know how much we were depending on her. 3. We show her all the things she's missing.

"So. Love, guilt and longing."

"Huh?"

"Never mind. Where do you suggest we start?" Willow might be12 chronologically, but Olive was smart enough to recognize an old soul when she met one.

"I forgot four. We need to knock some sense into Noah."

"Where did you hear that phrase, Willow?"

"My mom says that when Noah is being stupid. She says, I need to knock some sense into you, then she laughs."

Olive laughed, too. "Okay then. Let's start with the obvious. We text Alex everything that's going on here throughout our day."

"Noah's class! I'll do a Facebook live and send it to her. That will get her."

"You go do that. Meanwhile, I have another idea."

"What is it?"

"All I can say is that it's too devious for innocent minds." She leaned back in her chair and put her hands behind her head. "And it just might work."

"Perfect! Oops. Gotta go."

Olive wasn't sure how much time had passed since Willow left, but here she was once again, standing in the doorway.

"This is ridiculous." She sank to the floor, defeated. Juneau came out from under Olive's desk and curled himself into her lap. "She left Juneau! She just left him. How could she do that?"

"I thought—"

"Who does that?"

Meaning, she left Willow.

Juneau whimpered and Olive stuck her face into his furry neck. "Poor baby."

Olive thought: Poor Willow.

Willow looked up at Olive. Fierce, now. "Juneau is devastated. But don't go feeling sorry for him. He hates that."

After her grand pronouncement, Willow ended up crawling into Juneau's giant dog bed with him and together they fell fast asleep, Willow breathing gently and Juneau snorting like a NJ dock worker as the community center barge gently rocked.

Noah appeared in the door frame some time later and quietly surveyed the scene before him: Olive writing furiously in a notebook between sips of something that by now was cold, concentrating so hard that she didn't notice him standing there. And Willow tightly squeezing Juneau in her arms as they slept, wrapped around each other. He stepped back, closed the door, turned and ran right into a woman he'd never seen before and one who definitely did not belong here.

As soon as he had the thought, he stopped himself. Just because

Alex left, he didn't have to take it out on the next woman that stepped off the boat. At least this one had the sense not to fall in the water on her first day. And last day. He would have heard about it.

Olive looked up, taking note of how Noah looked past the new gal. Decidedly angry that another woman—an outsider no less—had shown up on our doorstep without warning. He would have denied it had she mentioned it. Or maybe she was projecting. She wasn't ready to like anyone new yet. It was like when her dad brought home that puppy right after their old boxer, Neville, blind and arthritic, had died when Olive was 13.

She took a breath, let it out and looked out the window at how beautiful the day was. The sun hit the water at just the right angle to turn the surface to diamonds and she could not find a cloud in the sky. She got up, ready to face the stranger.

Her first impression of Zoe was that she was a flower child out of time. She wore her straight plum colored hair in two Princess Leia type knots held loosely with strands of colorful, glass beads. Her embroidered peasant dress, shrugged carelessly off one shoulder, barely covered her thighs. She wore Birkenstock sandals and idly slipped one on and off as she explained to Olive that she was visiting from Seattle.

It turns out, first impressions lie.

In the music room, Noah began ticking off names on a class list that Olive had stuck in his hand at the last minute. One wall of the classroom held a wire rack with various types of tools, in multiples. Large pieces of freestanding equipment, including a table saw, grinder, belt sander and drill press, were pushed up against a second wall. An enormous ventilation system hung from the ceiling with long hoses that could be attached to the bigger tools to whisk away any dust and debris.

Noah had hung sample instruments in various stages of completion on the third wall. The fourth wall was comprised of a bank of windows with the second finest views around, only exceeded by the view from the top of the lighthouse.

Noah cleared his throat before introducing himself briefly because everyone in the class pretty much knew his whole life story, with the exception of Zoe. Afterwards each person had a chance to introduce themselves, except they didn't. All eyes were on Zoe.

"Fine. We'll start with—," he checked his list, "Zoe." He could ignore her no longer. "What brings you to class today?"

"Yeah. What did bring her to POW?" a local interrupted. "Surely not to take a class from a washed up old has been like you," someone shouted, followed by good-natured laughing by most of the class.

Zoe stood and silence fell. She definitely knew how to command a room. "That's exactly why I came." And she sat down.

No one spoke.

Finally Noah broke the silence. "Okay then. You all signed a letter swearing that you are proficient with each of the tools we're going to be using, so let's get started."

This was the first adult instrument-making class and Olive planned on using it as a test run. If no one cut off a thumb or impaled themselves with a nail gun, she had every intention of offering the next class to the local teens. People in town had been placing bets all week, waiting patiently to see if there were any ambulance runs from the class, as this would greatly affect their chances of winning.

Work started with students laying out their patterns for a small lyre and cutting the initial wood pieces as Noah stopped at each station, repeating directions, checking for safety violations and suggesting little tweaks. When he reached Zoe's work station, she was hand-sanding a wooden piece until it felt like a river worn rock.

"You've done this before." Noah said it half accusingly and confused simultaneously.

"I confess."

He rubbed his eyes. He didn't have the time or patience for games. Whatever. If a strange woman wanted to come all the way to Alaska and take his beginning instrument building class—or so she said—even though she admittedly didn't need the class, then fine. It wasn't any of his business.

"Aren't you curious?"

Another student called Noah over. As he walked away, he answered. "Not in the least."

"Really? You're not curious?" Olive asked later that day when she was sitting with Noah, Willow and Jackson at the cafe.

"Not even a little bit."

Ellie brought a tray of coffee and cocoa and joined them. "Curious about what?"

"About the new girl." Jackson

"Woman." Olive.

"She was in Noah's class." Willow held a cup of hot cocoa to her nose and breathed in the heat and fragrance. "She's from Seattle."

"Just what we need." Noah

"Just what who needs?"

Zoe had materialized out of nowhere and stood in the doorway with the sun to her back, looking like an angel.

"Nothing," Noah and Jackson parroted.

Ellie stood to greet her. "Welcome. Zoe? Right?" She put a cup of coffee into Zoe's hand, as if she had been expecting her. "Come sit with us."

Willow quietly made her exit with Juneau following. She wasn't sure how to act around Zoe. Was being friendly to Zoe betraying Alex?

Ellie made a place for Zoe at the table. "Olive, scoot your chair closer to Jackson. Noah, shove over so Zoe can fit."

Which meant that Zoe was now squeezed next to Noah, their shoulders and knees awkwardly touching, which might have been fine, except that Willow came out of the restroom and didn't register that Noah wanted no part in the cozy scene. All she noticed was that Noah's shoulder was touching Zoe's and that his knee was touching her knee and worse, that he wasn't moving away (not that there was a square inch in which he could move) and she lost it.

"What. Is. Going. On. Here. In the name to of all that is holy?"

CHAPTER 43

New Jersey: Hold the Dinner, but Keep the Cake

Were you serious?" Alex lifted her beach towel into the air and shook it, sending plumes of sand into the air. It blew back at them, as it always seems to do at the beach. "Sorry."

Phoenix rubbed sand from his eyes. "Serious about what?" He went about closing the large, striped beach umbrella and looked over at her.

"Ditching dinner with our parents tonight."

"That would make a great band name. Ditching Dinner."

"Be serious."

"I am seriousness personified."

Which made me laugh. It was good to be home.

"Happy?"

"Obviously."

"So, we're ditching the rents and—"

"Rents? Who are you?"

He sank onto the sand and pulled her down beside him. "When you left, I had a lot of time to think."

"Here." I reached into my beach bag and came out with a chunky napkin. He took the napkin and peeled back the top. "Seriously?"

"Peace offering?"

"You stole a piece of cake from the cake tasting?"

"Stole is such an inflammatory word, don't you think? Besides, it's delicious." He rolled in the sand, laughing joyfully. It was good to see.

"If you're not going to eat that—" I grabbed for the cake. It was this close to my tongue; I could almost taste it, when it was suddenly snatched away. Phoenix downed it in three enormous bites, then leaped up, grabbed our gear and took off, shouting over his shoulder, "Last one to the car calls and explains why we're missing dinner."

Which motivated me. I took off up the beach like the flare of a rocket (that's how I later described it to Olive, although I may have been more like a tortoise in a children's tale). We reached the car at approximately the same moment (I'm sure Phoenix slowed way down to make that happen) and crashed into each other, laughing and spilling our gear into the street.

I thought I heard a phone beep, but ignored it. We shoved each other out of the way to see who could get into the car first. I tripped Phoenix—all's fair and all that, jumped over him and threw myself into the car ass backwards, grinning like a Cheshire Cat, all bruised knees and elbows.

But I was in and he had to make the call, so it was worth it.

"If you want to play dirty . . ."

I ducked but I was too late. Phoenix had me out of the car in less time than it would have taken me to lock the door. We landed in a tangle of legs and arms, fingers and toes.

My phone chirped again and Phoenix managed to get to it first. An image filled the screen: Willow and Juneau. I sat back and brushed sand off my hands, expression grim. Phoenix caught it.

"Bulls eye!"

"What?"

"Guilt 101. Strategic perfection."

"Hmm."

"Do you want to talk about it?"

I wanted to talk about pus and bloody scabs a hundred times more than I wanted to talk about this.

"I'll take that as a no."

We got into the car, our exuberance subdued, but not completely obliterated. I had made my decision and for now it was the right one. Missing Willow, Olive and Juneau hurt, but like everyone else in this world, I can't have my cake and eat it too. That thought made me smile. It seemed the theme of the day was going to be cake.

We pulled into traffic and were driving down the boulevard when

Phoenix looked over at me. "What are you smiling about?"

"Cake."

His eyebrows went up. "You are an enigma, Miss Aerowyn."

"As it should be," I said. "As it should be."

"Where are we going?" We'd missed the turnout on the New Jersey Garden State Parkway that would have taken us back to our little town in the Middle of Nowhere, New Jersey.

"It's a surprise." He hesitated. "But, if you don't like it, we'll turn right back around."

"I trust you." I said it automatically, but it was true.

He squeezed my hand before returning his hand to the steering wheel.

I leaned back and closed my eyes. I could smell the salty air, exhilarating, like inhaling ginger ale or champagne. Fizzy, sweet and tangy with a dash of salt. No matter where you go, home is home. Home is part of your DNA. Mine, anyway.

"We're here."

I must have drifted off. The sun and warm air will do that. Come to the Jersey shore and you'll see for yourself.

I opened my eyes and looked out my window at a neat row of Victorian homes dating from the late 1800s and early 1900s. Gorgeous! We didn't stop there, however. Phoenix continued driving until we came to the end of New Jersey and the Cape May Ferry dock.

"The ferry!"

"I am officially taking you across state lines."

"I promise not to call in the FBI."

"Good to know."

Cars were already lined up waiting, so we joined the line along with everyone else. I had been on a ferry in Alaska, but this one was nothing like that. In Alaska, the ferries are called The Marine Highway System and they are considered a form of transportation. In New Jersey, the ferry is more of a tourist venture and it showed. There was live music, a cafe selling designer drinks and a gift shop, in case we wanted to buy an "I sailed my worries away," T-shirt as a gift for an unsuspecting relative back home.

Once aboard, Phoenix and I retreated to the uppermost deck and spent the rest of our time with the wind and sea-spray in our faces, letting our worries drift away. I did, anyway. His hand touched mine from time to time as we leaned over the railing, in our own little bubble, far from the rest of the world.

The ferry docked at Lewes, Maryland and we disembarked. Phoenix headed for a bicycle rental stand at the ferry dock. We picked out two old beach bikes with no gears, which reminded me of all the bike rides I had taken at the shore as a child. Phoenix went over our itinerary. We were headed for the state park bike trail which he informed me used to be the railroad tracks for the old Pennsylvania Railroad. As we rode along the trail, we passed WWII lookout towers, steered along the canal and under a large canopy of old-growth trees, past a horse farm, where two horses stood at the fence and whinnied a greeting to us. It was four miles to Rehobeth and after three miles, I heard music. Apparently, today was the Rehobeth Balloon Festival and yay, we were going!

I was busy looking up at the balloons when I bumped into Phoenix's bike. I swerved. He jerked his handle bars to correct and ended up spinning in a circle, barely avoiding landing in a ditch. Whew!

It was his own fault. What was he thinking riding so close to me?

"Still clumsy. I should have been thinking."

"Obviously."

Half of Delaware and New Jersey must have been at the festival; so many balloons were aloft that you couldn't see a cloud in the sky. Phoenix kept a loose grip on my arm as we navigated the crowds, knowing how I seriously disliked crowds. As we passed a small stage, a man announced the annual Rehobeth Beach Hot Dog eating contest. Phoenix put on the breaks. "We have to see this."

"Seriously? You want to watch people stuffing hot dogs in their mouths as fast as they can, to win what? A ribbon? A certificate?" I'd had my fill of hot dot eating contests in Alaska. Plus, it made me think of Willow and Juneau and my heart hurt.

"Apparently, you've been away too long. The winner gets a trip to NYC and participates in the national hotdog eating championship."

"Apparently, you've lost your mind." I pulled and tugged and cajoled until he capitulated and we continued past the event without me having to see masticated food spilling from the mouths of the many people who were mad enough to join the event.

"It's not all stupid human tricks. You do know the entry money goes to support school lunch programs."

I support school lunch programs, even so—

"Since hotdog eating is out, how about we do the next best thing."

I was afraid to ask what the next best thing might look like at that point.

"A hot air balloon ride."

Okay. I thought the balloon festival was so that people could show off their balloons. I had no idea there would be a chance in hell, I mean the opportunity, to go up in one. It's not that I was afraid. I wasn't.

It took no time at all for him to find a balloonist, pay and before I could come up with any kind of excuse at all—plague? rabies? heart attack?—he lifted me into the basket and off we went.

It wasn't as bad as I imagined. Our ascent was slow and the hissing of the fire was comforting in a way. Even so, I worried that a bird could hit us or we could snag a power line and end up in a big puddle on the ground. Although with a crowd of this size, the crowd might break our fall.

Phoenix put two arms around me, reminding me that we were

floating above the world. Not a cloud in the sky. No one to tell us what to do. No place we had to be.

I had to wonder: Who wakes up one morning and says, "I think I'll make a huge balloon and then I'll make it float by putting a big old fire beneath extremely flammable material. Then I'll affix a basket to it, hop in and take off for parts unknown."

People amaze me!

Phoenix was lost in thought when I interrupted. "Do you really believe it?" I asked.

He turned to me and leaned back against the aside of the basket, making my heart leap. I reached out to yank him back and he laughed.

"Do you? Believe all this stuff. About saving the world?"

"You felt it."

"It's possible I had the flu. Maybe someone drugged me. A Russian spy. The mafia."

"Okay."

"Seriously, doesn't it bother you how they're controlling your life? Like you're being punished for something you didn't do?"

"I would never call marrying you a punishment."

"It's just—"

"What?"

"Forget it."

I didn't think I would feel this way, but I was sorry when the ride ended. We came back to earth with a bump, as it should be. Life is bumpy. Get used to it.

My stomach growled and Phoenix must have heard it because he suggested we eat. No time like the present. There were food vendors of every culture and type of cuisine in booths skirting the edges of the festival. We went from booth to booth until finally settling on fried halibut with onion rings. It reminded me of Alaska. I shook my head, willing the thought to rise up and drift away with the balloons that were floating above our heads.

The food was delectable. We ate slowly and afterwards sat together, talking about this and that, nothing important. When we were ready to get moving again, our path led us to a pavilion where a band was playing. People were dancing in front of the stage, some in pairs, others alone.

"May I have this dance?" Phoenix put one hand on my waist, took my hand in his and pulled me in close. The dance was slow, the air warm and I relaxed into the music.

"We can do this for the rest of our lives if you'll have me."

He looked down at me. I looked up. It would be so easy.

If I answered, I knew I was going to be in trouble.

He looked away. "No pressure."

No pressure? Ha.

At that moment I looked up at the balloons and wondered: How much pressure would it take for a hot air balloon to explode into a thousand tiny pieces? How much pressure would it take for a Jersey Girl to explode into as many?

We arrived home at the stroke of midnight. Was it an omen? I was too tired to say. I lay in bed and checked my phone. I guess Phoenix had turned it off back at the beach, because the screen showed twenty-two messages. All from Alaska. I know I'm rotten, but I set the phone down without replying and fell right to sleep.

CHAPTER 44

Alaska: The Art of War and Cupcakes

She hasn't answered any of my texts."

"She's probably busy." Olive was trying to calm Willow down, but it wasn't working.

"We need to up our game."

"Up our game how?"

"Making her miss us isn't working. We need to guilt her."

"I'm not so sure . . ."

"We get Harry at the paper to write an article about how the community center is falling apart since she left."

"Except that the community center is doing great. All the classes are full and I have waiting lists out the door."

"She doesn't need to know that, does she?"

"Have you been reading The Art of War much?"

"What?"

"Nothing. I'm not sure Harry would be willing to fabricate an article for us, that's all I'm saying."

"Then we start our own paper. Easy."

"Right. Easy."

"Come on, Olive. Don't you want to get her back?"

Olive wanted her to come back more than she could say, but she didn't want to warp a 12-year-old's moral development in the process.

"What's next on the list?"

Noah returned from cafe's kitchen with a take out cup of coffee just then. "What list?"

"Nothing." Willow stuck her chin out as she shoved her list into her back pocket.

"I smell someone cooking up trouble."

"What you say about someone else is really true of yourself," Olive recited.

Noah stifled a grin and headed for the door. "Olive, I appreciate your offering to bring Willow to the community center for class. Just don't do anything that will land one or both of you in jail."

"You heard him. No jail," Olive said.

"Fine. I'll revise the list."

"You do that. Now eat your lunch before my mom starts in on you about not eating enough. You know what's she's like."

Willow took a bite of her sandwich, chewed and swallowed. She took another bite and asked Olive, her mouth full, "Olive. You know that new girl? Do you think she and Noah were getting a little too cozy yesterday?"

Olive tried to remember. Had Noah been overly friendly with Zoe? It was her mom who'd stuck them together at the table. Had Noah smiled too much? Laughed at a not-so-funny joke she made? She didn't think so.

She answered Willow as best she could. "I don't think so. Why? Are you worried she's going to replace Alex?"

"Of course not. That's ridiculous. No one could replace Alex. Could they?"

"Definitely not."

Willow thought about it all through lunch. Men were unpredictable. That much she knew. And Zoe was cute and friendly and she was interested in music, like Noah. It was a definite possibility that she could replace Alex. Except Willow had no intention of letting that happen. Not today. Not any day.

"What evil plots are you two cooking up today?"

Willow jumped before she realized Jackson was behind her, making rabbit ears.

"Hey, Jackson," she said. "I thought you were going to Kodiak today." "Cancelled. Which is why I can hang out with you guys. Any one for a walk?"

Jackson flashed Olive a smile that Willow knew said he wanted time alone with Olive. He'd only included Willow to be polite.

"No can do." Ellie arrived at the table with an arm full of dirty dishes. "Olive, I need you in the back."

Willow watched as Olive shrugged Jackson off and followed her mom. Score. Olive had left her laptop at the table. Better yet, the computer was open, so Willow didn't have to worry about a password. It only took her a few seconds to find the appropriate file and she was done. Now there was no chance of Noah replacing Alex with Zoe. Because Zoe was no longer going to be around.

She closed the file just as Olive returned from the kitchen and gathered up her laptop. They headed back to the community center where Olive printed off the most recent student list for Noah's instrument building class and handed it to him as he was heading into the classroom with Willow following. She was going to be his teaching assistant today and was bursting with excitement.

"It's not that I don't love seeing you smile, but you look suspiciously happy today. What's up?" Noah asked.

"You wound me." Willow put on an expression that read Drama Queen in Training.

He stifled a laugh. He'd find out what was going on sooner or later. Hopefully sooner. He looked down at the paper in his hand and frowned. Across the room there was a new student. One who was very pregnant. He went over and gave her a quick hug. "Marilee, does Joe know you're here?"

"Sexist any?" she replied.

"It's just that I don't think it's a good idea for a baby to come popping out around all these sharp tools."

"Smart ass."

"Seriously. You weren't on my list."

"Olive called. Someone dropped out."

Just then, Noah noticed Zoe walk in. He double checked the new list. Yep, her name was missing.

"Zoe. I thought you dropped the class."

"What? No."

"It looks like there was mix-up. Olive filled your spot. Sorry."

She gave him a look; she was as clearly confused as was he.

Willow! Wait. That was impossible. She was not a 12-year-old Machiavelli, he told himself. It was a simple computer glitch. Easily fixed.

"But don't worry, we can squeeze you in."

Willow threw her hands up in the air and was about to shout "What?!" when she realized that might be a giveaway.

"Great!"

Willow shook her head. Great! Noah set Zoe up at his table and now she would be even closer to him. How was she going to fix this? Worse, the universe was punishing her for her deception by forcing her to watch as Zoe and Noah got along great. Favorite music genres: the same. Favorite type of movies: the same. Favorite instrument: the same. Dang it.

By the end of class they had their heads together, laughing, so much so that Willow thought she just might vomit. Ooh, good idea. She could vomit on Zoe's shoes. That might work. But no, Noah was too smart for that. He was already looking suspicious. She would have to wait. Good plans require time and patience. That was the flaw in the current plan.

She'd do better next time.

Class was ending and Zoe took the opportunity to pull Noah aside while the rest of the class was busy cleaning up shavings from the floor that had escaped the ventilation system and stowing their hand tools and projects.

"Noah, I owe you an explanation." Zoe looked increasingly guilty. "Do you remember when Steve was teasing about how the reason I came to Alaska was you and I said it was and everyone thought I was being a smart-ass?"

"Um. Okay."

"Well, it was true."

"How would someone from Seattle find out about my class?" It didn't make sense. He'd have to ask Olive about her marketing strategy and if it included the entire pacific northwest.

She shook her head. "Not the class. I started an independent record company in Seattle a few years back."

He put up a hand to stop her. "No."

"I know you don't tour anymore. I heard the stories about how you're done with all that. But . . ."

"Willow. Can you please go to the office and help Olive for a bit?"

"No way. I want to hear this."

"Go."

"I knew she was up to something," Willow said.

"Please?"

"Fine. I'm going to find out anyway," she said as she turned to go. "You can't keep a secret around this place. Everyone knows that."

"Please. Hear me out," Zoe said.

"Zoe. That is your name, right?"

"Of course."

"I have a life here that I love. I have everything I need. I have everything that I want. You have nothing to offer me."

She turned away and thought for a while. "How about this." She turned back and faced him. "You'd be helping out a struggling record company. You'd be helping me. Give me twenty minutes of your time."

He checked his watch. "Start talking."

The offer was this: he'd do one record and a six-month tour in the US only. Willow could come with him when she wasn't home in New Jersey with her mom. After six months, that would be the end of it. In return, he would get the standard proceeds from his concerts and record sales. It would give her record company the momentum she needed.

Willow, who had sneaked back and was standing outside the shop door, heard the offer. Why was Zoe so desperate to get Noah? He was a great musician, but he was also her uncle, so of course she would think that. Not that it mattered. Because Noah hadn't said no. Now she had to ramp up her efforts to get rid of Zoe. There was no time for patience and careful planning. Zoe was toast. She just didn't know it yet.

"Owwwwww." Someone was yelling. It came out part groan, part moan.

Noah looked around to find Marilee bending over the table, hanging on with a death grip.

"Noahhhhh, I may be going into labor."

Looking down at a puddle on the floor, one of the guys joked. "Ya think?"

"Someone call an ambulance."

"Wait. There's ton's of time, only . . . ow, damn . . . I might need a little help getting down the ramp."

"Right. Guys. Get over here." Noah shouted. Everyone in the room, including Olive and Willow gathered around Marilee.

"I just meant I could use your arm to lean on, I don't need an entire football team."

Jackson showed up just then. "What's going on?"

"Marilee's having a baby. You'd better get out of the way before your tender eyes see something you don't want to see," another one of the guys in the class teased.

Olive chimed in. "If you're not helping, move." Olive pointed to a chair. "Sit," she directed at Marilee. Marilee obeyed because standing wasn't helping one bit. Olive directed Jackson, Noah, Steve and Harry to pick up the chair, with Marilee gripping the arm rests as another contraction hit.

"Put me down."

"Stop wiggling before you fall out of the damn thing."

The four of them, following orders, hoisted the chair up between them and began a slow procession across the community center, with Marilee protesting between moans, groans and expletives.

Olive had heard Zoe's offer, too, and couldn't hold her tongue a minute longer. She leaned across Marilee toward Noah as they walked. "So, nice friend you are, Noah, leaving us for fame and glory."

"Where did you hear that? Never mind," he snapped.

Willow, on the other side of Merilee, leaned over her to explain to Olive how it wasn't Noah's fault. "It's Zoe's fault. If she hadn't come here, we wouldn't be leaving."

"Great. So what happens to the community center?" Olive

"Olive, this is not the time."

"They all say that when they don't want to answer."

They had just reached the cafe entrance when Merilee shouted, "Will you all just shut the fuck up. I'm having a baby here!"

"Oops." Olive

"Sorry." Jackson said, even though he had nothing to be sorry for.

They finally arrived at the cafe without having dumped her out on the ground, fortunately. Everyone breathed a sigh of relief.

"God help me," Merilee said. "I'm having my baby in a freaking nut house."

Noah, Jackson, Olive and the rest of the men pulled up chairs, surrounding Merilee as they waited for the EMTs. Noah put his forehead on the table. Jackson put his head in his hands. Steve and Harry shot each other looks. Translation: "How soon can we leave without looking like we're complete jerks?" Someone across the room asked if he should be boiling hot water, as Olive patted Merilee repeatedly on the back saying how everything was going to be okay—although no one in the room thought it was going to be okay—when what she was really thinking was how she was never going to have a baby after watching Merilee, who apparently wasn't even in the hard stages of labor yet and still, it looked like it hurt like the devil.

Willow wasn't sure what she should do, so she did the best she could. She went into the kitchen and came back out balancing one of the cafe's largest serving platters.

"Anyone for cupcakes?"

Chapter 45

New Jersey: Grandma's Bright Idea

For three days, I didn't answer my phone. Not when Olive called. Not when Phoenix called. Not even when Willow called. I shut off text notifications. Email notifications, too.

"We need to have a talk." My gran came into my room one morning before the sun had a chance to edge into the sky and sat on the edge of my bed. I was still asleep, but when I heard the word "talk" I woke with a start and ducked further under the covers. I knew this wasn't going to be about the birds and the bees. It was going to be worse.

I peeked out of the covers at gran and shook my head.

"It's about your wedding dress."

I wasn't sure if I should be relieved or horrified. Which was worse? Wedding dress? Birds and bees? I tossed it around in my head for a while as gran waited and still I couldn't decide.

"GG." I used the voice my mom uses when she's setting down the rules.

"Don't GG me. If we don't get going on this, there won't be a thing left for you to wear. You don't want to march down the aisle naked as a jaybird, do you?"

Hmm. Were those the only two options? I had to smile, despite myself.

"Come on. We're going to Kleinfeld's."

How did GG know about a reality TV show where brides flock to a brital shop in NYC and parade around in high-priced wedding gowns while friends and family sling emotional arrows at them?

"I'm sure there are perfectly fine wedding gowns right here in New Jersey," I found myself saying. What was I thinking?

"Phoenix loved the idea of a road trip."

Of course he did.

"Your mom wasn't too happy about it, because she has a meeting and can't come along to supervise."

There was the rainbow.

"You'd better hurry." GG checked her iPhone. "Because we're leaving in 30."

As soon as GG left me alone to change I ran to the window and looked out at the deck below. I could duck out there and escape through the woods in the back of the house. I had a 30 minute head start if I left right this minute and didn't bother about changing out of my pajamas. That decided, I grabbed my keys and backpack and cranked open the window, stuck one leg out, bent over and pushed my head and shoulders through. One more leg to go. I hit the deck and was tiptoeing down the back stairs (this was going to be so easy!) when my pajama bottoms snagged on something, stopping me short. I pulled until the fabric ripped away, came free, wherein I immediately tripped over a pair of pink clogs I'd left on the stairs long ago.

"Good morning, sunshine."

Curses! Phoenix! He handed over a steaming cup of coffee.

"Seriously?"

"You've been avoiding me."

"I've been avoiding a lot of things. Don't take it the personally."

"Hey. A trip to Manhattan. When was the last time you were there?"

Never with parental approval. My parents believe NYC is rife with decadence and immorality and no place for, well, anyone.

He read my thoughts. "It'll be an adventure. What do you think?"

I think I had enough adventure. But then again, it was New York City. And it wasn't as if I was ever going to wear the bloody wedding dress anyway.

I shrugged my shoulders and sighed. "Fine."

"Trust me. It'll be fun." Phoenix took hold of my hand and pulled me back up the stairs. I glanced back as he was checking out my pajamas and bunny slippers. We reached the top of the stairs and he tugged at the torn spot on my PJ bottoms where bare skin was showing through and laughed.

"Go eat a lemon or something," I snapped. I mean, really. Enough was enough. "If we're going, I need to change."

He smiled again.

"And you are not invited."

GG had hired a driver, so we were traveling in relative luxury. I doubt mom would have approved, but I was pretty sure GG hadn't bothered to share our travel arrangements with her. Mom could be a stickler for not abusing whatever wealth we had; GG was the wild card in the family. Until I came along, that is.

Kleinfelds on West 20th St. was a short 87 mile drive from the New Jersey Pine Barrens, where we lived. Longer, thanks to GG, who was happy to prolong the journey in any way possible, I sensed.

"Driver, stop!" was becoming a litany. First we stopped at a roadside stand filled with fresh apples, blueberries, peaches, tomatoes and a plethora of kitchy, handmade items. GG came away with a bushel of apples she thought would help appease mom upon our return. I opted for blueberries, my favorite while Phoenix settled for snagging an apple from the top of GG's basket.

Back on the road, GG almost caused a five-car collision, when she grabbed the driver by the shoulder and shouted for him to turn immediately. Into Dairy Queen! I was happy to go along. I ordered a hot fudge sundae. On second thought, I added french fries to my order and when we all sat down (Phoenix with his plain chocolate cone), I proceeded to dip the fries in the hot fudge and ice cream.

"Try one." I dipped a fry in my ice cream and handed it to Phoenix

Phoenix screwed up his face, like I was suggesting he eat raw squid with frosting on top.

"Trust me, they're good."

I could tell he was looking for a way out. He opened his mouth to proclaim some perfectly reasonable excuse for not eating an ice cream-coated french fry and, obviously, I took that opportunity to shove the fry in.

"Hmph-grgle." He choked and cleared his throat, before chewing and swallowing.

"Good. Right?"

He was speechless, apparently.

"Here, try another. You barely tasted that one."

This time, he reached over, took a fry, dipped it and willingly popped it into his mouth.

"Well?"

He took another fry and held it out to GG, who downed it in one.

"I concede. It is good." I smiled and he added, "And a much easier way to commit suicide than the standard methods, if a lot slower."

"Ha, ha."

"I am nothing, if not hilarious."

"Okay, let's get this show on the road." GG had deposited her trash in the nearest bin and was heading back to the car. "Time's a-wasting."

Once in the back seat—GG insisted on riding shotgun—I leaned into Phoenix and whispered next to his ear. "Who is this and what have they done with my grandmother?"

We were only 20 miles from home. At this rate, we would get to NYC after the store had closed down for the night, although I wasn't complaining. Gran was quiet for the next few miles. We were reaching East Windsor, New Jersey when we passed a large billboard announcing the Englishtown Flea Market, Farmer's Market, Art and Crafts and Antiques Fair all rolled up in one. It was too good to miss, she announced, as she once again directed the driver to stop.

It turns out there are tons of flea markets all across New Jersey, but this one had been voted the best in New Jersey and even had its own tavern. It covered 40 acres and has been in operation for over 80 years, run by the same family. Their motto was "Shop 'til you drop", which seemed appropriate when we pulled in and saw about 1,000 cars already crowding a parking lot bigger than that of Yankee Stadium.

The driver dropped us off at the main entrance where I noticed a sign with the hours of the market. It closed at 4 pm, meaning there was still a chance we would get to Manhattan and Kleinfelds before closing. Phoenix noticed me looking at the sign, did the mental math and put an arm around my shoulders.

"It's going to be fine," he pronounced.

Of course it would. Things always work out in the end. Maybe not the way you planned, hoped for or expected. But they do work out.

I had to admit, this place was amazing. On the opposite side of the gate, we walked into an area that reminded me of a botanical garden. At least fifty tents housed vendors with long tables overflowing with every type of flower and plant you could imagine surviving in New Jersey and beyond. Sunflowers in great big tubs and taller than me leaned into the sun. Buckets of deep red, false goat's beards, bee balm and peonies created a path to the next vendor. I selected one of each to create a colorful bouquet. I felt I could have stayed there all day but GG was almost out of sight. My mother would never forgive me if we lost GG among the fried elephant ears, rusty antiques and giant pumpkins of central New Jersey.

I paid quickly, determined to keep up with her, I matched my stride to that of Phoenix. We came upon her stopped in the antiques row, which appeared to stretch beyond us for miles where she was fingering a crystal set of rosaries. When I got closer, I could see that it had unusual markings on the medal and that this was what was drawing her attention. She leaned across the table and handed it back to the dealer, reluctantly. "This is from the 1400's. It should be in a museum." Before the vendor had a chance to react, GG turned and was heading back into the fray of over-heated bodies and excited shoppers.

The sun was high in the sky by now and the ice cream and fries were doing somersaults in my stomach. I had only been away from the heat of New Jersey for a short while and already I was no longer used to it. I sank down on an old wooden rocking chair, leaned my head back and closed my eyes. Phoenix swooped in as if he were rescuing a baby bird from a hawk. "She needs water," he told someone. The next thing I knew, I was jumping up, screaming. Phoenix had poured an entire bottle of icy water over my head.

I shook out my hair and wiped water from my eyes. But I did feel better. The nausea was fading and I felt like I could walk again.

"Better?" He handed me a second bottle of water. "Drink up."

I shook my head but did as I was told. Drinking slowly so that I didn't vomit it all back up.

"You'll pay for this."

"I can hardly wait."

Smart ass. How can you not like him?

As we walked along, I wondered. How did GG do that? I mean, how did she find such a treasure amidst 40 acres of everything imaginable?

"You can do it, too."

I looked over at Phoenix. "Are you reading my mind?"

"Yes, and you're thinking I am delicious."

"Ha!"

"Delectable."

"In your dreams."

"Obnoxious?"

"Closer."

"Come on. Before she gets away." GG was receding into the distance. All I could see at this point was her red scarf flying behind her as she breezed down the row. I picked up speed, taking chase, flower petals dropping behind me like a flower girl in church. OMG. I had weddings on the brain.

"Taylor Swift must have a song for that," Phoenix said.

"Stop it!" I stuck a finger in his face.

He looked over my shoulder and reached for his cell, ignoring my puzzled frown.

"Hi, GG. It's Phoenix. Alex and I are in antiques row." Pause. "Where do you want to meet?" Pause. "When?" Pause. "Great. Row 7. 2pm."

We found GG moments later, looking skyward, dwarfed by a hand-carved totem pole so wide that her arms could not fit around it, had she attempted it. I stood beside her and followed her gaze up the length of the pole. Oddly enough, this work of art began its life in Ketchikan, very close to Prince of Wales Island, a sign read. It was created by Haida artisans. I ran my hand along the smooth old wood, fascinated by the carving of a raven holding a baby between its wings, the bear with a frog in its mouth and two small cubs. It was originally created to celebrate the adoption of a young local girl, all of which was included on the sign attached to the base of the pole.

The flea market owners' son had moved to Alaska in 1951 to run a deep sea fishing operation until the Exxon Valdez oil spill in 1989 put him out of business, driving him back to NJ where he married a nice Jersey girl and happily gave his parents three precious granddaughters, one who graduated from Harvard.

Another grandchild lived in Paris for a while until coming home to help in the family business. The entire family now ran the operation. And none of that was on the plaque! I yanked my hand back. Sheesh. I needed a guidebook for the incorrigibly crazy. What other weird talents did I have or would I possess next? If that was what this was? My brain was threatening to explode.

Phoenix, who had drifted off while GG and I were contemplating the totem pole, returned with the tip of a linen bag sticking out of his pocket. I'm observant like that. We left shortly after and frankly, I was ready to go home. But it was not to be. My eyes kept closing of their own volition; Phoenix pulled me over so that my head rested in his lap as he read from a pocket-size paperback, and when I opened my eyes again, we were being deposited in front of bridal hell. I mean, the bridal shop.

I like a pretty dress as much as the next gal, so walking among the bejeweled, beribboned and belaced mannikins wasn't entirely unappealing, although it crossed my mind to wonder why so many brides seemed to be going for the $100. hooker look. The tighter the better. The most boobage showing, the better. I hadn't seen so many boobs since, well, never.

Fields of snowflake white gowns complemented the polar bear white walls to create a perfect recipe for zoning out. I was brought back to earth by a very cheerful staff member who guided me into a room way in the back and began stripping me of everything I had on, like we had known each other forever and were besties and had watched each other's boobies come in, which we definitely had not. With the exception, thankfully, of my modest bra and panties, thank heavens. It was hard to believe I was semi-naked in front of a complete stranger and she didn't think there was anything odd about it in the least.

While I had been zoning out, she had spent her time being productive, namely selecting the first dress I was meant to try on, to "get feel for my style." She slipped the first dress over my head so fast I didn't even see what it looked like. She pulled the zipper up and it stuck. She reversed direction in hopes of getting it back down. When it didn't budge, she applied more pressure. The zipper broke loose and what with all that downward force the zipper ripped straight through the gown until I was once again partially nude and the gown lay in a fluffy white heap on the floor at my feet.

Dress No. 2 snagged on one of the eager staff member's 4-inch high heels before she even got the chance to force me into it. Needless to say, the gaping hole wasn't going to be a big selling point.

Dress No. 3 was the innocent victim of an over-caffeinated mom racing down the hall outside my cell, I mean dressing room, with an over-flowing cup of steaming coffee. We collided like peanut butter and chocolate. I felt myself shaking. It was getting worse and I had no idea what was happening to me, but I was definitely shaking. Phoenix arrived at my side just in time and laid a calming hand on my shoulder. GG showed up right after and took over, shoving the coffee mom—who appeared to be stuck in place like Lot's wife, her mouth set in an exaggerated O position— aside, then bumped past the appalled staffer to push me inside the cubicle and wrap me, coffee soaked dress and all into an all-encompassing bear hug.

It took a while, the hug feeling like a lifeboat in the Bering Sea, but I finally stopped shaking. When GG gently pealed me off of her, she shook her head. "This is a fuck up. A complete and total fuck up!" Stating the obvious, if you asked me.

We stayed in a hotel in Chelsea that night. GG called it a boutique hotel but it was wasted on me since I fell asleep before I had time to decide if the bed was soft, medium or hard. I woke to find no sign of Phoenix. Not that there would be. I was wearing all my clothes from the day before and I'm pretty sure I smelled as appealing as a regurgitated taco at the Balloon Festival.

Shower first. Teeth second. Hair. No, wash out undies first. Then shower. Check for hair dryer to blow dry undies. Then shower. Someone was making a holy racket in the next room. Forgoing the aforementioned bathroom to-do list, I peered out of my door to find GG slamming utensils into a kitchenette style sink and cursing like a sailor. Before I had to chance to stumble into the drama, Phoenix pushed me back and closed the door. I heard the lock click into place. He kissed me! His hands were in my hair, on my neck, arms and thighs. My back was pressed against a wall as the kiss deepened. His body was pressed against mine. My primal brain felt as if the stars and moon and sun were colliding inside of me. My logical brain worried that GG might come walking through that door. Phoenix pulled back. It felt like a cloud had passed over the sun on a winter's day.

"GG is going to tell you things I would prefer you didn't hear without . . ."

I barely had my breath back, but I managed to squeak out, "Without?"

"Without knowing how I feel about you."

His eyes met mine and it was as if we were talking to each other without speaking. Wait. We were talking to each other without speaking.

"We were separated before birth, but now we are united again."

He took the linen bag I had spied earlier from his pocket and opened a small box. Inside was a rhinestone pin in the shape of a dragon.

"What's this for?" I asked.

"So you will always remember how strong and fierce and wonderful you are."

A loud crash followed more cursing came from the next room. I was torn between staying where I was and checking on her. My good angel won. Phoenix followed me into the room where GG was uncharacteristically and loudly slamming pans into a tiny cabinet under the kitchenette counter. She noticed me and Phoenix and stopped suddenly then glanced down at the coffee maker that was now in shards at her feet.

"Coffee."

Phoenix decoded the message to mean, "You. Get coffee. Now," and left. I started to follow.

"Not you," she said. "We need to talk."

"I thought we—"

"Not about ridiculous wedding gowns. You clearly do not want to get married."

Oh, brother. The jig was up. She knew I was only going through the motions, waiting until an exit strategy became clear.

"Sit!" she commanded.

I sat. "Why are you so angry, GG?"

"You want the truth?"

No. "Of course."

"You left without a word. I thought you were better than that."

Ouch. Except Phoenix had said that they always knew where I was. "You knew—"

"Knowing where you were did not make it any less hurtful to me or to your parents."

Why were we having this conversation? I know I screwed up. I admit it, but why now? "I'm sorry, GG."

"I know. That's not what I'm really angry about."

I got up and started sweeping up the broken glass and bits of plastic from the coffee maker debacle.

"I'm angry because you felt you couldn't come to your family when you had a problem. You couldn't come to me."

That was worse than her calling me dishonorable.

"You don't have to marry Phoenix if it's really not what you want."

"What?"

"Dresses do not destroy themselves. Not three in a row and certainly not so spectacularly. I haven't seen so much mayhem since, well, never mind."

"But the universe. Our promise."

"Sit. Please."

I dropped the bits and pieces I held in my hand into the trash and sat across from her. She took my hands in hers.

"You lied to me. But worse, you've been lying to yourself. The question is, what will you do now?"

I had no idea. Go back to Alaska and let the world fall apart? Stay and marry Phoenix and end up hating him because I never got to find out for myself what I really wanted to do with my life? There was no happy ending for me.

"Your mother is going to kill me for this, but, everything Phoenix told you is true."

Great. No way out. I was right.

"Come." She led the way out to the balcony and leaned against the railing. "Tell me, what do you see."

"Um, cars. People. The Hudson River?"

"You need to talk with your mother." She handed me today's New York Times as the door to the suite opened with a bang. That was Phoenix making noise to warn us of his arrival. GG went back inside to greet him, leaving me behind to think.

I was feeling pretty grouchy at this point. What did the New York Times have to do with anything? I scanned the front page. Climate change was getting worse and the government was ignoring it. Someone had successfully stolen a Van Gogh from the Metropolitan Museum of Art. A politician was caught with a porn star. Same old. Same old.

Phoenix found me before my head exploded and handed me a cup of hot coffee.

"Thanks." I was on auto-pilot. Take cup. Sip. Repeat.

"It occurred to me half way to the cafe that coffee was a ruse on GG's part to get me out of the way. Sorry."

I shook it off. "It was weird." I explained the conversation I'd had with GG, but then remembered that he already had a pretty good idea of what she was going to say.

"She gave me a newspaper. Any brilliant ideas?"

"What else did she say?"

"She said and I quote, 'It's time to talk with your mother,' or something along those lines."

"Cue the spooky music."

"When did you get to be so hilarious?"

"Seriously. I'll come with you."

"Seriously, I can't do it. Our plan is working. There's no need to fold now."

I caught the look on his face. Was he going to try to stop me? "Don't. Just don't."

"I would never."

"Good. So we understand each other?"

"We do."

Today GG found a relic, Phoenix found a dragon pin and I found a new problem. Talk with my mother and find a wedding gown without blowing up the damn thing.

Chapter 46

Alaska: Laundry and The 80's

"Noah. There's been a minor problem." Willow was standing on the deck of the houseboat with her arms securely wrapped across her chest as Noah approached in his dinghy. He tossed the line to tie up the boat. "How minor?" he asked as he hopped out of the boat and onto the deck.

"It's nothing. Really."

He moved to enter the house. Willow jumped in front of him, blocking his entry. "Wait. Promise you won't yell?"

"You're starting to worry me."

"Don't be ridiculous."

"Fine. Then let me through. Juneau was firmly planted at Willow's side. "Juneau, move."

"Fine. Just don't get mad. Kay?"

He looked inside. Everything looked normal, as far as he could see.

"I'm going to take a shower." He'd been helping Ellie clean a load of fish and he reeked. "Before we head out for the baby shower." A baby shower had been thrown together faster than a lettuce salad.

"I don't think you want to—"

"What happened here?" he asked. The tub was full of soggy clothing.

"The dryer broke."

He pulled her into a hug. "This is what you were worried about?"

She nodded.

"Silly." He kissed the top of her head, went to check on the dryer and returned almost instantly. "I don't suppose you checked the plug."

Of course she'd checked the plug. She was the one who'd unplugged it, wasn't she? If he didn't have dry clothes, he couldn't go to the shower and hang out with Zoe, could he?

He went back to the bathroom to remove the clothing from the tub so he could finally get his shower, when he realized something. "Willow. Did you wash all my clothes?"

She patted Juneau's head and nodded sheepishly, thinking, good plan.

"Socks and underwear, too, I suppose."

"Of course. You wouldn't want to go around in day old underwear, would you? But don't worry. There's a box of old clothes in the attic you can use," she offered.

"If I recall, that box contains old costumes from when your mom insisted we throw an 80's party."

So true.

The light dawned. "You planned this!"

"What? How can you say such a thing?"

"I saw a copy of The Art of War on your bookcase."

"You wound me."

"Ha! You are evil."

"I'm 12. I'm too young to be evil."

He walked out to the boat and returned, swinging a backpack. "Your plot is foiled. Spare clothes!"

Rats.

"Don't think I don't know what you're trying to do."

She rolled her eyes.

"Look. I get it. You're threatened by—"

"As if."

"Listen up. The next time you pull something like this, I'm taking you back home. Let your mom deal with you."

Score! Noah and Alex would be together again, in New Jersey. This was turning out better than she had hoped for. Now all she had to do was think up—"

"You got that, kid?"

She decided to go with pitiful. "I'll be good." Juneau whimpered as if to emphasize how serious they were.

"Right. Been there, don't believe it for a minute."

CHAPTER 47

New Jersey: Just Don't Panic

It was inevitable that my mother would hear about the wedding dress fiasco, as I was now calling it. The entire family was calling it that, actually. I was avoiding mom and mom was avoiding me for her own reasons. Reasons I didn't care to bother figuring out. Maybe she was watching her blood pressure. Maybe she was regretting having a girl child in the first place and didn't want to deal with me until she had shoved that thought way down into that dark place, the one reserved for denial.

Life somehow managed to go on as before. I read the Times daily in the hopes that I would figure out the clue GG had so mysteriously dropped on me. Otherwise, her lips were sealed. When I asked—repeatedly—she would reply with, "I've said enough." Followed by, "Do you really want to give me a heart attack." Secrecy, guilt and manipulation. I should get her the T-shirt.

Wanting to get in as many nice days at the beach as possible,

Phoenix managed to whisk me away every morning without mom even raising an eyebrow. Phoenix, her last hope of getting me to comply with the family mandate, was the golden boy. Little did she know that he was on my side. No one wants someone marrying them out of obligation. I crossed my fingers, in case.

Today I settled in beneath an enormous beach umbrella, because I fry in the sun like a crustacean at a clambake, reading another New York Times. Damn it. I was going to read every word until it unlocked its secrets, even if it took until Christmas. But still, nothing. I tossed it aside. Someone was calling me.

I looked over at Phoenix. He was still absorbed in his book. There were other families on the beach, but no one was talking to me that I could see. The voice called again. Louder this time.

"Phoenix, we have to leave."

"Why? What's wrong?"

"I don't know. I think I'm hearing things."

He got up and started piling things in our beach cart. "Like what?"

I picked up my beach towel absent-mindedly and shook it out, sending a spray of sand up into the air. "Something about a song ending."

"Relax. Someone must be streaming a video. That's from Doctor Who."

"Trust me. Something is wrong."

"Okay. Wait. Let me check the news." He palmed his phone and looked up almost immediately.

"Okay. Don't panic."

"Whenever anyone says don't panic—"

"I know. But, just don't panic."

Chapter 48

Alaska: Prince of Wales Island Population: 5560

Doesn't the baby shower usually come before the birth?" Noah teased Merilee as she opened gifts at Ellie's cafe where the baby shower was happening in real time.

"Better late than never?" Olive was busy writing down each gift along with the name of the giver in a baby blue notebook while Willow collected the ribbons and bows from the gift wrap to save for some unknown reason.

Every table was filled with well-wishers who were passing Baby Noah, named after Noah because his quick thinking had made it so Merilee didn't have to deliver her baby in an old cannery, namely the community center, or in the local cafe. Baby Noah weighed in at a whopping 8 lb. 2 ounces and didn't mind being passed around, as evidenced by the contented look on his face, although the freshly changed diaper and his recent meal might have contributed to this in large part.

Ellie had made her Christmas cheesecake especially for the occasion. Olive had spent hours on an elaborate braided bread. Sam and several of the local firefighters brought crock pots full of clam chowder, planning on holding an impromptu contest for the best chowder of the day.

Food, friendship and a brand new baby. Welcome to the world baby boy.

With all the gifts now opened and safely tucked into boxes for Merilee to take home later, this was Willow's chance. She'd decided she was going to run away. Not actually run away. But disappear long enough to give Noah a tiny scare, although not of the heart attack variety. But a large enough scare that he would take her to New Jersey, where she would find Alex. She slipped out the door, followed by Juneau and no one noticed a thing.

She'd already decided that the safest place would be the community center. She would work on a project while she waited and it wasn't too far away, so she wouldn't have to wait long for someone to find her. When she got to the community center, she realized that it was actually a little spooky with no one around. The lights were off for one. She quickly flipped on the lights in Noah's classroom. It was smaller than the cavernous main room, so that the creaking of the barge didn't make her jump out of her skin every time it moved. She pulled out drawing materials so she could work on a gift for Merilee's baby as Juneau settled at her feet, giving her a look that read, We shouldn't be doing this.

She chose to ignore it, until the entire barge started shaking. She was used to earthquakes in Alaska. Small ones, barely perceptible, happened almost every day. She continued working until the shaking made her pencils skitter off the table, followed by several tools that someone had left lying around. She knew the rules. Get under a table. Stay put. Except she knew Noah would be worried sick. She had to get back to Ellie's before it got worse. She crossed the room just as the boat shuddered, knocking her off her feet. She tripped over a trash can and landed on the floor in a heap, her ankle aching. Another shake pushed a large metal cabinet over, blocking the door. She was trapped. Unless. She got up, limping toward the door. If she could squeeze through the small opening between the door and the cabinet—Juneau barked at her. She looked at him in surprise.

Get down, he barked.

"Fine. You do it, Juneau. Go get Noah."

Juneau slipped around the cabinet where there was just enough room for him to shimmy through the door and was gone, leaving Willow alone in the rocking boat, wishing she'd never had the bright idea of scaring Noah, because now she was the frightened one. Frightened and alone.

"Ellie, have you seen Willow?" Noah was clearing the wrapping paper and bits of food that had fallen under the tables when the cafe started shaking.

"I told her there was chicken in the frig for Juneau. Check there."

Noah checked the kitchen. No luck. He called out to her. No answer. He checked the upstairs rooms. No Willow. He was heading down the stairs when the entire building jolted.

"Olive, have you seen Willow?"

The shaking increased. Chairs rattled across the floor. Salt and pepper shakers skittered off the tables. Normally the shaking would have stopped by now. It was getting worse. Dishes flew from shelves and crashed onto the floor.

"Everyone under the tables," Ellie shouted.

"Willow!" Noah yelled. Ignoring Ellie, he ran outside. There was no sign of her. Panic was not an option, but if it were, he would be panicking, big time.

"Willow! Where the hell are you? Juneau."

"Quiet, everyone. There's an emergency warning coming in," Sam shouted.

The emergency broadcast system announcement flashed across the tiny TV Ellie had set on the counter. "Earthquake slams southeast Alaska at 5:09 p.m. Alaska time. Tsunami expected. All residents of the following southeast Alaska communities are advised to evacuate to higher ground: Kodiak, Ketchikan and Prince of Wales Island.

Jackson and his coast guard friends went into action forming an evacuation crew, while Noah organized anyone who was available to help look for Willow and Juneau. He was getting ready to send three groups of two in different directions when Olive intervened. "Let's think. Where would she go?"

Ideas came in from all around. "The ice cream shop?" "The pet store?" "The lighthouse?" and the three teams took off to check out all those places.

"What about the community center?" Olive asked as Juneau came crashing in, barking furiously, "Follow me, damn it. Willow is in trouble!"

CHAPTER 49

New Jersey: Cake Solves Everything

There's a tsunami warning in effect."

"In Alaska?"

He nodded.

"I told you it was bad. I have to go back." I turned to race up the beach. If we leave now, we could be at JFK in two, three hours, depending on traffic.

"Alex." Phoenix took my hand, stopping my forward momentum.

"You don't understand."

"Flights will be grounded. There's no way to get back there now."

He was right. But. "Well, do something. We can do things. So, do something."

He pulled me back down under the umbrella, I struggled to break free, but he held me tight. The confusion was suffocating. Why wouldn't he do something? He held the newspaper up in front of me. "Global warming. Wars. Poverty."

I gave up all my breath in an angry sigh. "So what? You're saying it's all a big fat lie." I shook my head, impotent, furious. "I guess that means I don't have to marry you."

"Found the silver lining, have you?"

What a jerk I am. "Shit. Um. God. I didn't mean it that way. It's just so damn . . ." I burst into tears. Frustrating. And confusing. Why would our parents insist the world depends on us if we have no power other than one, that of destroying wedding couture. I didn't know what to do. Willow was there. Olive. Juneau. Wait. "I stopped a storm. I created electricity."

"Alex, no one should have the power over life and death in that way."

That's what GG was trying to tell me. Not that it was bullshit, but that there were rules.

"That's crazy," I insisted. "I can't just sit here and do nothing. I won't."

"So you get to decide? Your friends live because you tried to stop a possible tsunami in Alaska, while thousands of people are dying in Afghanistan, Syria, Guatemala? Do you really want to play savior and executioner?"

I gave him I Hate You eyes.

I got out my phone and dialed Ellie's cafe. No answer. I tried Olive next. Then Jackson. Noah and Sam. And everyone else I could think of. No one picked up.

"Look," Phoenix held out his phone. "The local TV station is reporting cell towers are down. No fatalities reported across southeast Alaska."

"Really?"

"Really. They'll call you as soon as they can. They know you'll be frantic."

There was some small comfort in Phoenix's words. Olive would call me. Or Willow. Unless they were furious with me for avoiding their calls for so long. No, even if they never wanted to speak with me again, they would call me.

Wouldn't they?

That night, while I was lying in bed, unable to sleep, checking my phone every five minutes for messages, I heard from Phoenix.

"Are you asleep?" Phoenix

"Not hardly." Me

"I'm sorry." Phoenix

"I hate you." Me

"I know." Phoenix

"Not really." Me

"I know."

"So, it was a bunch of lies?" Me

"It's complicated." Phoenix

"So un-complicate it." Me

"Alex." Phoenix

"Phoenix."

"Everything I said was true."

"To a point."

"To a point. It boils down to differing beliefs. Our parents feel that we made a commitment and we must uphold it. Some younger members have left, and needless to say—"

"Our parents are blaming them for everything from global warming to the opioid epidemic. Thanks for being honest with me. But I still hate you."

"What do you want to do now? Now that you found your loophole."

I put the covers over my head. It felt warm and safe. A perfect hiding place. Was it really a loophole? No one could prove one way or another if Phoenix and I marrying would truly make a difference, but they also couldn't truly predict the consequences if we didn't. What if our kind died out on earth because the younger generation, my generation, decided to go our own way and leave things to chance? What if our kind married "earthlings"? OMG. I made myself laugh and this is so not funny. But really? What if we intermarried?

"Are you still there?" Phoenix

"I'm here." I yawned, big and loud.

"You're tired. Go to sleep."

"I still hate you." Code for I still love you.

"I know."

"Night."

"Goodnight."

I awoke to GG and mom having a screaming fight, one that reached all the way upstairs to my bedroom. The universe was collapsing. No one had ever raised a voice in anger in this house, in my memory.

"You had no right to do this." It sounded like my mother was about to hit something.

"She has a right to her own life," GG answered, slamming something down on the kitchen table.

"I'm her mother."

"Well then, act like it."

The back door slammed. I looked out the window. Mom had the pruning shears and was now pruning an over-grown lilac bush into oblivion. I went in search of GG and found her sitting at the kitchen table in front of a pile of mail.

"What's all this?" I went for a cup and filled it with coffee, cream and honey before sitting next to her. She pushed the pile of mail over to me.

The return addresses shocked me. Oxford. Yale. Princeton. Cooper Union.

"Catalogs?"

"Open them."

I opened the one on top: Cooper Union, an art college in NYC. "Dear Miss Aerowyn. We are happy to ..."

Oh my God. I was lucky mom was going after the lilacs with the pruning shears and not GG, who had sent off college applications for me. Is that even legal? But, wow.

"GG. What did you do?" I asked, not like mom, but with enough love to last most people a lifetime.

"You have the right to your own choices."

"Thank you."

"I am still furious with you. And with your mother. She should never have forced you to run off like that."

"I'm sorry."

"You said that before. Now it's time to decide what you want and then stand up for it."

Right. If I knew what was the right thing to do.

"I didn't say to do the right thing. I said, to do the thing you want to do."

This thing with people reading my mind was seriously getting old. I wondered how many times they'd used it on me when I was growing up. Alex, did you leave fill-in-the-blank's bike in the driveway? No, mom. Are you sure? Because I think you did. Etc.

"Mom will kill me."

"She'll get over it."

Easy for her to say.

"Here, open the rest."

Yale, Oxford and Cooper Union accepted me for this fall. Nearby Princeton wait-listed me. A good thing, because if I did decide to go to college, I might need to be further away from mom than Princeton. Self-preservation and all that.

"Anyway," GG added. "There's nothing in the rule book that says you have to marry when you turn 18."

"What?"

"It is the custom, but technically it's not an absolute and irrevocable requirement."

I blinked. Or choked. I don't remember which.

"Here, your mom made cake. Have a piece."

Chapter 50

Alaska: Seriously!

You are dead to me, young lady."

"Very funny."

"Seriously, Willow, you could have been killed. Then I would have had to tell your mother and she would be really, really mad at me."

"You're such a comedian, Noah. Har har."

"And you, Juneau! You let her sneak off and didn't even tell me, which means you're dead to me, too."

"Just tell me. What's my punishment? Are you sending me home?" She ducked down to pat Juneau, trying to hide a smile.

"You look entirely too happy about that option. Wait a minute. Did you plan this? You run off, I find you, you're in trouble, I send you home. And bam. You find a way for us to go see Alex and your devious plot is realized."

"Seriously, Noah, you've been watching way too much TV."

CHAPTER 51

New Jersey: A Shaky Balancing Act

As loopholes go, this one was excellent. I could go to college. England. NYC. Connecticut. California. I could even go to the University of Alaska, if I chose. I looked it up. They have open enrollment. Saving the world could wait. Now that I knew Willow was safe—and actually back in NJ because Noah had said enough was enough and he was done. At least for now.

I had options.

The door bell rang and something told me it was Phoenix. Actually, I knew it was Phoenix. We were going to GG's house today. In what felt like minutes later we stood together in front of a baby blue door, hand in hand and knocked.

"Ahh!" My screams could be heard all the way to Philadelphia as the door flew open and a big ball of fur launched itself at me.

"Juneau!"

He leapt into my arms and wrapped himself around me, as if I was the last corn dog in New Jersey. Olive came out of nowhere and grabbed me, completing the Alex and Juneau sandwich. "Olive!"

"Don't look at me. It was all Phoenix and GG," she said when she finally pulled herself off of me and we were settled on GG's wraparound porch, looking over a glorious stretch of the NJ Pinelands.

Juneau, who hadn't strayed from my side since our reunion, was spread out across my lap like a well-loved wood blanket on a cold winter's day. I looked around for Willow.

"Willow's with her mom. She was supposed to come see you too. It was all planned," Olive said. "But now she's grounded for life." She leaned back in one of GG's whitewashed oak rockers and sighed. A cool breeze was blowing softly through the trees.

"So, you get me and Juneau instead."

After visiting with GG, Phoenix and I bundled Olive and Juneau into his car for a tour of the Pinelands and a bit of the Jersey shore. We arrived at my house hours later and, truth be told, my mom hadn't exactly been happy when a wolf-hybrid had come charging into her house, all paws, tail and tongue. Olive, on the other hand, she treated like she was a long-long daughter. Gracious under fire.

Aliens are friendly that way.

"How long can you stay?" I asked, dreading her answer.

"I got early admission to University of Alaska, Southeast, so I have to be back—"

"Don't say it."

"If you come back, we could go together. Not that you'd give up Yale and Oxford and Princeton for—."

"Princeton is wait-listed."

Olive smacked me on the shoulder, like I'd stolen her cotton candy at the state fair.

"What?"

"You're stalling. No decision is a decision."

"Where'd you hear that? Dr. Phil?"

"Tick tock."

"No matter what I decide, someone ends up unhappy. If I go to Alaska, it's Phoenix. If I marry Phoenix, it's GG. If I don't marry Phoenix, it's my mom. If I go to away to college, it's also my mom."

"Okay. Okay. I get it. You're screwed."

Great.

"What are the top ten things you would do right now if there was no one and absolutely nothing to stop you from doing it."

"More Dr. Phil?"

"For instance, you could sail to Antarctica. Or apply for an artist internship at CERN in Switzerland and get to see the supercollider, for example. Those sound like you."

It had taken every last ounce of courage I had to go to Alaska and that wasn't even my own idea. Great-gram had orchestrated it. That night I fell asleep thinking. I really only had one dream up until now. To be free.

The best part of Olive being here was Olive. The next best part was that her presence delayed a confrontation with my mom. GG and mom were currently engaged in a cold war the likes of which I had never seen. Meanwhile, all pretend wedding prep had been cancelled. My dad was making himself scarce. We were all in a balancing act that everyone with a shred of sense knew could not last.

And it didn't.

It happened the night Olive and I tearfully parted at the airport in Atlantic City, having spent out final day together with Olive rhapsodizing about how great it would be if I came back to go to college with her and me deflecting her at every turn.

Long story short? Mom slapped GG. I packed a bag for me and one for Juneau and walked out.

Mom is not generally crazy. Possibly because she's always gotten her way before; therefore, now faced with having absolutely no control over me or GG, she cracked. At least that's what GG says. Me? I'd had enough. And Juneau agreed. Phoenix patiently listened as I ranted and raved and cried on his shoulder after Juneau and I arrived on his doorstep, soaked to the bones. Of course, it rained. The universe is twisted that way.

"We could just leave."

Phoenix's suggestion seemed a bit like déjà vu to me. Done that. Was dragged back by manipulation and guilt.

"Really? How'd that work out before?"

"I know. You tried. I didn't help any. But I understand better now what an untenable position they'll put us in if we stay."

"So you're saying you've grown up." I was only half teasing. We'd learned more about our families and ourselves in the past few weeks than some people manage in a lifetime. "Where would we go?"

"For tonight we head for my grandpa's place in Cape May."

"And tomorrow?"

"Tomorrow we consider our options. That's the best part. We have options."

My eyes filled with tears. I had GG and Phoenix on my team. Phoenix was wrong. The best part was that I wasn't alone.

Phoenix wiped away his own tears. What a pair. You think your life is going one way and suddenly it takes a sharp left turn. Optimists say that can be a good thing.

I'm starting to agree.

CHAPTER 52

Alaska: How to Fry an Egg

I miss Willow." Olive was sitting at a table back home in the cafe. "And Alex."

Noah, who was sitting between Olive and Ellie, didn't bother to answer. They all missed Willow and Alex. And now Zoe was gone, too, realizing finally that trying to get Noah to leave Prince of Wales was a dead end. No need to go over and over and over it. Olive jumped up suddenly, like she'd stuck her finger in a socket, and blurted out, "You know, if you don't stake your claim, you're going to be out of luck, stuck here all alone, growing into a cranky man who's butt twitches every time someone looks at him."

Noah scrunched up his forehead. Definitely not his butt. He hoped she wasn't talking about Alex, because, for one, Alex always seemed to be mad at him, not to mention that she was eighteen friggin' years old—17 when she first arrived—for crying out loud. Not that he'd ever considered dating her in the first place. He hadn't. If that was what Olive was talking about, because who knew what Olive was talking about half the time. Most of the time.

"It's too quiet here." Olive sipped her chocolate milk and sighed.

Ellie gave her a quick hug. "You'll be off to college soon. Then we'll really see what quiet feels like."

A herd of firefighters poured through the door. Perfect timing.

"You were saying?" Noah said.

"I was saying, do you know how to fry an egg? Because this crew isn't going to feed itself."

CHAPTER 53

New Jersey: French Fried and Ice Cream

"Since we're already heading toward Cape May tomorrow, going right past Willow's home town, there's no way we can drive right on by without seeing her," I told Phoenix. We were lying side by side in the twin beds he'd slept in as a child, holding hands across the expanse.

"Resistance is futile," I informed him.

"You need to know that you have been watching entirely too much TV lately."

"I have eighteen years to make up for, so excuse me if I happen to LOVE Star Trek."

"And Doctor Who."

"It goes without saying."

"I'm noticing a theme here."

Yep. Fascination with aliens. Who would have thought it.

The alarm went off early the next day, much to my disgruntlement, which lasted through my shower and all the way through teeth brushing as I pulled a hair brush through my tangled hair and as I dragged my backpack across the walkway to the car and tossed it in.

"Wait. Do you have the car keys?" I asked Phoenix after I slammed the car door.

He nodded. Good.

"Where's Juneau? Oh. There you are. Wait. Did you pack Willow's gift? Did you pack the cooler?"

"What? Are you my mother?"

I sank into the front seat of the car. "Sorry. I'm nervous." He got in on the driver's side and took off down the driveway and before long, we were flying down the Garden State Parkway.

"Which of our many, many problems are you nervous about?" he asked finally.

"Very funny. Willow, of course. You've noticed, haven't you?"

I wasn't a hundred percent sure that he would acknowledge the weird things happening with Willow or if he had even noticed them. He hadn't been around her as much as I had, after all. I looked over at him. He was looking away. Was that a guilty look or had my imagination gone all wonky on me. "Phoenix?"

"You're not going to like this."

Sigh. Where was a cast iron frying pan when you needed one.

"I should have told you."

I crossed my arms over my chest. Better to keep my hands occupied so that I didn't reach over and attempt to choke the life out of him, which wasn't a good idea considering as how we were going at least 60 on a major highway. "What?"

"Let's just say that our families know each other."

"God, Phoenix, you sound like a crime boss."

He wasn't answering. Waiting. For what, I couldn't say.

"Wait a sec. If our families know each other—then. Holy. Oh. No."

"I wanted to tell you."

"But you were protecting me? Protecting our parents? Protecting the whole alien-save-the-world thing? Stop the car!"

"Alex, I'm not leaving you on the side of a highway."

"So, you're saying Willow is in the same boat as we are?"

"Maybe. Maybe not. Just because two families . . . it doesn't have to mean that . . . I never asked and no one ever said."

"Where's the maybe in this? She has powers. I've seen it." We passed a sign saying we were two miles to the next rest stop. "Take the next exit."

"Alex."

"Stop the car at the next exit, or I jump out right here."

Here are the things he didn't say, fortunately for him: Calm down. Listen to reason. Everything is going to be okay. Take it easy. We'll discuss this when you are thinking more rationally. Put on your big girl panties. He didn't say any of those things, which saved his life. Or at least it felt that way to me at the time.

We pulled off the highway and stopped next to a concrete complex. Inside was a food court with at least six different restaurants that you pretty much see all over New Jersey, and probably the entire US. I settled on coffee and a buttered croissant. Phoenix got french fries and ice cream. We took our food outside and silently sat under a tree far from the tourists that converge on the Jersey shore every summer.

I pulled my roll apart and with each piece that I ate, I found a reason to calm myself down. 1. Phoenix was right. He didn't have proof. 2. Phoenix had come clean when I brought it up. Another point in his favor. 3. If he had told me earlier, I couldn't have done a damn thing about it; if I wasn't able to help myself, how could I help her. And 4. Maybe the timing was perfect. Phoenix and I were now in a better place to help her. I looked up and met his eyes.

"So?"

"Sorry."

He moved closer on the bench so that our shoulders were touching.

"We're a sorry pair, aren't we?"

"Pathetic."

"I know."

"Fry?"

"You have to ask?"

I took a fry, dipped it into his vanilla ice cream and popped it in my mouth. Yum. He held out the container and I reached for another. "So, what now?" he asked.

I thought about it. "We keep with the plan. Go to Cape May, but first we visit Willow."

"Are you going to tell her?"

"We're going to tell her that we're here for her. We're going to tell her that any time she has a question about anything, she needs to pinky swear that she won't believe the first thing she hears and that she calls us."

"She won't know what we're talking about."

"This is Willow we're talking about. She already knows. Maybe not the who, what, when, where and why's of it, but she knows."

One hour later we turned down Willow's street. Phoenix pulled over, stopped the car and looked over at me. "That's settled. Now what about us?"

Wasn't it clear? We were in this together. Til death do us part, even if marriage wasn't on the immediate horizon. We were peanut butter and chocolate. A shell and a hermit crab. Two spoons in the same drawer. French fries and ice cream.

CHAPTER 54

Willow's Blog: December 21, 2021

To everyone who is out there reading this blog, this is the final day of my grounding for running off during a tsunami threat and scaring the bejesus out of everyone—Noah's words, not mine.

In fairness, my grounding was well-deserved, but I have served my time and I am now free, which explains why I have my iPad back and am allowed to start this blog and why I am having a weekend sleepover at the lighthouse with Alex and Phoenix, who are back for Christmas, along with Olive and Jackson, who will be here too.

To get you up to speed on everything that has happened since the summer, I'll start with Olive's happy ending. Her mom finally won, because Gabe, the Harbor Master was offered a job in Maine, someplace he'd always dreamed of going and now Olive's dad is once again the harbor master. The good news? Ellie says she no longer has dreams about going after him with a cast iron frying pan, which everyone thinks is funny, because Ellie wouldn't disrespect her cooking utensils that way.

Jackson is happily studying at the Coast Guard Academy in Ketchikan. Nothing new there, except I caught him and Olive holding hands earlier this winter when they thought no one was watching.

Zoe left POW, rightfully, after Noah made it clear that he had no plans to go on tour with her and that nothing she could say or do was going to make him change his mind. Only now he has gone "outside" (being anywhere that isn't Alaska) to visit her once a month. And it's not about music, from what I can see. I'll keep you posted on how that turns out.

Olive is attending The University of Alaska Southeast, majoring in journalism. They don't have a major in world domination.

Phoenix is currently studying astrophysics at what Noah calls a fancy-pants college, namely, Princeton. He lives in a historic loft above a hundred-year-old bookstore and cafe in downtown Princeton. Interestingly enough, Alex lives on the floor above his, which she has converted into a studio/living space, foregoing college to continue working on the things she loves best—besides Phoenix and Juneau, which, obviously, is painting. Can you say happily ever after, even if I haven't heard a word about—"

"Willow! Put that thing away and get over here."

That would be Olive.

"These marshmallows aren't going to toast themselves, are they?"

"Be nice." That's Alex. The camp fire is making loud snapping and crackling noises as Alex, in her winter parka and a thick wool scarf that I knitted for her for Christmas, holds two sticks with marshmallows that are clearly on fire and hands one to Phoenix.

Phoenix and Alex have been watching over me as if I'm a newly hatched baby turtle, trying to make my way from the sand to sea. Can you say, obvious!

I humor them. It's so sweet. Completely unnecessary, but sweet. Because I made a decision as soon as I figured out they were hiding something from me, to find out what it was. And what I finally did find out—they're not nearly as sneaky as they seem to think—was, wow, we're freakin' aliens, our parents have an agenda (albeit one coming from commitment, loyalty and good hearts) and that Phoenix and Alex are determined to be there for me. Another thing they don't know? One day we're all going to be living in Alaska again, in the lighthouse. If I have anything to say about it.

My favorite story in the world has to do with a devil. He's large and fiery and he's telling a young girl to back down. He says there's no way she can survive, that there's a powerful storm coming her way.

Her response to the devil? Which I love. I am the storm!

That's me! So you can just stop worrying, everyone.

"Willow!"

Oops. Alex is calling.

"Willow!" Now it's Phoenix.

"On my way!"

Marshmallows await.

The End

ACKNOWLEDGMENTS

I am enormously grateful to my family and friends who have supported and encouraged me in my writing career. And a huge thank you to every one of my readers.

ABOUT THE AUTHOR

Izzy Ballard grew up at the Jersey shore. When she moved to Alaska, she traded sunny beaches for snow-capped mountains and moose who love to eat her garden.

She is the author of Alaska Virgin Air, Fearless in Alaska, Temptation, Alaska and The Alaska Girl & The Spy.